Litany

Litany

A NOVEL

MARY TRAVERS

FREE TREES PRESS

ISBN: 978-0-9831458-0-6
Library of Congress Control Number: 2011921100

Published and printed in the United States of America

Cover drawing by Pam Keeley, Seattle, Washington
Photograph by Dana Schuerholz, Vashon Island, Washington
Cover and interior design by Sonya Unrein

Free Trees Press

Seattle, Washington

Contact: maryptravers@gmail.com
Website: marytravers.net
E-fiction review site: thebookreviewforfiction.com

This being a time confused and with few clear stars,
Either private ones or public,
Out of its darkness I make a litany
For the lost, for the half-lost, for the desperate,
For all of those who suffer, not in the flesh.
I will say their name, but not yet.

—Stephen Vincent Benét, *Minor Litany*

CHAPTER ONE

Rose
Entering the Garden

If I got to live one more stinking day like this, somebody's going to get hurt, Rose threatened nearly out loud. Clouds formed inside her head, bolts slamming the backs of her eyeballs. She placed the rough, cracked chap of her hands along her temples. Her eyes wrinkled into the droop of an already fallen face. The sun was sharp. She was stupid hot.

Or maybe me, maybe I'll hurt me and get beyond hurting. Her hand ached for the heavy metal of the.38 buried in her belongings and wandered toward her two bags, which leaned against each other like drunks. Make a damn end of it.

Out of nowhere, maybe from the slightest blush of spring still in the air, she realized she'd missed the lilacs this year. Just hadn't noticed them. What the hell was she doing in May? It was only last month. She got quickly mad and slowly sorry. How did she turn out to be a person who let spring pass by when she wasn't looking?

As one puffy eyelid slit open to the unforgiving shimmer of Chicago sky, a flash of cornflower caught her eye from the yard across the street. It was struggling in a massed mound of wild growth. She didn't want to go there. The hell with that. She had no ambition, which was fine with her. But it was as if a traction beam pulled her bulk up from the somebody's front steps where she'd been sitting for an hour. Without will, in an unsteady arthritic shuffle, she was brought across the street to the slipped boards of a weather-beaten fence.

Her practiced fingers reached through and pinched a spent red rose from its straggling stem. As it was destined.

She'd been gardening like this, like a penance, for ten years already. In passing. Ever since she gave up her own garden.

She resettled her tapestry cloth bags, grown grimy year after year until their design had become a smudge, against the fence. Rose stepped back and stared at this yard, which used to be an orderly riot of a garden, a favorite of hers long days ago. In a city where flat-faced lawns stood tired watch out front of brick and frame bungalows, this lot was fenced off from the unbending cement ribbon of sidewalk with a ramshackle attitude. By taking some chances, the gardener had changed the nature of a rectangle. Even in her madness, Rose continued to admire a well-planned spot.

Then, a few years back, the tended order of it began to fall apart when no one did the autumn cleanup. The spring after, Rose knew trouble had entered that house. No hand was put to the garden. It became a tangle of choking weed. This was coming to be its third full summer without intervention.

"Hello," a man passing by on the sidewalk startled her. He was in his forties, dressed in clean clothes, beige cotton workpants, his yellow nylon shirt, top unbuttoned, showing his white dago T at the neck. He wore sandals with black socks, the summer look for men in their part of town who were not young, who were from the old country no more than once removed. The newspaper was tucked under his arm. The headline was bold: "RFK Fights to Live."

What the hell was that about? JesusMaria, they didn't. Ya, of course they did.

The man had stopped with a smile. What he wanted to know was who the hell she was. She was used to that from people. What he saw and must assess was an old woman without a neck, just a lot of shoulder with a head popping out the middle. Rose was broad across the back, in hip as well as torso. Her waist, which had not much been there even when she was little, had disappeared into a girth. She was layered in clothes, any piece of which by itself had once been a respectable housedress, a decent blouse to go shopping, an apron for making soup, but when taken together made a motley tarantella of an outfit. Her slippered feet were covered in dirt, and she wore her nylons rolled at the knee. Her short hair was the color of steel and stuck up in uneven tufts, giving her the look of a lopsided bird. She was missing a lower tooth, just to the right of center.

She ignored him.

"I'm the neighbor next door. I'm Stan," he said. "Can I help you?"

Ya, she thought. You could tell me about this Kennedy brother. When? He was winning in California, she'd heard it on her transistor radio on the bus last night. But she couldn't ask.

She turned her back to him and simultaneously flicked a few inches of the dress that made up her outer layer. In heavy-accented English, she said as one word "Kissmyass."

"*Pani*," he said in Polish.

"Never mind, *'Pani'*," she deflected his attempt at respect with her English. She tried not to register a bit of surprise that he spoke her language. She was in her own neighborhood. Why shouldn't he?

"Look," he said, "I don't mean to bother you, but..."

"Then get the hell away," she said with Chicago's dull "t" and her thick Polish accent. She said it mean as it was ever said to her.

He backed off a couple of steps, not quite willing to turn his back to her until he'd put some distance between them.

She'd seen that before. She laughed to herself. He was a little scared of her. Go run to your house, she mumbled at him under her breath. She supposed he'd call the cops, but that didn't bother her. Cops didn't care. And they'd have to get in line not to. If Grace was still around, well, then, things would be different. Grace and Rose, little twins, Grace and Rose, sisters living their lives together. Two, two. Two kidneys, a set of lungs, day and night, right and left, dialectic. Diametric. Dichotomy. The binary. Base two. Stupid man, stupid Stan, he made her think of Grace. She glared toward his house. She didn't have to reach far for Chicago's time-honored dismissal. "Asshole," she said out loud, "a" as flat as the lake, and turned back to the hole in the waist-high fence.

No longer satisfied with the little pinch-prune that had started her off, her hands grabbed at the weeds surrounding the struggling rose. She pulled them top-first through the gap in the fence and tossed them on the sidewalk. Then she reached in, lower, to go for the roots. Disturbed bees worried her head, her arms. She pushed at the next few fence boards. They broke off from where they were fastened, the rusty nails beyond use in grayed wood. She hunched and stepped through the rails into the space she'd just created, intent on finding the base of the plant. Her skin tore where thorns of the spindly, leggy whips had mixed in with weeds. She was glad for the familiar pain piercing her fingers, her palms, the soft underbelly-like skin of her upper arms. Later would come the dull irritation of thorns beneath the skin.

Damn everything. JesusMaria, Bobby Kennedy shot? Just like his brother? Her mind popped back to her sibling. They'd had a good life together, her and Grace. Peas in a pod. When Grace thought of a joke, Rose was already smiling at it. When Rose was about to have an itch, Grace had the scratch ready. Even long years and thousands of ocean and mountain miles, Grace still over there and Rose here in America—streets paved with gold, ya! —even when they lived so different each could not have imagined the details of the other, still each knew the deep interior of the other. Two from one. They knew each other from before they were born.

Rose pawed the soil. Clumps of dirt stuck to root balls. A spurt shot into the air as a tall dandelion flew in an arc onto the growing pile outside the fence. She was rhythmic in her work. Bending, pulling, twisting, tossing, turning, bending.

Death was nothing, just another trick. Zero as placeholder. A terrible trick played on Rose.

Now. Damn now. When Rose dared look in a mirror, a paper cutout shined back. If she yelled in a canyon, her echo would be swallowed. She had no shadow. Every day had an awkward yearn about it. A listening. As if her heartbeat were missing.

Her mind pined, and she moved all the more furiously in the garden. Her eyes were intent, deciphering weed from flower. They had the code. They spoke to her in a way only gardeners and farmers, people who are primitively intimate with plants, can understand. Her hands, cut and clumsy, often grasped a flower stalk instead of a weed, not having got the eye's, the mind's, message soon enough. She tossed them with a detached regret that she wasn't more patient, slower. But with no time for remorse she turned back, bending, pulling. She had all the while a dim smile on her face.

Some part of her registered that she didn't belong in this somebody's garden, that she was going further than she ever had before in touching someone else's garden, but she refused to allow that thought exactly in. Gardeners, more than anybody, know that what you toss is only gone, but that what you allow in can take over. You need to be exquisitely selective.

Before long the space she'd created was the size of a small room. June's humidity and her own sweat made it a sauna. Her face was freckled with the fine dirt that had been liberated with each flick of roots into the air. The pile outside the fence was as wide now as it was tall, measurable in feet, not inches. She noticed it with satisfaction. What a great pile of work! Then a panic welled.

She'd better get out of here.

She bent to step out between the fence boards but was caught stooped over, midway, by the sight of two solidly shod feet planted just beyond the pile of green.

Oh, no. She hated people. And here was one.

She backed into the yard and straightened up to see a woman's face surrounded by a fuzzy head of salt-and-pepper hair, still more pepper than salt. Was it her curly younger doppelgänger?

"What are you doing?" it said.

Rose turned away and fumbled for the gesture with her dress. "Kissmyass," she said halfheartedly, knowing her position inside the yard, facing the woman, made it laughably less belligerent than it should be. She was cornered by her own work. Where could she go?

The woman was taken aback for a second, but made a quick recovery. "Pleased to meet you, too," she said. "Now, please, what are you doing?"

Without knowing it, Rose counted on people kind of having seen her around the neighborhood. She'd been on the damn streets for all these years, had sat across on those same steps many times, many times. Where had this one been? Rose turned back to the face, not sure what to answer. Shit! She'd got carried away. She didn't mean to make a mess. Maybe, she thought, she could still pretend not to have any English.

"*Co?*" Rose asked simply in Polish, as if she hadn't heard the question.

To her surprise, Sophie answered in Rose's native language. "What are you doing? *Co ty robisz?*"

"You speak Polish," Rose responded in Polish, shaken. *Psia krew.*

"Yes."

"You don't look Polish."

"I'm Polish. Jewish. From Poland," Sophie said. "You're having a hard time answering a simple question, no?" They continued in a language common to their childhood.

"I'm weeding this garden."

"Don't you need permission?"

"Go to hell with permission," Rose answered. "Anyhow, I just started to pick at that climber, Blaze, and then I got in." She paused. "It's a sin to let such a garden go," she said with vehemence, meaning her own.

"Maybe someone has a reason to let it go. Maybe that's easier than the way it used to be." The woman seemed angry—quiet, but angry.

Back to English. "Maybe. If someone's happier with a mess. If someone wants to look at a mess instead of monkshood or even, for Chrissake, mums." Now Rose was starting to steam. This was bringing back the time when she had been lost in her own garden, the time after Grace. The idea made her livid. She bent toward the fence. "I got to go."

The woman, with her foot, nudged a corner of the green pile away from the hole in the fence. Rose steered herself through it with a groan and came face-to-face with her.

Rose's face, covered with the dust of the soil, had run, was smeared by sweat. The crevices in her forehead and along her nose were lined with dirt, presenting an odd emphasis, an outline drawn around nothing in particular.

"Zosia Warshawsky," said Sophie, using her Polish name and sticking out her hand.

Rose glowered. She spit English: "I'm out of your somuvabitch yard."

"If you're going to work around here, you'll have to stop being rude," Sophie persisted with Polish.

"Who says I work here? I don't work for nobody. I ain't got no job." Rose would not be taken in, Polish or no.

"You just did work here. And it's good you have no work because then you'll have time to put things back in order."

"I got to go." Rose said, reaching toward her bags.

"Wait," Sophie said, with her hand up as if she were stopping traffic. "One, you made a mess." Her hand went down and her voice quieted more. "Two, I need some help."

"Wait a damn minute," Rose persisted in English, trying to grasp at something just outside her reach. "You said you don't want the yard nice. You just said. What are you, crazy?"

"Let's not stand out in the sun and discuss it," Sophie continued in Polish. "Come inside and we'll have some iced tea."

This *babka* was nuts, Rose thought. Crazier than me.

Rose hadn't gardened this way in years. Working wholeheartedly like that, being slippery with new, fresh sweat that came from gardening, Rose liked that. Okay, so maybe she would take a few minutes with this snotty one, Zosia, even if she acted like a bosska. What the hell? She could get cleaned up. She was itchy. Rose jostled her bags, her life, along the fence and through the gate. She settled them just inside the enclosed back porch, on the indoor-outdoor carpet, near the door.

"Come into the kitchen," Sophie offered, leaving the harsh Chicago sun blaring outside as the wooden frame of the screen door gently tapped, tapped the green jamb.

Rose looked at her dirty shoes, one with a hole cut out on the side for her bunion. Should she take them off? But her stockings were ripped; they were as filthy as her shoes. What was she doing? She didn't need this confusion. "I got to go," she said out loud and rustled her bags.

"Don't be silly," Sophie said. "Just come in." She'd worn her own shoes in, though they were dirty from the mess outside the fence. "Tonight's housecleaning. I'll be washing the floor."

The itching was driving her nuts. "Maybe ok. I need to wash up?" Rose asked.

"Of course. Help yourself. It's right off the back porch here, this door."

Rose went across the porch and into the room.

There was a little wall sink, an old-fashioned claw-foot tub, a painted wicker hamper with its top full of magazines and newspapers. There were towels hanging on a rack next to the sink and a pastel disarray of folded clean ones covering the oak dresser in piles. They toppled against a little doll with a hand-knit dress that stretched over an extra roll of toilet paper, giving her huge rectangular hips. The dolly stood next to a toy, a fortune-telling eight-ball that, if you rolled it like dice, it showed answers. Rose shook it and the up side said: "Guess what?" There was junk on every inch of the dresser, on the shelves above the toilet: little faded soaps, toilet waters, folded fancy towels on top of old terry towels, Fels-Naptha, Calgon. An infinite number, she laughed. A series of odd numbers is infinite, but the sum of the first n numbers is n^2, her brain went on. Rose washed the itch off her arms and made a pass at her neck and face. She didn't want to start on the grunge at her feet or she'd be in there all night. She started mumbling to herself about this garden. Blah, blah, she mocked herself. I don't need this crap, she heard bouncing in her head as though in an audio infinity of mirrors. Get out of here.

She moved down the glossy-walled hall, through the kitchen doorway, just making it. She used the walls to walk. Years of gardening had shaped her body into a big rock washed by rain and wind. Her joints were stiff with age and lack. Rose leaned on the back of a chair when she got in the kitchen, where Sophie was fussing. A pile of newspapers and mail was on the ground next to that chair, the only one outside of Sophie's that was not crowded with things. With effort, she settled herself at the old-fashioned, wooden table. It was warm-colored and had designs painted in red and green, a bit of yellow along its edges. In the midst of small stacks of bills and junk mail, empty Tupperwares, crystal ashtrays and relish trays and bowls scattered across the table, there, right in front of the window, was a vase on a doily placed in a space carved from the junk. It held a handful of zinnias.

A clock was ticking in another room. The house was cool and dark from the Venetian blinds being down all day.

Rose rolled her nylons down to her ankles. Sophie was at the fridge bringing out a pitcher. She set out two tall glasses and poured.

"Do you like lemon and extra sugar?" Sophie asked.

"Yeah, sure," Rose said, as if it didn't matter.

Sophie looked around distracted.

"I have a sugar bowl here somewhere, with pincers to take up the cubes balanced through one handle," she said, her fingers meeting in a delicate arc. She moved a few leaning piles, glanced behind them. She shrugged distractedly, opened a cabinet and pulled out a pound box of C&H, which she placed on the table.

"Shall I let the heat in?" Sophie asked, without reaching for the cord of the blinds.

"Sure." Rose shrugged.

Sophie drew the cord and the late afternoon sun pierced the room. Rose was startled by the light. Always, the sun indoors was a shock, not at all like the outside's. A spotlight.

It reminded her that she didn't belong there. "I got to go," she said.

"Can't you stay a little? Because it really is time I get the garden going again," Sophie said with a hint of sigh. "I don't know much about it."

"I threw all that crap outside your fence. I'll come back and clean up tomorrow."

Sophie waved her hand as if brushing away a light cobweb. "That doesn't really matter. You also opened up a space inside. I needed a kick to do something about it. It's been a while since I even looked out there."

"It shows. Things are choking to death," said Rose with her big mouth.

The corners of Sophie's mouth turned down and her cheeks went slack, her face in struggle. In a second, she had it back under control. "It wasn't so much my garden. It was Barbara's." Her hand waved toward a framed photograph lying on top a pile of magazines. "It's been hard to go out there."

"It's almost impossible with everything growing on top each other," Rose said in another burst. She was nearly sorry she couldn't keep her mouth shut.

"Never mind," Sophie said, though it was clear she did mind. "I need to get going with it, I guess. Do you think you'd be interested in helping me clean the yard up?"

Rose didn't answer.

"I'd pay you, of course."

"Go to hell with that," Rose burst out. "I don't need your damn money." She scrambled toward the porch door and pulled her black leather double-handled purse out of one of the cloth bags. She was scratching at the clasp.

Sophie was stunned. "You don't need to spit at me."

"No one tells me what to do." Her knotted fingers struggled with the opening. "I don't need your goddamn money, if that's what you're thinking," Rose said. "My cousin leaves my checks stuck on a nail on the porch for me to pick up."

"I don't mean to offend you. It's traditional to pay for labor, you know."

Rose sat back in her chair, her fingers still fumbling with the clasp, but less urgently now. "I don't like to get paid. It makes people bossy. I don't mind a couple of days helping out. I made a mess."

"I'll feel bad if I don't pay you."

"You see?" Rose said. "You feel bad or you pay me. You pay me, you don't feel bad, you feel like telling me what to do." She pushed her hands away from her chest, shoving the idea away, and expelled a breath through her teeth.

She knew her face had a lopsidedness to it—right side gesturing—left side free of passion. Sophie looked her in the lively eye. "You think I'll tell you what to do, eh?"

Rose glared back without an answer.

"Then I know we can work something out. I don't know the first thing about a garden. I've no plans for it."

Rose crossed her arms across her huge chest.

Sophie went on. "You can have carte blanche. Anything you'd like." Rose relaxed her arms a bit. "You don't know me, but when you do, you'll see it's not in my nature to be bossy. It's just that I came home early because I have to go back for a presentation later…. Well, never mind that. Anyway, you caught me by surprise. It's a practical matter. I need something you already started. So you can finish if you want and you'll be doing me a favor."

Rose moved slightly in her seat. She was back to working the clasp.

Finally, it gave way. She jammed the jaws of the purse open. Fat and glossy in the center lay a pewter handgun. Sophie twitched.

Peeking out of a handful of torn-open manila envelopes were the hard, neat edges of green government checks, the booty that finally came through Social Security after a lifetime of pitiful wages. "These checks, they come by my old house."

"Good," Sophie said, relieved, maybe, that Rose was not going to shoot her. "Good, you have checks."

There was a knock at the back door and Sophie went to answer it. That guy Stan was there, Rose recognized his voice. Their conversation was blocking her exit route.

Then Sophie was coming back with a sleepy little boy. "My neighbor just asked me if he could leave his grandson over here for a while. He has to run an errand. Do you mind if I tuck him in for a nap?"

Rose wasn't used to all this commotion, people talking to you, asking you questions, people knocking on doors.

"I got to go."

At the door, she gathered her bags in a fumble. "I come when I want. If I want."

Sophie stood in the kitchen with the little boy pulling at her arm. "It's already been a long time. I'm in no hurry."

Two hours ago, Rose was ready to take a bullet to her heart. The gun was going nowhere. "I think I'll come back," Rose said. "Maybe okay."

"Okay," said Sophie. "So. Is there anything I can do to return the favor?"

Rose saw herself as a Möbius strip, topologically complete. There wasn't much she wanted out of this kind of life. Her habits had grown close to her. All she ever wanted anymore was exactly what she had. Or less.

"Leave me alone."

CHAPTER TWO

Sophie
The Flood

Imagine coming home unexpectedly this day, drawn for a rest
between the day's administrative work and the night's overseeing.
Poets, tonight. Usually, when there was going to be a reading
or lecture at her branch in the evening, Sophie stayed on, went
out somewhere nearby for dinner alone, and saw it through. But
this blistering day, she'd given herself a little break.

"Can you stay, Virg?" she asked the other librarian. "I can be
back around 6:30."

"Go home," Virg said. "Put your feet up. Read a while."

Sophie pulls up to the curb. Here's a pile of weeds outside her
fence. Her heart contorts in a clutch. She'd tried that first summer as Barbara lay dying to keep the garden up, but instead she
would picture her—Barbara—bending over to dip the algae from
the pond. Stretching from Barbara's arched hand were the rest of
her years alone. Defeated, she couldn't budge a dandelion. The
poor fish in the pond died later, of course—from strangulation
or lack of food or a neighborhood tabby or, if they made it that
far, from the first freeze that came that winter.

Someone's in her yard. Vegetation is arching, flying, landing
outside the fence. Who in hell has the nerve?...

She peeks in to see a comical mountain of an old woman bent
into the yard, musty-looking drawers showing and her hands
a blur, flinging vegetation past her own behind and at Sophie

like a tiller. And oh Lord, she feels puzzled. There's something about the woman, hunched over to herself, mumbling and working, that makes Sophie more curious than angry, somewhat less than aggravated.

The home, not the garden, had been her palette. In her home, in the many years past, each room had always calmly showed the prettiest, the most dear elements of her life and her family's life, displayed just so.

These past seven hundred odd days though, her living room, doused with stately pools of light from homey floor lamps, suddenly, oddly, became littered with detail upon detail. Photos, for example, began to simply bob up. Barbara's nephew, Alex, beaming from his school picture from five years ago, stands cheek-by-jowl with Sophie's World War II Great Uncle Harold saluting in British-soldier crisp. He shadows Aunt Lettie and Uncle Myron looking as somber as their cloth coats, the fact of them mere photographs that had been tucked in wartime letters full of measure, letters that avoided hysteria even as the reason for it slammed down their doors. Until the letters came no more. Behind them are her parents' wedding photo in a beautiful pewter frame and another picture of them laughing, taken by their friend, Howie, on his aunt's farm in Wisconsin, its friendly silo in the background.

The photos made their way out of long-sealed boxes, from cardboard containers, from rubber-banded portfolios. Sophie became helpless against them. Her cousin David, proud before his almost-new 1953 Dodge; her mother's best friend Aunt Sarah, leaning intimately toward the camera from the arm of the chair in which her sour mother sits; crazy Hirsh, one of the few men she did not call uncle growing up, hamming it up in women's clothes at a costume party; high-school friends, all done up in black sweaters and pearls for graduation portraits; classmates from

Northwestern in every possible combination—pretending to make a diving catch for a softball, losing a debate with this particular speech, sleeping in the library over *The Importance of Being Earnest*. Edging in everywhere is Barbara: in a hand-tinted portrait taken at Our Lady of the Angels, where she'd taught fifth grade; Barbara, sun-bathed in bronze, leaning against a palm tree with a lei around her neck; Barbara, a little frizzy-haired girl in plaid jumper looking confused before the camera, her foot tucked behind her leg. The front room is crowded. Every horizontal surface is filled with framed and frozen people jockeying for the few thin inches they need to present themselves.

Sophie had been set adrift in the jetsam of her own life.

It wasn't only the photos. Seeping out of the same closets and basement and bottom drawers were, too, things—things that belonged to her mother and the few distant relatives who had made it to Chicago and things passed on from her parents' generations of friends who had no living children. Silver chafing dishes and porcelain egg coddlers with hand-painted columbine; a star-blossom crystal relish dish; demitasse, deep-red sherry glasses; a Waterford bowl with gold rim; silver fruit spoons; cake forks with cutting edges—the necessary glories of entertaining as it was done a generation before. What place did they have here? She wondered.

The house continued to generate wave after wave of goods. Out came acres of tapestry fabric, matelassé coverlets, doilies by the drove, birth certificates, warranties for appliances long-forgotten, maps from ancient vacations, a tiny spoon from Mexico City and an ashtray from the Wisconsin Dells, Irish linen and damask tablecloths. No amount of glaring or distress could make them recede. Flotsam settled on the dining-room table, on the kitchen table, the counters, the padded seats of all the chairs save one. The piles of stuff swelled from annoying to cumbersome to precarious. When she went to reach for something simple as a salt shaker, first the slide projector, then a neighborhood newspaper, then a half-dozen daily papers might tremble or totter or slide. What had been beautiful or precious and quietly stored took charge of the house. Her loss bobbed among them.

Without bearing, Sophie had coursed from room to stuffed room, drowning in goods, wondering at a place to light, at where she could place another thing that might force itself into her hands. Like a good librarian, she had an idea where nearly every item settled as it came out. Her mind catalogued them as they passed through her hands. The trouble was, they drifted somewhat. Sophie, whose mind was one with the Dewey decimal system, who admired the poetics of railroad timetables and was at peace with stress equations and architectural form, swam in a cancer of memorabilia. This almost-knowing where things were and not being able to reach them, along with this being unable to turn the tide, threatened her existence. Her look had become, more and more, the fish-eyed look of a person underwater.

Here's this wandering pile of an old lady who had taken it into her head to weed and pull and transplant, and mulch sense into the garden. It would be a start, she shrugged to herself.

In the meantime, she had Frankie, Stan's grandson, to keep her quiet company for a little bit.

By the time Stan got back, the boy had awakened and they'd been playing the three-year-old's version of War. When he could identify the numbers, he won.

"Sorry. Hope I wasn't gone too long. I had to stop down at the soup kitchen where I work. You know, I was on the highway and it seemed quicker to shoot down."

"I didn't know you do that. You still work at the Sparky's?" He managed a diner there at Six Corners, at Clark and Fullerton and Lincoln, for years.

"Oh, yeah. Sure. I just got involved with this other thing. It's a place to go to."

"That's nice, Stan. You weren't gone so long. This guy was sleepy. He just got up."

"Two," said Frankie.

"You win again," Sophie said.

"You know that lady?" Stan asked, motioning his head sideways to the outdoors.

"She was in my yard when I got home."

"I tried to talk to her—she's a little…" he made a corkscrew sign near his temple. "She gardens around. Some people from Stan's B&M know about her, St. Gen's, too. Used to live over on Altgeld."

"It would be nice to get the yard cleaned up."

"Well. She's Polish at least—"

"I asked her to come work. Who knows if she'll come back."

The doorbell rang. Sophie, about to leave for work again, made her way through the front room with Stan and the boy just behind.

"Excuse me, *Pani*," said the tall man who had rung. "My father lives next door…" He stopped when he saw Stan.

"Zbiszu," Stan said. "I'm sorry, Zosia. This is my boy, Stan Jr."

"Pa."

Frankie ran to him and jumped into his arms. "Papa."

"I had to go somewheres. I'd forgot about it," Stan said, "So the Skipper here came over for his nap. He's been having a good time, eh?" he winked at Frankie.

"Where'd you go, Pa?"

"Some errands," Stan started to say, but the boy started, too.

"Djia-Djia went by Blessed Mother," Frankie said, patting his father's hair.

"Oh, cripes, Pa," Zbiszu said, "you still doing that?"

He had told Sophie a bit about it. How he'd lost faith and hadn't been to church in a long time. Then some fellow he knew started seeing the Mother of Jesus at St. Adalbert's Catholic cemetery. There was quite a following, especially in summer when the weather was good. Stan hadn't seen her himself, but he said his rosary and he went every month.

"Yeah. It don't hurt nobody, Zbisz. I'm sorry I had to lose out on time with Skip, though," and he grabbed sweetly at the boy, who pretended to dodge.

"Hey, if it's how you want to waste your time, it don't worry me," Zbiszu said. The way he said it showed not worry, but contempt.

The three trundled out the front door, the young man inviting his father over for *pierogi*, Stan making his excuses. Family.

Sophie waved them off as she headed for her car.

Her parents, practically children themselves, left Poland in 1929 with their little Sophie, age three, before her memory had a chance to set in.

They lost nearly all their family in the old country during the war. "You must plan," her mother told her over and over as she grew up, Papa nodding behind her. "Then you can hold on to life." Sophie took the lesson, living her life consciously and without drama, inspired to nothing much.

In their time—maybe a little earlier than if they'd lived without suffering, without emigrating to a place where they knew only a few people, without learning a new language at gunpoint, as it were, without being shocked at the magnitude of what they'd escaped—her parents died. Just like that, her mother, from cancer and, four months later, her dad, from a stroke, they said. She saw it in his eyes. She wasn't going anywhere without him.

When they died, Alan, with whom Sophie had had a standing date every Friday evening for more than five years (neither of them ever having been motivated to change the comfort of that), spoke the magic words that made Sophie realize something had to change.

"Why don't we get married," he'd said more than asked. Dumbstruck, she didn't respond. "I know that's all you girls think about." She had never. "You don't need to look so surprised." She didn't know what she looked.

"That doesn't seem possible," she said.

"There's no reason not to. We're good for each other," he'd said.

"Shouldn't there be something else between us?"

"Whatsamatter you? We're not getting any younger, you know," he tried to laugh it off.

"I can't," she answered.

He stared down at the table. "Why?"

"I don't know."

"That's better," he'd said, looking her in the eye.

"No. I don't mean I don't know if we can. I mean I don't know why I can't."

"Maybe it's 'cause you're rigid," he said, smile fading into an edge in his voice.

Well, Sophie had thought to herself, he'll think what he wants to think, so be it. "Maybe," she said. She knew at that moment that he wasn't going to forgive her for turning down the offer of his life. There'd be no more nights spent at his house, no more dinners, no more talks.

It wasn't until a while later, when Sophie met Barbara, that she knew what had been missing. She passionately, surely, with no doubt, wanted to be with her. She didn't know what to do with that.

Yes. She was not in the habit of going against custom, especially her own. Yes. There was no one left to disappoint, no one looking over her shoulder with hopes for her. Maybe that's why she let herself get involved so far outside her expectation. Yes. Yes, she would marry her.

Sophie discovered she'd never been an indifferent person. Until that point in time, nothing had captured her interest. She had been quietly waiting. With Barbara in the picture, Sophie became vivid at work, vibrant with her acquaintances.

"Zosia," said a friend, one of the women she'd played cards and gone to movies with, complained over work and family life with, "is there a new man in your life?" Sophie looked down instead of toward Barbara. They teased her and cajoled her and she looked away and turned the attention to the bridge mix, how tasty the cashews were. As if a light turned on, they stopped. Or they might have to recognize something about their old friend that they could not. They calmed down and let it pass and invited the two of them to dinner, out to a movie. Just lady-friends going out.

She and Barbara were together, as a couple, for nine years before breast cancer put its tentacles on Barbara and took her.

A thousand layers.

After the death, Sophie's habit of indifference returned, underscored by a deep aloneness. She often felt it would have been better to have never participated in life. Drowning in loneliness was something she'd never noticed before.

Why was she thinking all this? She felt like someone had overturned a rock and stirred things. Prancing around was that large, dusty unkempt old lady.

CHAPTER THREE

Zak
Whose Child?

Across the city, a pale girl smoothed her long self onto her pint-sized foam mattress. She liked to lie out flat when she wanted to mull over things. From the next room, she heard the easy shuffle of the deck, the flick of cards being dealt among friends.

She had better come up with a plan pretty soon. He must could be looking for her now. Her mama had told her he was starting his pestering even back in spring. She shook herself loose of the thought of him as if she were cutting kudzu off a shed. No sense in letting him put a worry on her. It was her situation she better worry on. Her mind was going two-forty, but she let the hum of the next room lull her. She had a lot to sleep about.

In her first dream, she started off rushing out of control downhill on a cart that looked like it was going to blow apart any minute. Running from something, but fast, too fast, like a waterfall. At the bottom was a guy in a suit with a smarmy grin on his face and papers in his hands and she was, pure and simple, on a collision course. "Wake up, little pearl," she heard.

In a stuporous struggle, half asleep, quiet words burst out of the murmurs from the kitchen and startled her awake.

"What is that white girl Zak doing here?" a woman's voice asked. Zak's exhaustion was gone in a flash. She elbowed herself up so she could hear better.

"Living, same as you."

"Girl, you know what I mean."

"She got some trouble. I don't know what it is." Zak held her breath.

"Her people from around here?"

"Hell, no. She stay somewhere on the northside. She at Macy's school."

"Why don't she stay with somebody up there?"

"My guess is she don't have a place up there. She staying here, Renee." She used her friend's name like a period, a stop sign.

"I would call that school and find out what's going on," Renee said anyway.

Zak's heart stopped. Goddamn, don't let her. Please, I'm sorry, please, God, don't let her. Zak was at the edge of a crumbling cliff. Time slowed as she watched earth clods turn over, bouncing down. She waited there for years.

Finally, Suzee said, "Hmh. What'd they do to Marcus when I called?"

"Marcus different." Zak stretched into the quietness, a moment before the fall. "What she doing here?" She emphasized "here" as if Zak had landed on the moon.

"I been knowing the child, Renee. If she don't say, I don't need to know."

"She white. You understand?"

Zak heard a hum out of Suzee. "She is."

"They different. You understand?"

"Not yet. She's same as Macy. Fourteen."

"That's the age," Renee said. Shut up, Zak thought. Shut your big blathering hole. The age for what? She wondered. "You understand?"

"Renee." Suzee said it like a full sentence. "I understand."

"You should be scared."

"Scared to death, even she don't mean harm." Harm? Zak was a danger to Suzee? She didn't know that before. "Scared better not keep any one of us from doing. She must not have family worth going to. Do you understand?" Suzee emphasized that "you."

There was a sound of reserved agreement from Renee.

"She's not staying here for the room service," Suzee added.

They laughed kind of quiet. Zak listened hard.

"They bring trouble...you know that. Even a girl."

Suzee said nothing. Sweet Jesus, Zak thought.

"All right," Renee said. "You ain't got enough to do, you need to raise other people's children. I suppose you know what you going to do. I will stand next to you. Like my father used to say to me, I am your main boon coon. Raising other people's children, you don't have enough to do."

"Just in pieces. I can't stand to see some child go to waste," Suzee said.

"So long as she don't waste you," Renee said. "They kill people. JFK, the King , God rest him, and now this."

Zak held her breath. Suzee, she reached to some religious place, do not forsake me.

"You don't think she shot Bobby Kennedy, did she?"

"May as well. These people can't let a good thing be."

"Oh, Lord."

"You know what I'm saying."

"She got to have a place," Suzee said. "She staying here. You don't need to bother yourself. That girl going to be all right," Suzee said.

Suzee might liable to know when a kid was going to go bad. Linda Lee, Zak's own mother, was losing big time. She didn't mean to, she just wasn't good at getting by. Was it in the blood? But Suzee just said the opposite. Zak breathed out.

The night wasn't being kind to her. But she talked herself back into sleep, back into a hammock of illusion.

Now she was in disguise. She looked like herself to herself except she was in a bathing-suit outfit that looked like an animal skin, an outfit she would never in real life wear. She was carrying something weird, like an alien flower, and walked around the edge of a party, looking for someone, she didn't know who, someone important. Someone else there was out to protect her, too, she could feel it. One person in the room knew who she really was, knew, even, what she was doing there. That person was dangerous. She was scared awake. Again.

The low voices in the next room were gone. There was nothing but the sound of breath in the room. And again she tried to sleep, this time conjuring mental pictures of the future. Art School. Brilliant paintings with unbelievable colors. Delicate line drawings. They almost made her too excited, but her growing body was crusty and uncomfortable and it demanded rest.

As her eyes fluttered, she saw her mother, looking haunted as a graveyard. Zak started to get sad and wake herself, but Linda Lee, completely out of character, told her that she needn't to fuss, that she was without sin, that peace was within her grasp. Amazed as she would have been to hear that awake, in the dream it was perfect sense. Her mother talked that talk to her all the rest of the night.

Zak slept.

CHAPTER FOUR

Rose
The Dancing Bear

That very night, Rose made her way, a healthy walk west on Fullerton, past the grocery stores and hotdog stands, the Walgreen's and the fancy car showroom. St. Stan's Bishop and Martyr, all the way out at Central, is the place she stayed.

Rose bounced her bags down the steps to the doorway at the back of the parish hall. The old nun was waiting to take Rose's things inside and lock them up for the night. A while ago, she'd offered Rose the janitor's room, since the parish could no longer afford to keep the man on. But Rose slept outside at the top of the stairs, off to the side, nestled among the hosta, under the eaves. She had a light by which to read and when she wanted to, she turned the bulb to the left and she was alone with the night.

Rose liked sleeping in the dirt. Even tonight, when it smelled like rain. She was not about to be beholden to the wives of the Lord. Or the Lord himself for that matter. The stars were barely visible, their light diluted by the lampage of the city sky. The air was thick with heat. Between this surface heat and the cauldron of molten rock that made up the earth's core was sandwiched the cool ground and its long history with man. Its thin mantle provided food and beauty, shelter and the tomb. Even at this time of year it was cold to the bones. Rose had come to a discomfort with the interference of timber or carpet. The dank chill would spread into her knees and hips, would settle into her uterus. In the morning, inevitability would be in her. She felt every day begin as part of the continuum of sun-life-warmth and death-cold.

Rose made a bed with the sacks and raggedy cloths that were her blankets. She had had no time to read today, she thought with regret. But, too tired, she tucked herself in, and stared up at the night. It was nothing new, this feeling of falling up, unfathomably far. It was not the stars she wanted, but the between— the deep blue of a trumpet's note, the blue-black of summer's night mountains, the velvet of a heart at rest. To melt into that.

Before long, though, it was constellations that she saw. She'd learned them from her books and her father and the knowledge danced before her eyes. It was a trick of uncertainty that kept her naming stars. Maybe that was how they were ever named, she thought. Long ago, perhaps, the sky's ebony answered a depth in someone. A man. Rose pictured him. Quietly, studiously, he moved toward the restful intensity of the between. But just as he thought to touch that reality, it changed. An illusion, she knew. The black he sought became empty space, what looked real were the stars. Distracted, he named them. In contradiction to himself, responding to his own naming, he denied the true reality, the blackness. He might have touched paradise, nirvana.

She spotted them. The constellations her father had pointed out when she and Grace were girls: the Pleiades, the Archer, Ursas Minor and Major. The ones she never got to teach her little Grace.

She thought: we've thrown our nets into the pure eternity that lay all around. The catch is charts and graphs and constellations.

This was the way with her, too. Sure of herself in one moment. Then possibilities, sullen and sibilant, gathered at her feet. She became tangled in that-which-might. Hesitancy took the place of action. Finally lurching free, her mind's budding elegance, her delicacy, the mental seamless pirouette of Margot Fonteyn, collapsed upon itself. And her thoughts became the clownish plodding, the tumbling tango of a dancing bear.

It was a mercy to sleep.

With the convention coming, though, the cops were going way out of their way to be nasty. An hour later, she was poked awake.

"Hey, hippie."

Rose turned her face into a flashlight beam and felt the end of a nightstick some punk cop had jabbed into her shoulder. Jesus-Maria, now what?

Her eyes barely open, "Kissmyass," she said. One thing she spoke clearly were words that got people to back off.

"It's a old *busia,*" the young one said, laughing. "With a mouth on her."

"Oh, shit. That's Rose," the older cop said. "Let her alone." The youngster protested. The older cop gave him a slight shove. "Good night, *Pani.*"

"Good night, goddammit," she said. Jacinskis, she thought. It was only June and they were at least 65 blocks from the Lake, which is where Daley kept saying all hell would break loose. The most disruptive element on the northwest side, Rose mumbled inside, would be a random drunk Italian. That made her laugh. She was old. She was already crabby. She had work to do in the morning. Work to get a good garden to come back. Somebody was always aggravating her. JesusMaria, what the hell was the matter with people? "That gets my ass tired," she said to herself. She repeated the phrase to herself. She liked to get the tone right. Crudities, that's what she had to say to this smartass world. In her head, big ideas ran like a possessed hamster on a wheel for her amusement alone. The muddled ideas of a crazy old lady. In Polish, yet.

Grace. Two crazy ladies who had started as one. One gone. One left. One.

CHAPTER FIVE

Rose
Herself Revealed

The very next morning, after washing in the parish hall and bundling up her belongings, she was glad to get on her way to this house and to this work. It hadn't rained, her good luck.

The long walk on heated sidewalk, city traffic at her side on the four-lane road, didn't provide much to look at. She noticed the corner tavern at Kildare. The sign in the little bar window said "*Cerveza Fria*" instead of "*Zimne Piwo*" as it had for the last twenty years. When did that happen? The changes in the neighborhood were as thick as the humidity.

She moved to the side street north of Fullerton. As she passed these struggling yards, she would, just at the fence, tie up a beginning rambler here, pull a weed there. An old lady, Rose's own age, when she stopped to think, who doesn't seem at all shocked to see her touching her flowers, says, "Djien Dobry." She answers with a nod, says "*Pani*." It's all they need to say.

For Rose, a garden was a necessary part of life. As long as a garden existed, she literally had to have her hands in it. Here and there, just a touch. She could not live without it. Since she'd lost her own, necessity had made every garden hers.

Rose had worked her little plot of land behind her two-flat for more than twenty years—mulching, planting, composting.

Her displays were gorgeous, handsome, romantic or fragrant as the mood struck her at planning time. Anything she saw in a book, she could bring into her garden—a walk-through trellis, a picket fence with peaks and gullies like a mountain range along the top of it, benches made of slabs of oak under her arbors, rounds of maple to pave the paths—all with an eye to arranging beauty. She had divided and replanted, sometimes ripping out whole beds to redefine a space, to follow a hunch.

For all those years, she'd tended her garden with the same devotion she and Grace individually gave to her reading, to the education of herself, and later, to their discussions, as their father had taught them. Until tragedy struck.

Grace weakened. Whenever Rose wasn't at work, during Grace's ever more frequent naps, she wandered into the yard. Her hands automatically reached out to pinchprune an impatiens, to slap at a weed. If string was at hand, she might secure a vine to a trellis. As Grace's mind began to trail in the dust, Rose began to lose the big picture. The delicacy of the mallow escaped her. The beauty of the larkspur escaped her. Her own logic escaped her. There came to be little peace in the flowers, in the hearty vegetable garden.

The beginnings of grief.

Sophie was already gone to work when Rose got to the house on Wrightwood. There was a note tucked under the hoe lying in front of the back door. "Here is the key. Come inside. I will check in later." What the hell was the matter with that woman? Leave a key right here? Didn't she know people are dangerous? And even worse, mean? I could be one of them, she thought with no malice toward herself. This Zosia was not so smart in that department. Rose hid the key. Far, far from the door.

She was not going in to somebody's house and sit on her fat ass, that was for sure.

She got to work.

Her mind could not wrap around all the mess, but a gardener's habits can often save her. Her eyes saw a lumpy area, full of weeds. Her mind's eye saw the possibility of a patio underneath. An hour later, she had removed enough to spot the first piece of flagstone. Aaah! Pure delight. This knowing and not-knowing.

While she'd had the tender job of caring for her sister, Rose had turned to her world of books, where she could slip into a familiar solitude. When her little Grace, her daughter, her future, had died, she couldn't touch a book. She couldn't eat or breathe. Nothing, nothing could she do then. When sister Grace was ill, books were her shield. At first, she read medical books, books about the terminal illness. And then, treatises on the soul—seeking a logic, a philosophy. All she read was elusive and intellectual, mute in the language of her desolate heart. Finally, when the boredom of fact and logic had beaten her down, she turned to the fleeting order of a novel. But. Too sensible, too planned, that. She doused herself in truth, in poetry. That, also, failed her. She finally washed herself in the stark truth of mathematics. There, she could be lost.

With books to accompany her, at least, she'd been able to hold on to her sanity while her sister sank.

It was an hour until lunchtime. She had to think about lunch, about finding a bathroom. Lunch. She could head over to St. Stan's Kostka, two bus rides, but there was the matter of needing a john pretty soon. She could go get a hot dog and fries (59

cents) on Cicero—five, six blocks walk. Two birds with one
stone. Yet she needed to get a bathroom quick. You need to set
aside a lot of time when you don't have.

Or.

Rose pulled back a wall of bramble, the elderly rose bush at
the corner of the yard opposite the door, where Sophie's key
swung softly from a rusty nail.

As she approached the door, she began to tremble. It was a long
time since she had access to a real house without a guard dog,
even if it was an unimposing nun. This little key, so heavy. Still,
she felt something familiar as she stood on the top stair. Even
from outside, she smelled the Eight O'Clock coffee.

The lock turned. The door gave way.

When she stumbled out of the bathroom and into the kitchen,
she saw the large note tucked under the coffee maker: "Prosz´
bardzo." Help Yourself. No one said that to her. Beside it were
a couple slices of pumpernickel bread, a ceramic butter dish and
knife, some cheese in SaranWrap.

The cozy kitchen hummed. A huge cliff of fear towered over it.

The countertop around the coffee percolator had been cleared,
and next to it were a little pitcher with half-and-half in a bowl
of nearly melted ice and its matching double-eared bowl toppled
full of sugar cubes, silver pincers balanced through one handle.
So, she'd found them.

Rose poured herself a cup of the burned coffee, made her way
through the kitchen, past sleeping-cat salt-and-pepper shakers,
German porcelains of large-headed children dressed in old-time
clothes, a unicorn music box. She picked it up as if it were a newborn, wound it, and heard a pretty little song. It said "Soon It's
Gonna Rain—The Fantasticks" on the label. The steaming cup
warmed her work-swollen fingers.

Among the jostling photos in the living room were some of a

smiling Sophie with a broad-grinned woman. Like the one in the kitchen. Barbara, Rose was sure. On the end table next to the slip-covered couch was a larger photo, a studio portrait, from Sears, maybe. The woman looked about 35, with light brown hair and green eyes, unless that was a trick of the photographer. This was Sophie's gardener. She was gone from the earth. She was gone. Grace was gone. Little Grace was gone. Her little girl, her own. Her self died twice. Rose struggled every day. She could not fathom it.

Rose was helping the lady's garden come back. That much she could do. She lifted her cup slightly to toast the portrait.

By now, a deep cold was at her center. She shivered. She was pushed back to the kitchen, where she took a slice of bread and a hunk of cheese. Hurrying to the back door, she nearly tripped, but caught herself in time. She felt more than heard the screen door tap closed behind her. She was outside again, her heart making a racket.

Rose lowered her bulk onto the stair third from bottom. A bite of bread, a sip of coffee. Her hands lost a bit of their tremble. The key was still in her right hand, with the cup. She tore at the bread, the chunk of cheese. She laid the key on the stair. It was dark green. The key was silver.

She remembered one day at Tillie and John's storeroom, their little store on Elston Avenue. Tillie was one of her oldest friends. She had married John because of course she would marry, and he was a good man. Their kids were still some in elementary school, the oldest in high school then. This was back in the early days after she'd left her place. They could see I was on the fritz, she thought. I had gone round the bend. They must have been on the near side themselves at times. If she got there before they closed, she could stay. Though I didn't like to get caught inside in the spring or summer, even then, she said to herself, and I never would take their key. Still, sometimes, when it was cold and she'd been careless about time, she would go around back in the dark, bitter night and try the alley door. Of course, it would be open. They took chances for her. They knew her in some way.

She remembered that night how she'd watched for hours, a leftover summer fly ramming against the glass pane of a slightly ajar window. So intent on getting out, it couldn't stop battering its head against the glass, couldn't fly two inches out of its way to see that the window was open. Tears came to her eyes. Angry, she pushed the butt of her hands against them.

She finished her lunch and climbed back up the few stairs to lock the door. Then back across the yard. A thorn ripped her as the old rose sprung to cover the key.

She was exhausted. The yard was nearly living. On life support.

Rose began again clearing the paths, adding to the piles of discard. Not strong enough to move them at once, she figured to take them later in bits out to the alley, next to the garage. The day had cooled down. The smell before rain was in the air. She'd have to call it a day soon.

All of a sudden, Zosia was standing in the back door looking out. "*Dobry wieczor,*" she said.

"*Czesc.*"

"How did things go today?"

"*Dobre,*" she said. Then she brightened, throwing in a phrase she'd heard. "Comme ci, comme ça."

Sophie said to come in. Rose came through the door for the second time this day.

She was uncomfortable about the key, about having come in when no one was home. "What's wrong with you?" she said in Polish.

Zosia looked surprised. "*Co?*"

Rose continued in Polish. "I hid that key far away. You just left it where any body can come by and break in your house?"

"Technically, they wouldn't be breaking in if they had a key. I didn't think anyone would come looking except maybe you."

"See? Are you nuts? I put that key across the yard, behind that overgrown rose at the garage. It's on a nail there, see?" She made Sophie acknowledge the plant. "I'll go get it. I was afraid someone could come and go in when my back was turned."

"You think it's safe there?"

"Ya. That's why I put it there." Rose realized that everything she said came out flat and mean. Well, that was okay with her.

"Let's leave it then. It's good to hide a spare in case you want to come in. Or I could lose my key."

"It's stupid to leave it for me, too. You don't know me."

"I know I don't have anything to steal that I'd care about, really. Sometimes," she said, looking around at the piles, "I think you'd be doing me a favor."

Rose was insulted. She would never steal anything. Why would she, everything she had, she had in her bags. "Go to..." she started. Then she realized that it might be a joke, a pale joke. She shut her mouth, which was nearly a smile for her.

Sophie gestured her into the kitchen. "Want to split a Schlitz?" she said.

"Sure." And they sat, dipping their stick pretzels in the little pot of mustard Sophie put between them.

"Why don't you stay for dinner?" Sophie said. "Tom, my coworker, caught this Coho at the lake. It's too big, even if I give some to the neighbor. I hate to freeze it. It's fresh caught, that's what's so great about it."

Her immediate reaction was to say no to anything nice people offered. But she wanted something and this might work out just right.

"I like to take a bath," she told Sophie.

"So, you'll stay for dinner?"

She could not remember when she last had a long soak. She hadn't completely unclothed her body in much more than this little month. There was a craftiness to washing parts of your body in stores in public toilets where the sinks are far from the stalls. You had to keep an eye for a manager, underpaid and crabby, who would grab you while you were rinsing out a washrag. "Oh no, you don't," they would say, as if they'd caught you with a purse full of jewels and they were Tiffany's.

A bathroom to herself. A frightening luxury.

"Of course. Maybe."

"Perfect. There are towels..."

"I seen them," Rose returned in English. "They're all over the place."

Sophie took a breath in. "Yes. Help yourself to a couple. Just leave them on the floor when you're finished. In the meantime, I'll cook up a fish."

The room steamed with hot water and the tub half-filled before Rose began to peel off her final layers of clothes. She'd taken the black polyester pants from under her dress while she worked in the sweet sun that little while in the afternoon. Still she had on three pairs of underwear, a large sleeveless blouse she used as an undershirt and a cap-sleeved dress on top. She stuffed them into her bags.

She let herself down in the water by inches. Her skin, not used to immersion, crackled with pain as if a low electric charge were spreading over the hundreds of thousands of follicles. She stopped short of letting her head slip under, waiting for her skin's riot to subside. Finally, the back of the head lowered, the ears filled with water, the scalp prickled, itched, set her hairs dancing and she lay, suspended, only her nose and her enormous belly and breasts breaking the quiet surface. This was not the awake sleep of a usual night, not the dead sleep of exhaustion, not the fitful sleep of the terrorized doorway. It was awake comfort.

Her mind, too, was at peculiar rest. Rose drifted through plaster, the lath, the roof, to feel clouds almost within reach, split above her. She hated her substance, which kept her from going there, kept her from leaving this, going where Grace was. Little Grace,too. Oh, she moaned. She had started to think about her daughter more and more. Could she just leave here?

Her lids closed, she was propelled into that space. Coming toward her was a young girl, not anyone Rose could identify, but she was as familiar as her own hands. She was carrying a flower stalk. Gently centered in its bowed head was a single blue eye, its botany forgotten in a heroic effort at biology.

"What does it mean?" Rose whispered in perfect Polish.

The girl looked at her with full attention, like a bird surprised by a sound new to the world. "It can be your third eye, and mean everything to you." She laughed. "Or nothing—an oddity, if you prefer." She floated toward a door with no lock, no key, no handle. It opened by the suggestion of her breath. Rose moved toward the doorway, but could see through everything, the walls, the door. Was it the back of her sister's head? She stretched her neck for a look. The head turned slightly with a terrible laugh and Rose saw that this was not Grace. This was a hideous caricature of a woman, if, indeed, it was a woman. For it bore a large, overbroad face and the hint of a shadow of a beard, but its lips were slashed with a violent red and when it laughed, they heaved back over large horse teeth. Danger. There was danger here.

The slight youth, her eye flower raised delicately, stood at the doorway, looked back to Rose, looked to the hideous harlot who would have impersonated Grace. The girl raised an eyebrow and smiled with a corner of her mouth, as if mocking. Yet her eyes were innocent. That innocence was all the world Rose needed to live in. Danger like danger, Rose thought. What was danger, after all? Wasn't it dangerous to open your eyes every morning?

While Rose's mind had floated for only corporeal minutes, her habit of fear took hold of her body. She shot up like a whale. Where were her clothes? Oh, yes, in the bag. Was someone coming in? No, she saw, the door was locked. The door was locked. The goddamn door was locked. How should she believe she was sitting in a locked room in a tub full of steaming water?

She felt like she had a hangover, though that little beer couldn't have done that. She'd had a stroke, maybe. Something, something had scared her, gripped her heart and her head. She felt what little control she had slip from her. Frightened, wary, like a nervous robber with a loaded gun.

Rose had no time for such a luxury, to dwell on things. Tasks were what she knew, what grounded her. She went about checking her swollen ankles, her cracked skin, her too-long toenails. The great toenails were blackened from God knows what. Maybe she had diabetes. Maybe not, too. The minutia of her body was not interesting to her. She knew it in a familiar way, from use, but she was not on intimate terms with it. The water grayed as she washed. She lathered and rinsed and wiped every hair and inch of skin. As she let the water drain out of the tub, she showered with a rubber sprayer she stuck on to the nozzle of the tub. Good idea, that.

She was clean.

Now, as she stepped from the tub, she saw a full-length mirror attached to the back of the door. It was clouded with the moist heat of the room. Her hand reached out to it, smeared a clearing. Her hand still suspended, she saw her fingers, etched with tiny cuts, webbed with deep dirt, the nails split, a thin line of soil beneath them even now. She had not seen her body in its entirety for many years. She was afraid to wipe away the veil that kept her from herself presented. In a small circle in the glass, she saw wet hair flopping like smelt around her enormous face, her flesh like putty below her eyes. She turned slightly and saw jowls lining the rim of her jaw, more than one chin.

"Enough," she said out loud and turned her back on the vision.

There was a polite knock at the door. "Did you find everything you need?" Sophie asked. "Is there anything you'd like to launder?"

"I have what I want," Rose whispered back in harsh Polish. "I'll talk to you when I'm through."

She found some clothes that were not bad. They must have been washed out recently. Her nose, insulted over the years, had lost sensitivity.

The bath had made her relaxed and drowsy. She was weak with dreams and fear. She staggered out of the room carefully. Sophie sat in a crisply tidy kitchen. Different than only this afternoon.

"You look pale. Heatstroke? Are you sick?"

Sick? Or crazy. All the years of acting as if she had nothing to do with this world might have finally made it true. Rose felt too tired to keep one foot out the door.

"*Niecz*. I'll eat with you," she said. Sophie looked surprised, but bustled to get dinner on the table.

The two of them sat down to a meal of fresh Coho salmon.

The table was clear. There were cloth napkins and a new vase of fresh zinnias. A cross-stitched tablecloth lay diagonally across the square oak table with its merry little colors along the edges. A bowl of new potatoes and one of fresh green beans steamed. With a gesture from Zosia, Rose cut the bread, laying her napkin on her chest, tucking the loaf of rye against it, and sawing with the knife's blade turned toward herself, until it was a breath from her breast. She placed four slices of homely rye on a little blue bread plate. Eating at restaurants and at soup kitchens and back doors had made Rose accustomed to food that came on one plate. She helped herself carefully to some of everything. She could not remember to make dinner conversation. The sound of the forks touching against the plates was their dinner music.

"You okay?" Sophie asked while clearing the dishes.

"I'm okay," she said in English. She realized she didn't have to and went on in Polish, "I think I was in the sun too long."

Sophie sat down across from her, pouring rose-garlanded cups full of good, new coffee. Rose was not able to focus on so direct a face.

"It's getting some order," Rose said, remembering the garden. Polish was a comfort. When she tried to speak English at any length, her muscles became sore, her jaw began to hurt as her mouth wrapped around words she found unpronounceable. Her brain had learned so much in written English, but she couldn't say it out loud. She thought in English, because she had so over-educated herself in that language all these years, but she was pretty sure her pronunciation was mangled. Her "th" came out like a "t," and she knew it was because her tongue had learned Polish first: there was no "th" in Polish. It made her sound dumb, along with the wrong stress on words she knew perfectly well on paper. "You know there are some unusual perennials out there. And there was a pond."

"Oh, yes. Barbara loved her pond. Her koi were beautiful. The whole yard, really, was striking and original. She won prizes for her dahlias." She spoke this almost sacramentally, as though she were whispering her confession to a priest. "She was the steward of this garden, that's what she said."

"And then what happened?"

"She died. She just died and I didn't know what to do in a yard."

"She died?" Rose looked as though a sword cut through her.

"I tried that first year. The vegetables went brown. And by the next year, I didn't care to bother with the flowers either. Things just grew. I haven't looked out there. I just could not."

"She was your sister?"

"No, no. She was my friend."

"Oh." Rose looked sick. She stood up and held to the back of the chair to steady her mass. She could not let there be talk about sisters or about death. She would be sick with the grief. Rose appeared to float in spite of her bulk. "I got to go," she said.

"We don't have to talk about Barbara," Sophie said.

"I got to go," Rose said, getting her substantial self upright.

To hell with this, she thought. To hell with it.

CHAPTER SIX

Sophie
Help Arrives

That was the last Sophie was going to see of Rose. The old lady waddled off like an elephant with canvas shopping bags to its graveyard. Didn't look back.

"We don't have to talk about Barbara," Sophie had said, with the familiar sinking feeling. No one. But Rose said nothing. She gathered her things and walked out. No one to talk to about her. Not family. Not anyone.

Only two days after she'd watched her lover take her last breath, Sophie had been back at work.

"Hey, Sophie," said a coworker. "Took a couple days off, eh?"

"Yes," Sophie answered with the quiet that shudders from a numb heart. And then, in a moment of near intimacy with herself, she said it, and not much of it at that: "My friend died."

"Oh. That's too bad," he said, shying away as though death might be catching. "Was she sick?" he added, clearly not interested, but stuck in the courtesy of the conversation.

Sophie could taste the antiseptic smell of the medicines, the sweet rotting of the last weeks. "Yes," she said.

He nodded.

"She was my roommate," Sophie added. My love, my life, the reason I took a breath of air. The thrill of thinking it made it exquisitely more painful.

"Oh," he nodded, like a spring-headed papier-mâché donkey in the rear window of a car.

And they both turned to their work with relief. She didn't say it. He didn't have to hear it. Chicago was chock full of nice people who understood. As long as things weren't made clear.

Nothing to worry over. She was at a loss speaking words like "lover" or "partner" or "mate." And Barbara would have been outraged at the thought of them. They were simply two women who loved each other, she would put it when they put it at all. Perhaps they were hard-headed and denying. But in gentler moments, Sophie thought that they were simply modest, not in a sexual way, but afraid to speak it out loud and break the spell. Afraid. They never talked about the sex between themselves. But isn't that what other people were celebrating when they got together, when they married? That they'd found a partner, that they'd formed a sexual union with Someone Special? It was. Only after Barbara was gone did Sophie realize she'd wanted to tell everyone: "Look, I've found my happiness. Be glad for me. Here is my girl, my dear, my heart." Unspoken, outrageous and secret: "A great lay." That made her blush and laugh. It wasn't even her language.

Sophie's loss remained private, as their life together had been. She was too responsible to grieve in an unseemly way. Her black humor about it was secret, too. Barbara wouldn't have thought it was funny. So now, with even a mention of her beloved, she'd scared the old lady away. "*Merde*," she thought, because it sounded so much less vulgar in French.

For the next few weeks, she went to work, came home, saw her lady friends. Some days there was evidence that Rose had been there. Most not. A couple times, she saw her as she was leaving and they'd exchanged a few words.

Then, one day, she pulled up and there was Rose, in all her glory. And a big white cast on one foot.

"*Dobry wieczor,*" Sophie said. Rose nodded. "What happened?"

Rose made a noise, a cross between a "p" and "ach." "The toe got infected and then the bone. They put me on antibiotics. This is to protect the foot."

"Is it serious, then?"

"I don't think so. It hurts. I'm on the verge of diabetes. That's not good. So they watch it."

"Come on inside. Have some iced tea with me, eh, *pani*?"

Rose nodded. She began to tidy up her garden rakes and hand trowels.

"Leave it, Rose. It's hot as hell out here."

Rose glared at her. "It's important to put tools away," she said.

Sophie wondered again what she was getting into here. She rolled her inside eyes. A bit touch and go. "Come in when you're ready, then. I'm going to put the air conditioner on."

"How did things go in the yard today?" she asked after Rose got herself into the kitchen.

"It's getting there," Rose said.

"Maybe I can bring someone in to help with the heavy work, with your foot and all."

Rose furrowed her brow, but then, perhaps reality set in, and she agreed it might be okay. "If I come back."

Right. Hang loose, Sophie heard the phrase from the TV. Why was she doing this? "Good. I'll look around. I don't know who, but I can find somebody. The kids are out of school now." She poured their glasses full, offered a plate of cookies. Change the subject quick. "Tell me a little bit about yourself, your life."

"Life like life," Rose answered, in English, looking away.

"Come on, Rusia," Sophie said in Polish. "You said you were from around Haczów. Tiny. Southern 'Little Poland,' they call it." She caught Rose's sharp look. "I looked it up. I don't remember Poland. Tell me something."

"It's funny, something I could tell you," Rose said back in her native tongue. "But it's stupid."

"Don't be silly."

"It's really bad, how ignorant we were. Not that we didn't read, anything we could read, we did—theory and art and science. Papa would trade anything for books. It was the everyday world I knew nothing about. I mean, the farm, yeah, but the world? Nothing. You know, when you said you were a Jew, I thought, well what is she talking about, she's Polish? I never knew a Jew in my life. There or here."

It was interesting, how formal Rose's Polish was. Sophie realized suddenly—of course, it's not formal, it's old-fashioned. She spoke a Polish from 1913, maybe to 1915. She brought it with her and, along with the other immigrants, the Polish part of their language was frozen at best, deteriorated at worst. Only the English side grew. Well, it wasn't so different from her friends, who learned and read in college and their knowledge just stayed at that level—nothing much new except in their jobs. "You lived in the country. Different worlds, maybe," Sophie said. "Your parents might have known some towns that were Jewish."

"*Tak*. But do you want me to tell you a story?"

Zosia nodded. "I'm going to throw something together for a little dinner while we talk. Do you mind?"

"No. I don't mind to tell you, I'm pooped."

Sophie laughed. It was funny to hear Rose talk in so many ways, sometimes stiff and formal and sometimes colloquially, English slapped into the middle of the Polish. "Go ahead with your story."

"The year before I came to America, 1912 it was, my father had made a speech to the neighbors—farmers, too, like he was. It was against a priest, who was working with Germans, the ones who started off forbidding us to build houses on our own land. The Church was the center of Poland, you know, surreptitious, working against the *Kulturkampf* of the German Empire. Hell, my ship came from Hamburg, the Germans were like our bad uncle. In public meetings, the people would talk by drawings because we were not allowed to speak Polish and some of them, of course, could not learn German."

Sophie made a sound to indicate her surprise. "I didn't know that."

"Yes. Yes. They tried to take away our culture. They knew that would break us. Our church, before this bad priest, used to hold secret classes to teach Polish to the little ones. My father kept a grammar book hidden in a vase on the mantel. We were not allowed to tell anyone."

"Unbelievable."

"Believe it. So, this bad priest tried to add a moral burden to us, poor people scraping existence from dust, that under yoke of sin we must provide shelter and food for the Germans studying 'agricultural production' in our region. But my father spoke against this priest, because, he said. 'He is not the Church. He is wrong.'"

"Your father was a man of courage," Sophie said.

"Maybe," Rose said. "Or bound to the truth or beyond caring. Our harvest was found wanting, of course, in retaliation, so no pay. They took it, but no pay. My father explained: 'We might have hunger all winter, but right is right, no matter who tries to fool you.'"

"Our neighbors, can you believe it, they came and left rye, potatoes, even butter and milk, beer even. They were generous toward him."

Rose slipped in and out of Polish with no resentment, just landing where the words were. Sophie knew from herself that people who live alone are in the habit of keeping everything inside. When they finally talk to someone, they might talk a blue streak. She was happy to be the ear for this.

"After I left, after they sent me away from everything so I could start a new life for us in America, the Germans, with the help of Poles like that goddamned priest, passed an expropriation law that made Polish peasants give our lands to the Germans. My parents lost their land to those bastards."

In English, again: "We already lived through the Russians, who were no kinder. Just they were more to the north, we got the Russian dregs by us."

Sophie nodded as she placed a couple grilled cheese sandwiches with pickles on the table. A sweating 40-ounce bottle of Meister Bräu was in the middle, two pilsner glasses fresh from the freezer, next to it.

"The Church was our leader. Not the priests, who made devil's deals like politicians, but the Church. Here's the funny thing, our parents taught us that when we were asked what nationality we were, we should say 'Catholic.'"

Sophie smiled at that. Rose did not.

"And here is the part that will show you how ignorant I am. I thought that everyone in Poland is Catholic."

Sophie looked about to say something but Rose shushed her.

"In spite of Auschwitz, which I thought all my life, even since the war, was a place taken over by Germans to bring Jews from Germany, in spite of whatever is known in the world today, it never occurred to me, until the day I met you, that you could be Polish and a Jew. Period."

Sophie didn't know what to say. Then she said: "I've always been both."

"Yes, I see that," Rose said. "I'm telling you how stupid I am."

"You didn't know about the Holocaust?"

"Sure, I knew of it. Who didn't know? Felt terrible about it. But knew about it in Poland? No, nothing."

Sophie was silent.

"I don't like history," Rose said, embarrassed. "Then a couple weeks ago I brought a book from the library about Poland during the war. About the camps. I started to read." She stopped, finished her glass of beer. "Zosia, the Poles were terrible. If I were a Jew, I would hate the Poles."

"We were Poles, too. I'd be hating my self."

"Terrible. My people."

"My people, too. Not you."

"Not your people, they were Jews. But for all I know, my family."

"I can't imagine."

"I can't imagine it, but could anyone imagine her family brutal? Someone's father is a rapist, someone's mother turned in her neighbor and stole the silverware, the cloth from the table. Someone moved into the Jews' apartments and when the war was over wouldn't give them back. My parents had to move from the farm to the poorest part of Warsaw—not even our Krakow, but north to Warsaw. They were kicked like shit off German shoes. Where they lived couldn't have been so far from the Warsaw ghetto. Did they help anyone? Did they harm anyone? In the filthy dark, did they hear the terrible sounds of *Krystallnacht*? Who knows?"

Sophie waited long minutes before answering. Rose looked out the darkening window and Sophie looked there, too, where she saw only her own reflection.

"I'm not about to hold you responsible for people you haven't seen in fifty years," Sophie said. "Who are dead."

Rose made a noise, a puff, as if to dismiss Sophie's excusing them. As though she wasn't sure she could.

"Do you hate Jews?"

"Of course not," Rose said in a huff, "I don't even know any."

Sophie laughed. "Yes, you do."

"Me? I hate you?" Rose said. "Of course not. But you hate me? That makes sense."

"No, *Pani*. I do not bear a secret grudge."

"I'm a stupid old lady. I didn't know about Jews in Poland. I can't even keep a house."

A bridge, delicate as a silkworm's new thread.

"You do wonders with a yard," Sophie said.

Rose yawned. "It does wonders to me," Rose said. "I better get some sleep."

"I'm tired, too," Sophie said. "Stay in the back bedroom. It's a little musty, but we can air it."

"No. I am not able to sleep in your house."

Sophie looked hurt. "Rose. Why not?"

"It's a casket. A small room, a tiny bed."

"You can have my room, then. It's much bigger, with a full four-poster bed. I don't mind sleeping in the other room."

"No," Rose exploded. "It doesn't matter how big the bed is, or the room. It's a box. I like to sleep in the deep dark. I sleep outside, under the sky."

"What is that about? You don't have a house?"

Pugilistic English surfaced again. "I don't want to go into that shit now. I quit all that life one day and thought it would do me the favor back. But here I am, you see?"

"It's far to go, all the way, what, to Central Avenue? Just to come back…"

"Maybe. Maybe I come back."

"Well, tomorrow you mean to, didn't you say? Such a long walk tonight. Or I can drive you there. But we're both tired. You can stay here, too."

Rose looked suddenly proud. "I have my own things, my blankets, my clothes—all with me." She seemed to be arguing with
herself. "I am independent." Rose stood up.

"You want to see the room?"

Rose gave her a thunderous look.

"Let me drive you." She wondered whether the old girl could
make it back tomorrow.

"Okay."

Sophie dropped her off on Lorel, near Hanson Park. She didn't
have the energy to argue with her. Rose was a far-past-grown
woman and daily, Sophie realized that she was of sound mind. Her
spirit had been sandblasted, but there was nothing wrong with
her mentally. A very unprofessional opinion, but there you go.

The next morning, Sophie left the coffee brewing and a couple bagels and cream cheese out; who knew if Rose would even
look at them. She thought twice, and decided that a note would
be okay. "Have fun, Rose."

She headed off to the Rogers Park library, where she'd worked
for a good few years. They had been hinting that she could take
an administrative job, which would put her out of public contact.
She was trying to decide how she felt about it. The drive along
Lake Shore Drive was a pleasure, with the sun slapping the Lake.
It was a good place to get some distance on a turn of events. So,
she thought about Rose, too. She liked the old woman. Maybe
she didn't have enough trouble in her life since Barbara was gone.

She opened the door to find that Virg had got there earlier still.
And "their girl" was there. She'd noticed her for several months,
even before school had let out for the year. The skinny girl sat
quietly every day, read the newspaper, went outside and smoked
(far too young for that), came back in and bulldozed through a

novel. Lately, she'd discovered Shakespeare and was devouring his work piecemeal. Sophie knew because the librarians picked up the books throughout the day from where they lay. People wanted to put them back, but there were signs everywhere begging them not to or they'd be here all night correcting mistakes. The child must have a reason to hang around, day after day. She looked bored at times. Sophie had seen quite a few people go through this phase of life. It's not as if she were causing a disturbance or damaging anything, she was just reading, waiting for her life to happen. None of her beeswax.

While she was in the back doing some paperwork, Sophie saw a bit of something through the one-way window that made her change her mind.

A lady had left her personal stuff on a chair while she wandered off to the stacks. The girl, who had been sitting with a big volume of the Complete Works got up, apparently to stretch her legs. She stretched them right over to the lady's purse, swooped her hand down and came up with something worth putting in her pocket.

"Excuse me, miss," Sophie approached her a few minutes later.

The girl looked up to Sophie's face, and centered on her dark-on-dark eyes, almost as if they were one color entire. She looked innocent as a newborn.

"Yes, ma'am?"

"Can we talk for a minute, if I'm not disturbing you?" The girl was leaning over the newspaper at the moment. "LBJ Crime Law," the headline ran. A gun bill is all they were talking about since RFK was shot. And MLK and JFK and just everybody Sophie cared about in politics. Not a word lately about the convention and the fact that Chicago was going to be torn apart by hoodlums.

"I like to keep up on the news." The kid folded up her paper. "You never know." She laid it on the chair. "Okay. Shoot," Zak said. Sophie lowered her brow a bit. There was no one else around.

"I noticed that you spend a lot of time here during the day."

"Yeah," said the girl, one eyebrow lowering, her mouth remaining a bit open. "It's cool in here."

A little tough, that could be good. "Are you new in town?"

"Yes, ma'am," she said.

Laconic. That could be good, too. "So that explains why you haven't been in school these last few months. Your parents didn't want you to start in a new place at the end of the school year? And now the year is done." Sophie was relieved at her analysis. This needed to make sense and she was not beyond helping it do so. "My name is Sophie."

"Pleased to meet you, ma'am. I'm Zak," Zak said, putting her hand out. Sophie was surprised by the gesture, but took the girl's hand.

"So, Zak." What a strange name. "Are you interested in a bit of a job?"

The girl sat up a little.

"It seems that you might need some money." No hint of nerves after what Sophie had just seen. A cool customer. Sophie waited for a response. When none came, she went on. "I have a yard being cleaned out by a lady friend who can use some help. She's older. It's not difficult work, but it's too much for her." She stopped speaking and looked for long seconds over to where the lady's purse still was. Zak did, too. "That way you could earn some money." She emphasized "earn." "Today, if you want."

Zak stood up and walked over to the purse. The lady had returned, but was just at the moment over at the desk, talking to the other librarian. Zak fished in her pocket and put something into the purse. Or at least it looked like she did.

"You would help her. Carry vegetation to the alley, anything else she needs. We can call your mother and let her talk to me if you'd like."

Zak slapped on a smile. "Well, ma'am, my mother won't be anywheres you might reach her," she said, her child's Southern drawl crawling forth. "But I'll be pleased to come with you, if I might could make some money working."

"Great," Sophie said, glad to wait for lunch. She was worried about how Rose would take the girl, yes. Still.

There wasn't much conversation on the way over. Sophie wondered if she might be one of the hippies or Yippies that Hizzoner, the mayor, had started warning the citizens about. She looked like she could be.

"Do you know anyone coming here for the convention?" Sophie asked. Not that Rose would care, but the kid had just behaved like a hoodlum.

"It's for the Democrats, right, ma'am?" Zak said.

Sophie assented. The child wasn't near old enough to vote, what was she thinking? Her only relationship to kids had been to help them find what they needed. None of the girl's clothes went together: blue jeans, the bottom of them frayed, a shirt that looked like it came from some other country with a cheap cotton suede-look vest over it.

"Are you against the war?"

"I never thought about it until lately." Zak was blank, as if she were talking about Mars. "The *Sun-Times* seems to be printing some stories where things don't sound so great." She was just making conversation. "How about you?"

Sophie had no idea. She didn't expect the child to ask back. World War II was necessary to stop expansionism, an international hysteria. How much of that mess was really about being Jewish? As soon as the war was old enough, in the past enough so people could analyze, research, do anything but live it, Sophie had read books about the Holocaust. They themselves hardly qualified as Jews, her parents had shrugged. But her aunts and uncles there had disappeared. No cousins, no grandparents, none of them left. They were not a religious family, her parents said. They said this with such innocent perplexity, so often, that she eventually had to stop believing it. How "religious" were the ones left behind? How Jewish might they have been in a different world? A world not forged by the white heat of Nazi Germany? Even if you ran an ocean away.

Even though they were not so Jewish, "Learn it," her parents said. "You should know, in case it ever happens again." As if it were a snowstorm that would be forecast and she could bundle up against it.

The Holocaust books reassured Sophie that she could not affect her universe, that the indifference that had been taught to her, that been woven through the meeting of her days, was not a choice but the only action available to her.

The evil picked Jews that time. Someone, somewhere, will pick them again in a terrible tradition. Time-honored, historical.

She'd managed to ignore Korea altogether.

And this. She didn't know why we were in Vietnam, why all the dying while the young men's graduation pictures hung fresh in their hallways. She would say, if anybody but a child asked her and not unless, that all war was about greed, power, and about the rot people carry in a righteous cloak and put on others, not about Jews or Communists or unstable leaders.

"I guess I don't understand it," Sophie said in full honesty. She'd just given herself a headache. "That's an unusual name. Zak."

"My mother picked it," Zak said, as if she was the first child in history for whom that was the case. "It's short for Zakaria, which is spelled with a "k" and without a 'h.'"

"An 'h,'" Sophie corrected. It was a habit of working with kids.

Zak smiled at her, which disarmed her. She had planned on giving her a mini-lecture about stealing, but the girl had returned the money and there was no opening and her head hurt. She fell silent for the last few blocks.

When they pulled up, Sophie left the girl at the car having a cigarette, while she went around back. Rose was sitting on the bottom step of the back porch, dividing a huge mass of iris. She obviously wasn't expecting her peace to be disturbed.

"*Jak sie masz*?" Sophie asked.

"Okay. You're early."

"Late lunch." Sophie looked shy. "Rose, you need some help with the heavy work."

Rose's hands continued separating rhizomes and roots. "You? Okay, better change clothes first."

"No, I'm not staying. I have to go back to work. There is a girl, a teenager maybe, who spends a lot of time at the library."

"Ach," said Rose, "I don't want somebody here. I like to be quiet."

"Well, she is very quiet. She has never caused any trouble." Well, she hadn't really. It's not as if she were inviting her to live there. "I thought she could move some of these piles to the alley for you, help you a little."

Rose looked up from her work.

"It's a record heat today, Rose. I'm not sure you should even be out here." They were dripping just standing still.

"So you came home early to tell me?"

"No. I thought you might want to meet her."

Rose threw a dark look from under her eyebrows. Sophie already knew Rose didn't like to meet anyone. Rose put the iris down, looked down at her dirt-covered shoes. "You want me to go with you?"

"No. Is it okay? Will you meet her?"

"Is she Polish?"

"She's just a girl."

"I don't know. I like to be by myself."

"Just for a few days, to help you. There's all this stuff." She waved her arm to the yard, which had large mounds of vegetation around. "There's your cast."

Rose looked around the yard. There were piles of weeds and junk kids had, over a couple years, thrown over the fence. "Yeah. I can meet her. Maybe tomorrow. I don't know if I want her help."

"I brought her," Sophie said, ducking back down the gangway without giving Rose a chance to say no.

Within a few minutes, Sophie came back from the car with the youngster. She was gawky, long-legged and pale. She looked like a wind could blow her over unless she stood sideways—then it wouldn't have anything to catch. She had an ease to her movement, like a juggler. When Sophie looked at her objectively, she saw that something in the way she presented said she had a chip on her shoulder.

In Polish, Rose said, "She's a little girl. How old is she?"

Sophie asked. The girl said, "Sixteen." Sophie looked long at her. "Almost. I'm going to be sixteen."

"She's a liar," Rose said in Polish. "She isn't fifteen yet."

"I don't know," Sophie answered, still in Polish. "She's tall."

"Tall," Rose said, exasperated.

The girl looked back and forth. "What are you guys?"

"Polish," Sophie said in English.

"Man, don't she speak no English?"

"Doesn't," Sophie corrected, "Any."

"Okay. Doesn't she?"

"Yeah," Rose answered. "I speak English."

"Oh, that's cool," the girl said.

"You are not sixteen years old," Rose said.

"Not yet," Zak said. "I said that."

"Not yet, not next year. You're a liar," Rose answered.

"Go to hell," the girl said and started to turn away.

"Wait," Sophie said. The girl stopped a few feet off. She lit a cigarette. Sophie turned back to Rose in Polish. "Rose, look, what difference does it make? She's at the library all the time. She can use something to do. You can use help. Why not?"

"She's a liar," Rose said in Polish. "She has a snotty mouth."

"She won't hurt anything. At worst, she'll walk away. Why don't you try her just for a little bit this afternoon? I'll be back in a couple hours."

Rose glanced at the big piles, at her foot, with a look that said, Maybe I could put up with her, enough to clear the junk out.

"Okay," she said in English. "You. You want to stay today?"

The girl said, "My name is Zak."

Rose looked at Sophie, her patience thin. She turned and addressed the girl. "What kind of name is that?"

"My name. Zak. Z-A-K. That's my name."

Sophie interjected. "Zak's short for Zakaria. She's from the South," she said, a bit too brightly.

"Zak." Rose said it as an amen. "Are you strong?" Rose asked. "You don't look strong."

"Yeah? You look like an old fart."

Rose glared at Sophie again, but spoke to Zak. "I can be a old fart. You got to be strong to do this," she waved her arm to the yard. She didn't seem to require the girl to be respectful, just accurate.

"I can do it," Zak said.

"Okay," Rose looked through Zak. "Okay," she said to Sophie.

"Good," Sophie said, relieved. She thought she'd better get out while there was a tentative agreement. "I'll check in later. If you need me," she said to Rose, "you know my number at the library. To Zak, she said "You, too, you can call me if there are problems. And please try to be helpful."

Then, "Rose, there's a reading at the library tonight. I'll be introducing them and I'll stay to close up. But I'll come home in between to drive Zak to the El at Logan Square. Is that okay with you, Zak?"

"Yeah. But you tell me how to get there, I can take the bus."

In English, Sophie said, "It's just the Fullerton bus to Logan Square and a walk—about a block, to the El. The Northwest line, not..."

"It's okay, ma'am. I know the El lines."

In Polish, Sophie said, "That seems thoughtful and polite, no?"

"To you," Rose said.

In Polish, again, Sophie said, "I'm going to put some money inside, by the coffee pot, in a can. You can pay her. We'll talk on the phone in a couple hours. I can come home." Then to Zak, "Maybe you can do that. I'll check in later. If you change your mind, I'll come drive you."

Rose could take care of herself.

The girl got to the library every day. She wasn't polished, but she was certainly astute, in a smart-alec way. In spite of her palming the cash, she did at least wince. She seemed to return it. Should she tell Rose about that? That would do it. No. The child didn't seem dangerous, though there might be a bit of Uriah Heep in her.

She left them to each other.

CHAPTER SEVEN

Zak
The Book of Zak

Zak came to Sophie's strictly from hunger was how she thought of it. She needed her some money. She did not mind taking something when she needed it. If you'd got caught in the taking, trouble; it was always best to work for it. She had chastised her lame self at the library when she heard her real name pop out of her mouth. All the same, she hoped she knew better than to turn down some good luck when it slapped her in the puss.

Zak started sitting at the library when she had to stop going to school which, she reminded herself, was quite a bit after she stopped staying home with Linda Lee. She felt like a fucking astronaut, on the move from one planet to another most of the damn time. She carried her notebook and pencils, charcoal, whatever she had to draw with. Her consistency. A girl needed that. At the library she drew the bookshelves, which was no challenge, the people who came in for company under the guise of a book, and now and then she walked outside and drew a garden with a house behind it. She saw in color, hell, she heard in color, she just couldn't put it down in color. She was learning to shade in the narrow palette she had, black and white. It still looked like color to her.

Sophie seemed correct and righteous, even if she did dress older than an old lady. And she hadn't scolded Zak about the purse thing, and Zak was pretty sure she'd seen it, which was to her favor. She wasn't sure exactly how, but Zak thought she'd be able to use her.

Once she met Rose, Zak was about ready to go back and sit her butt down on her hard wooden chair and forget the dough. She thought Rose was a weirdo and mean as a snake. She didn't like the way she treated her, but she knew how to just get along for the money. She'd hauled the heavy stuff out to the alley and she pulled the good stuff into a compose pile, whatever that was.

She could handle people and whatnot and everything else, if there was a paycheck at the end of it. She didn't have to marry her. That's what she and her best friend Macy always said about someone they had to put up with, like that crazy Sr. Antonisia at Trinity, who thought all the girls were walking breasts and all the boys were giant penises. "I hate her," one of them would say. And the other would say, "Well, you don't have to marry her." They cracked themselves up.

So she kept showing up and getting paid.

This Sophie might could have something Zak had been look-ing for. Zak could read just fine and could memorize like any-thing, but observation was her keenest quality. She observed that Sophie was not big rich and seemed to have no special skills, but she had a home and she was educated and she had a good job. These were more things in her favor. Working against Sophie in Zak's estimation was that the house was all crowded with stuff so much you could hardly find a place to sit down. She saw that when they had to go inside from the sun. Still, she must have had a plan. Linda Lee's problem, as far as Zak could see, and her own current one as well, was that she didn't.

Well, Mama did, on occasion. But...

"You, my girl, are going to go to Art School." Linda Lee had always said it like that, in capital letters. She was looking at a pretty fine portrait of herself with a little bit of Zak peeking around her head—just her left eye and part of her hair, with the top of her cheek showing a smile. Zak had copied herself out of the mirror, with her head turned a bit askew. "You definitely, very definitely, have a touch for drawing and color. I don't know how you see so different than me. But we are going to get you into Art School where they will teach you what you need to know."

"You think I got talent?" Zak asked, more because she wanted to hear Linda Lee say it than because she cared if it were true.

"Talent!" she exploded. "You make things look more real than they are in front of my face. You are my own bones, but the Lord made better of you." Zak glowed.

"Do you think you could find a place for me to go?"

"Sure, little Pearl," she said. "I'm going to get on that tomorrow. Let me see, where to start? We can find a nice two-bedroom place, so you have a room of your own. A Art Room."

Zak pictured having a room to herself, not just the daybed that doubled as a couch in one of their living rooms.

"I never had any kind of talent I heard about," Linda Lee said. "I didn't get anybody to give me a foot up. When I was a kid, it was get to school only so you could get home and help with the others. My mama and daddy were always at that damn glass shop, then I was supposed to go glaze my life away with them." Zak pictured their little place down in Henry, where they tried to stay before they hightailed it to Chicago. Zak didn't hate it. She kind of liked how everything was put away and there were rules about this and that. Dull, but more something.

Linda Lee looked like she might slip down into her own self, but then she rallied. "I'm going to try to get a better job tomorrow," Linda Lee said, warming to the subject. "I want you and me to have a decent life with good stuff, not this crap we're living with." They spent the evening laughing it up, Zak doing impersonations of the nuns, which she was famous for. Zak could get somebody's mannerisms down so well, they were more than the original person. Linda Lee giggling. And they sang "I Want to Hold your Hand" and she let her smoke a cigarette together with her.

That next morning she got up early and informed Zak that she'd called and quit her job first thing. It put a worry on Zak, but she kept mum. Linda Lee'd already gone out and brought the paper home to see how she could do better. When Zak left for school, it was turned to "Help Wanted: Women." She left Linda Lee sipping coffee, a red pen in her hand. All day at school Zak thought about their new start. The Art Room.

When Zak come home, Linda Lee was spread out over the daybed, asleep, a pack of cigarettes down to its last few on the floor and, on the coffee table, a half glass of Russo red, deep and dark red, the color of blood left in the air. The cold coffee still filled half her cup, had left a dark ring at the top. The paper was turned to that same page of ads, with three of them circled in puny red ink. Zak poured the coffee down the sink, making a brown stain on the porous cast iron. She took her mother's shoes off but didn't stir her. There was that plan. Drownded in a bit of wine.

All that first afternoon, Rose had walked, walked, walked through the garden, muttering to herself as if Zak wasn't even there. That garden looked like a bunch of sad cases for flowers to Zak. Zak did this and that as she was directed and thought that was the end of it.

At the end, Rose said, "You come tomorrow?"

Why not? she thought. "Maybe," Zak said.

"JesusMaria. What's maybe?" Rose said. "You come, you don't come."

"Maybe. Yeah," said Zak.

"That means yeah?" Rose was giving her the evil eye.

"Yes." She also decided right then and there that she'd wear her cowboy boots tomorrow. Her shit-kickers.

For every step she tried to take, Zak moved backward. The hottest summer in Chicago, streets full of hippies, protestors, believers and promisers and engineers of a new time. And Zak had no future at all she could see.

It was how she was brought up.

And who brought her up. Linda Lee active and lively, her own woman—a pistol. Zak's happiest possession was pride in her mother.

On that dripping-hot summer day back home,'cause she still thought of Georgia as home, the babysitter, Agony Rust, called to say she was sorry but she couldn't make it to sit with four-year-old Zak. Before the call, Linda Lee had been fussing with her own hair getting ready to go. Zak sat on the toilet seat and watched. Linda Lee had sprayed Aqua Net until they both were near-asphyxiated. Zak looked up at that hair like a trophy her mother had won. It was shining blue-black. The conversation on the phone was short. It ended with Linda Lee's kind of hyperbole: "I have an appointment that's extremely important. How am I ever going to trust you again, Agony?"

As soon as she hung up, she gave Zak the once-over. "Now I'm going to have to gussy you up, little girl, little pearl," Linda Lee said with the quick change she was famous for. She stood Zak in front of the bathroom mirror. Zak could only see the top of her own head. But she could see Linda Lee's slight worry in the little lines at the top of her nose. "You're coming with me," she said, twirling the child back toward her and smoothing her hair as if she were her hairdresser. The motion in her emotion made her exciting. She swirled out of the closet a nice light blue dress with two-inch black-leashed Scottie dogs scattered on it, Zak's favorite. "We're going to meet my friend at Eckert's," Linda Lee said, as though she were talking to herself. It was the only store in town with a second floor. "It has a moving staircase to take us to the restaurant." She wrestled the dress on, wiped the smudge off Zak's cheeks and stood admiring her work, lost a little in the fussing. "You look pretty enough, Zakaria." She said, brushing Zak's white hair with smooth, kind strokes.

As suddenly, she must have realized she'd spent too much time. "Just sit here, child, and don't put a worry on me." She ran to the toilet to splash on her makeup. "Jesus jumping Christ, we are going to be late," she roared. And they tore out the house.

In the car, Linda Lee kept up her one-side conversation. Zak loved, loved, loved the excitement in her mama. She made everything seem like a party. "You know, now, not to call me Mama nor anything like it when we meet a stranger, though he's not a stranger to me, but he don't know a thing about you." Zak had been taught to call her Linda Lee by name from a baby. "Maybe you can be my older sister's daughter. Or just a neighbor child I'm helping out with. I don't know how he would be if he knew I had a child," she fretted.

As she took Zak's hand to help her out the car, Zak was thrilled to smell her mother's sweetness, the taste of lilacs.

Zak walked her proud walk next to Linda Lee once they got downtown. Linda Lee had on her red heels. She was in a shiny black skirt that tugged at her hips. Her buttonless blouse, a favorite for Zak to snuggle against just for that reason, was whiter than clouds, with cream shadows in the folds that ran across the space above her breasts. She walked tall with her red nails hanging carelessly just beyond Zak's soft and chubby hand, which rested lightly in the spoon of Linda Lee's.

When they got to Eckert's, Zak felt her mother's hand tense over her own. A gentleman stood smiling. He was in a clean shirt, collar open at the throat and he had some nice dark pants on. His shoes were shiny. She saw his eyes wrinkle deeper as he put a light arm to her mother's waist. Zak knew she wouldn't be introduced unless the man asked after her. She didn't mind it a bit. She didn't know another way.

He had a broad grin that showed his teeth, including two that were crooked in the upper bunch just to the side of middle. He said something into Linda Lee's ear. Zak could see his lips brush the edge of her ear. Oh, jealousy. Zak felt the same when Linda Lee sat on the couch focusing on the TV so that Zak had to squeeze onto her lap. "Jellyfish," her mother would say, grinning. Right now, though, whatever the man said to Linda Lee upset her. She dropped Zak's hand and flustered over to the plate glass window. The window reflected her and, in her background, the gentleman and Zak. The backdrop for all three of them was a sleepy downtown street in midday, with a big-finned, iridescent-green car parked right at the curb. In the hollow of each of Linda Lee's cheeks was a red circle the size of a nickel. The color was happy. It matched her mother's shoes. Linda Lee fumbled in her purse, coming out with a Kleenex. Zak watched with disappointment as she wiped the colorful blotches from a circle of bright red into a faint shadow of pink. Linda Lee walked back to them slow, rolling her hips, a laugh on her lips. As the smiling proud gent turned ahead of them to go in toward Eckert's, Linda Lee took Zak's hand and jerked her arm nearly out of socket.

"You're useless as tits on a bull." Linda Lee whispered violently. "Why didn't you tell me I forgot to smooth out my blush?"

"I thought you was made up special. I thought you was going as a clown," Zak explained quietly to the black eyes that glimmered at her.

In a split second her mother turned her attention back to the gentleman with a broad, sweet grin on her face. Her face didn't match the anger vibrating in the hand that held Zak's. How was Zak supposed to know that Linda Lee was supposed to look different than she did?

Linda Lee needed Zak to keep an eye out, that was clear. A place in her heart opened and shut over this seed: I don't have any idea what I should be looking out for.

On the way back from another work day with Rose, Zak's heart took a detour she damn well knew it would. She needed to see how things were at home, where Linda Lee was, where Linda Lee would be right now. Zak hadn't been there in more than a month. It meant a lot of bus transfers, but Sophie's house was nearer to it than Macy's or the Rogers Park library either. She needed to get near her, even across the street from her, even for a minute.

When the bus pulled up at Humboldt Park, she got off, looking around at the familiar stores, the *wedlinys*, the taco joint, the polka tavern.

Her apartment building looked the same, papers cluttered at the outside door, a Reese's peanut butter cup wrapper crunched in the corner. It was probably the same one there when she'd left. She was scared her key wouldn't work. It did. She laughed inside. The landlords wouldn't take the trouble to change locks if William Speck lived there. She climbed up the paint-chipped steps hadn't been washed in ten years, the dust as thick as the music pouring out of a second-floor apartment.

And there she was. In front of her own door. She didn't know if she was going to knock or use her key or what. She stood staring for minutes outside of time. She leaned her forehead against the door. She turned her ear to its bumpy surface. No sounds. She leaned her forehead again. If she just walked in, unannounced, would Linda Lee be beside herself to see her, put her hands over Zak's ears and look at her, kiss her cheeks, tell her.... What exactly did she want to hear? Zak and Linda Lee, one-on-one. One. She stepped back from the door, walked a few steps away, thinking what to do.

The door opened. She didn't know yet if this was actual or a dream. The man coming out was not a man she knew, not the one who was there the night she left and not Eddie. He didn't even glance at her, said nothing back into the apartment. He locked the door with a key. Oh, yeah, it was real. Zak stood soundlessly.

Before the lock clicked shut, this flowed through her head: Push him aside, run in. Linda Lee loved her in that mother way, where she cared for her like breath, didn't she? She did. They both knew that—whenever she broke out of her orbit, the gravitational pull that centered on pills that knocked the sense out of her, pulled her to liquor and tobacco and brown powder and men who groped her daughter.

Zak waited until the man went down. She approached the door. She needed to take care of her mother again. She needed to fucking see her. She took a long time trying to smell the lilacs through the rust-brown wood. The wood was cool in the stifling hall.

Zak kissed the door. It smelled of knuckles.

She reached her hand toward the knob. And let it fall.

Down the dusty stairs to the street.

In the light of the street lamp, Zak studied her bus map. The South Side was a long journey yet, she had to get back to the El. She rummaged her pockets for change and called Suzee to say how late she'd be. Suzee raised hell that time she stayed for dinner with the old gals and came home late. She didn't expect anybody to make no nevermind over it.

"Where in hell are you? You better get your butt home," Suzee said tartly. Suzee liked her children home before dark. Then, "Call me from the El when you get down here and I'll come meet you with Macy." Then, with more love than she owed her: "You be careful, baby."

Suzee was Macy's mother. Macy was Zak's best friend at school or anywhere and the only one Zak could turn to when she needed a place to hide out.

Zak used to stay over at Macy's sometimes before it became semi-permanent like now. Those old days were days when she couldn't face the storm of Linda Lee's wild mood swings edged to full force by the prescription pills she always had too many of.

That first time, when Zak came over and let it get later and later and finally Suzee suggested could she stay, Suzee had said "We got to call your mother first, Zak." There'd been other kids staying there when she used to just go over for an evening. Suzee somehow raised up kids who weren't hers along with her own, which was amazing to Zak since her own mama couldn't do one or even her own self. Zak already knew the jumble she'd get for an answer. Suzee'd called and stood listening to the phone, looking at the yellow kitchen wall with its apples and oranges in a painting, and took Linda Lee's rambling as a conversation. "Your mama didn't say you couldn't stay," she told Zak, "so I guess you can." Instead of visa-versa. Zak had appreciated that.

Macy was one of two Negroes at Holy Trinity, in what used to be "Little Poland" around Milwaukee and Ashland. At the school, Zak and everybody else, including the teachers and janitors, were all different kinds of white—mostly Polish but some German, even Italian, some Ricans, too, but they were even white compared to a Macy. Nobody from Georgia, though, she was the only one. Zak didn't come from anywhere but the South, no matter she been living in Chicago for five years. She didn't count the time as anything down in Henry, Illinois, that little grandma–and–grandpa town couldn't hold their big selves, Linda Lee said. Linda Lee counted up their money and said, we got enough to get us to Chicago or Louisville and flipped a coin and here they were. When a little bit of phrasing come out of Macy's mouth that sounded like Wake County, Georgia, Zak felt like a bird inside a window just heard one with the same song singing outside. Macy wasn't from the South, but there was something about her talk said South. And that outsider thing, too, they had that going. From when they met in grammar school and went into the all-girls high school crost the street, they got to be best buds.

The first time they got together, they went to a nearby "smoking place," the nuns called it. The neighborhood around Trinity was getting more Rican than Polack and Leo's Steakburgers was going to make the transition, a rock in the stream, didn't seem to mind who swam by. Zak pulled out her cigs and offered one to Macy, who took it and proceeded to wave it around like the leader of a band.

The two never hung around in school. That would be trouble. Some things you didn't have to ask nobody.

"What're you doing at Trinity?" Zak asked.

"My mama made me come." Macy forgave her an obvious question.

"Mine, too," Zak said.

"I got some scholarship from the CIC." Zak didn't know what that was. "Catholic Interracial Conference. My mama says this is the best education. Catholic sisters."

"You like it okay?" Zak asked.

"No and no. Make me come all this way." She blew smoke up in a stream. She didn't inhale, just used the cigarette for a prop.

"From where? Where you live?"

"South Side. It's exactly nothing like my old school. I don't know what my mama thinks I'm learning, but it ain't worth all this."

"Worth what, man?"

"Like when I make a mistake, it's all about 'how you were brought up.' When I do something smart, they are so surprised, like I'm a hound talking. They don't even want to look at me. Never ask me a question."

"They" were the nuns. They were white, not white like from the South, but a quiet mean.

"That'd be okay with me," Zak said. "They just want to teach you to be a good mother." They both snickered. "And a good wife." They choked more laughs out.

"What are you?" Macy asked the Chicago question. Nationality, religion, whatever.

"I'm just Zak," Zak said. "I'm not Polish nor anything. I'm from Georgia. I don't know how the hell I got here, just Linda Lee, that's my mother, says I got to go." It's the one thing her mother kind of kept together. It had been a constant struggle for Linda Lee, how to pay the tuition. But once you were already through the grade school, they pulled you on, got kind of lenient about it. Zak was months behind as she spoke.

"Man. What about that thing with Jimmy this morning?"

"Lord," Macy crushed her cigarette into the ashtray as if she'd been doing it all her life. "If that was me, I'd be six feet under tomorrow."

"I was all, Jesus, call me a preacher."

The whole school went to confession on different days, and their class, all girls in the high school, was Wednesdays, right after the seventh- and eighth-graders. Even the heathens had to come to the church and sit while everybody went. Jimmy Przybylski, class clown and general disrespecter of values in the seventh grade, went into the confessional in his turn. A few minutes later, Father Grabowski came roaring out of his priest's place in the middle and reached into Jimmy's sinner's place. Father pulled him out and grabbed him by the front of his shirt, brought him up to his eye level, slamming him against the carved grapevine on the dark wood of the confessional. "You what?" yelled the priest. "You did what?" Jimmy's face was bright red. He had on a small grin that had got to come from not knowing what else to do with his face.

"What could he do that made the priest go nuts? Kill his parents? I can't think of nothing," Zak said.

"He just a kid," Macy said from her lofty, older-girl place. "Probably something nasty. These people are nuts about, you know—" it was clearly hard to spit the word out, "sex."

"It didn't make me feel too good about going to confession when we get Catholic," Zak said. Zak could say that she did evermore love the Lord but she was not in the least bit interested in being a Catholic. "But Linda Lee says I'm just here to learn math and history and all 'cause they're good at that. She says it's okay to lie when I got to confess."

"My mama's down on lying. But I bet she'd say so, too, if she saw that father today. And I don't think she really want me to go Catholic. We at the AME church."

From that time on, after CCD classes which were Wednesdays at 2:15, when all the real Catholic kids got off early and the pagans like themselves had to stay for catechism, after class, they would get the hell out of there fast as their feet could carry them and meet at Leo's where they smoked Kools and drank Cokes. Sometimes, Zak would head down to the South Side and hang at Macy's.

In April, Leo's was where Zak had presented her problem.

"So this guy's coming around our house. He's nutty as a pecan pie, and mean, too. He's supposed to be Linda Lee's boyfriend but he hates us both, I don't even know why he comes. He treats her like dirt. And. He's giving me the eye. It's scary."

Macy twirled the air with her cigarette. "He permanent?"

"Nah. Fuck, I don't know." Zak smoked. Macy waved her cigarette with dramatic flair. "Eddie shows up now and again. I don't know."

"Eddie, he your daddy?" Zak nodded. "You tell your mother about this guy?" Macy asked without hope.

"Uh-uh! What is the matter with you, Macy? She is zonked out. I'm more worried about him hurting her."

"No, you ain't. You worried about he'll come after you and you stab him and end up in Juvie." And, they both knew, that would be the most successful scenario.

Zak was about to argue. This was one reason she needed Macy. Macy knew better than she did what she meant. She couldn't explain how her heart was torn. Take care of Linda Lee. Take care of her self. Why couldn't she take care of them both? If she could keep these guys out, they'd have a shot.

Would not, maybe, but that's what she was selling herself today.

A couple days after that conversation, Zak grabbed Macy. "We got to go to Leo's."

"Maybe. But I got to get home quick. It's mama's birthday." Macy looked at her. "You a mess."

"Shit." Zak abandoned the idea of going to Leo's. "I slept on the landing downstairs from my apartment last night. This guy had glass in his eyes and he came after me like a mummy." Zak acted him out, arms ahead, no spot of light in her eyes. She meant it to be comical. Macy didn't take it that way. "I didn't take a chance to get to Linda Lee this morning, just snuck in and grabbed some clothes, headed for school. He was in there, in her bedroom. I grabbed ten bucks on the floor must have fell out of his pants by my bed."

It had been easier to raise herself when she was little than it was getting to be. For one thing, most often no one, like Social Services, used to stick his nose in their business, and, when somebody did 'cause of some busybody neighbor, Zak had learned real early how to play them so they left her and Linda Lee alone. This was true in Wake County and Cook County.

Like that time with the smoke in the kitchen. Linda Lee was going to make a chicken soup "from scratch." She took some liquor to help her "get creative" and that pan smoked so bad, the neighbors called the Fire Dept., who called the police, who called the social worker, for whom Zak had answered the door. Linda Lee had rousted awake by "all this fuss."

"Mama sick," the five-year-old said, reverting to her idea of baby talk.

"You're coming with us," the stick-your-face-in-it lady said. It might have occurred to somebody that the kid hadn't eaten, but no, it's a couple hours past feeding time and everybody's do-gooding and forgot to hand her a Twinkie nor anything. Even as a five-year-old, Zak could see that was about the way it would go.

"Mama," Zak said, dramatically reaching for the couch. "Daddy!"

The social worker looked alarmed. "Is there a Mister Stone?"

"Yes, there is a Mister," Linda Lee slurred.

"Daddy," cried Zak. "Come home." She was looking hard at Linda Lee. Thank God and all the angels, she figured out what Zak was doing.

"My husband," she said, raising her sitting position perceptibly, "Edward Jefferson Stone, will be here presently."

You could see the social worker lady conjuring up in her head the reports and follow-up she'd have to do if there was an irate husband in the picture.

"Daddy," Zak said. "Where's Daddy?"

Linda Lee looked at her watch. "Soon, baby. Mama should have waited before she took her medication."

"I don't know what soon is," Zak said. "I'm just little." And with that, she twisted away from the lady and buried herself in her mother's arms.

"You're a sweet, girl," the lady said to Zak. "Are you sure you'll be okay?" she asked Linda Lee.

"Um-hmmm," Linda Lee answered. "We'll just stay right here 'til Eddie comes home."

And suddenly, the police were leaving and the lady began backing out.

As soon as the door closed, she and Linda Lee laughed at the thought of Eddie saving the day. And Zak was able to go about getting her dinner, which was Hostess Cupcakes and Ruffles 'cause there they were and not an adult to show her anything else.

If somebody's little and hungry and doesn't have any money or is trying not to spend what she's got, she could ask anybody at the store to please get her a treat. Sometimes, people weren't around or the guy behind the counter would tell her to get out and stop bothering people, but treats was still all Zak had the change and idea for, so she'd pull out her cash and buy it herself. When she got old enough to figure out how to work the can opener, she would heat up pork and beans or chicken noodle soup in the can because no use in messing up a pot and she'd eat standing on a chair over the shut-off burner so she didn't scald herself trying to move that little can. A new dawn broke when she was six, and a neighbor fixed a sandwich for her. She didn't know why it'd never occurred to her before to stick some things between two slices of bread. That opened a world of dining pleasure, she would tell anyone. After that she joined her two talents—opening cans and laying out bread—and she'd spoon cold SpaghettiOs on bread. It was a convenient little sandwich.

And it filled her right up.

That all was simple next to now.

"You can't go back there," Macy said.

"I don't know what the fuck to do."

"You come by my house."

"Now?"

"What else you going to do?"

On the way they yelled intimacies over the El noise. Best thing was for Zak to keep going to school for now. She could kind of stay at Macy's.

"Just keep quiet with my mama," Macy said. "Don't lie. Just stay quiet."

Macy told her Suzee'd tried to be an official foster parent, but they didn't approve her. So she was one anyway, with not the blessing nor a dime of Cook County's. Zak was her new temp kid.

That night they had cake and sang and went to bed early. It was hardly light when they jostled on the El, transferring twice, to get to the Milwaukee Avenue stop to Trinity in the morning. Macy lived all to hell and back from the school.

That first morning, having abandoned her mother, Zak was sick at heart, full of yearning to be with Linda Lee as the El moved north. The baked brick and the peeling, faded, clapboard tenements lining the tracks were wet, muted, the colors sealed in by the morning's cold drizzle.

Though it was near the end of the school year, Zak knew she couldn't keep going to Trinity, even if her tuition had been all paid up. Could be Linda Lee would lose her mind and tell Social Services she was gone or tell Eddie where her school was. Could be a lot of things that wouldn't add up right for Zak.

After that first week, the girls decided Zak better stop going to school. Every morning they left to go to Holy Trinity together. Then Zak cut out and headed for anyplace else. She could travel the El all day, transfer from one to another all on the same transfer. Usually she took the Ravenswood to the far north side, like Rogers Park, where she wasn't likely to run into anybody who knew her. Finally she settled in at that library.

Two weeks before school let out, Zak met Macy at Leo's on pagan Wednesday before they headed south together. Zak lit up a Kent. She'd switched because the ads were better. Macy waved it off.

"A guy came around looking for you," Macy said. "How come you ain't coming to school anymore?"

"What's he like?" It could be Eddie.

"His shirttail sticks out under his jacket. Tall. White, of course. Dark hair, kept short, but not like a crew cut."

He sounded creepily familiar. Zak blanched. Wasn't Eddie, though.

"You know this guy?" Macy asked.

"Not to call his first name. His last name is something like a president or a general. I'll think on it."

"Don't have to. He ask most everybody do they know you, you got any information, call this number." She handed a card to Zak.

"Charles B. Emerson, Department of Social Services" she read. That was their old social worker, she remembered with a quiver.

"What'd you say when he asked you?"

"He asked *most* everybody. Didn't ask me nothing," Macy said.

Right. They looked right past her, like she wasn't there. So she didn't have to lie. Macy already knew not to bother even having opinions out loud.

"He talked funny, like he's laying in wait for you to say something wrong. Didn't anybody like him."

Zak nodded. He was a creep. Zak had to lay low. The South Side was a far unlikely place for anybody to look for her, especially since it was nowhere near Bridgeport nor the University of Chicago, which is where the white people lived. The cops, Social Services, they all stayed out of the Negro neighborhoods. Especially since the riots last April. When that Dr. Reverend Martin Luther Jr. King was killed.

Here it was, weeks later, and Zak was getting more guilty she ain't told Suzee the entire true story about her mother. And she was coming home late causing Suzee more aggravation. She was scared she was screwing up royally. Still. You had to do what you had to do.

When she got to her El stop, she called Suzee, who came with her downstairs friend Renee to walk her home. Suzee said it was too late for Macy to come, and gave Zak that look that said they would talk about this coming in late tomorrow. They warmed her something to eat and Suzee told Zak to go to bed. Suzee kissed her forehead, even though her look wasn't soft.

Now she lay awake all night, thinking about the things that could go wrong. Macy had thought with her that it was smart to get so far from Trinity, but staying here, in a colored neighborhood on the South Side, made her stick out like a sore thumb, Renee was right about that. CPS might could find her at Suzee's, because some well-meaning Renee wanted to save Suzee trouble. Or somebody not so well meaning wanted to cause her trouble. Or Suzee could get nervous and decide that Zak wasn't worth it. Zak agreed with Linda Lee that you don't go visiting deception upon people who are truehearted. Yet she hadn't told Suzee a whole truth.

Zak didn't want to get nobody, especially her own self, in trouble.

She had deserted Linda Lee. She'd done her best, but she couldn't keep her mama safe. If she stayed, she thought she'd go nuts, end up raped or in kid prison or some fucked-up foster home. Or the both of them with Eddie, since he seemed to be around in and out again. Linda Lee needed her. Zak missed her crazy self. In love with Linda Lee as she was, Zak never needed much back. She couldn't go back to Trinity unless she went back home. Where was she going to go to school come September?

The night folded on her with a weight beyond her fourteen years.

Night had never scared Zak that she could remember.

Maybe when she was under three, maybe, her earliest memory. She woke up starving in the night when she heard a thud on the other side of the wall. She struggled out of the seat cushions of the couch, pushing her straggling hair back of her ears. In the bedroom, she pulled on her mama, "Get up. Get up." She threw a screaming tantrum fit that made no difference whatsoever. And there was blood coming out the back her head where Mama hit something on the way down. Maybe then, in the night, she wondered if her mother would ever get up again. How long would her short self have to wander around like she was, looking on the floor and the coffee table for crackers and things to eat and wishing for something clean to drink, not the beer in the brown bottles, which tasted like feet and was all she could reach? She wondered if she would be able to find something night after night. Her first concept of tomorrow.

Maybe night looked long when she was six back in Wake County and for far too long that ugly-assed, puke-smelling bastard, Eddie, stayed with them. "This is your daddy, sugar. Don't be shy." Zak wasn't shy about him but that didn't mean something was right about him either. Something too much about him, like a false mustache. He was all sunshine and my-little-girl all day, while the liquor got in them. Then mama passed out. He came back in the front room and hung all round her studio bed like kudzu, smacking his flapping lips to make rude sounds. Zak had to press herself against the wall and push that couch-bed with her feet from the wall just far enough to squeeze her tiny self through and under it to keep away from his waggling fingers. Him saying "Don't you want to be my little girlfriend?" And her not answering. "I'm your daddy, you better show some respect," he was saying with a mean little edge and grabbing half-heartedly at her until he passed out on her own bed and she kept put under it until it was light enough to go to school. Praise the Lord she had her clothes on and could just wash her face and go.

Maybe night started seeming impossible that other year when they moved to Henry and Linda Lee started into crying deep into the night. Zak would rustle up off her couch and put her arm around her mother and stand next to her. Mama needed her. Linda Lee sobbed a litany of unhappiness, of need, of grief. You didn't need to know what all the words meant, the rest was clear. Zak saw the snot glistening where it hung from her mother's nose and wanted to wipe it away, but just could not because it was so private, like her mother's sorrow dripping out.

Zak pulled on her mother to make her go to bed and she got up, her shoulders slumped, staggering against Zak. Her mother lay herself down on top of the covers. Zak covered her by folding the edges of the blanket over the periphery of her. Zak always, always took off her mother's shoes, because shoes on the bed made her feel like it was a dead person or a person with no manners was lying there. So she'd always taken off the shoes.

Pretty often Zak fell asleep on the couch to her mother's sobs and woke to her mother's sighs, to the permanent night fixture of mother sitting, mother weeping.

But, mostly, night didn't scare Zak that she could remember.

She lay on her little foam bed on the floor next to Macy. She couldn't stay at Suzee's forever, that was for sure. She didn't know what the hell she was going to do.

Except she would wear those boots tomorrow.

CHAPTER EIGHT

Rose
It's a Fence

"Read," Rose said. It was a library book. It gave basics of carpentry.

Zak didn't seem to like the tone of her voice. Rose said everything flat out, no sugar about it. Certainly in English, where everything came out awkward.

The girl showed up this next day dressed somewhere between a hippie and a cowboy, jeans frayed at the bottom, some kind of vest with stuff hanging down—and boots—in a garden?

"Make the fence," Rose said. There was a hammer, a tape measure and a hand saw on the ground next to some nails and a few boards of new wood.

"Fix it?" Zak didn't like to be told what to do; anybody could see that, even Rose. They both stared at the broken pickets, Rose's lopsided portal to the garden only a few weeks before. "What if I don't?"

"Sommabitch. I don't need you," Rose said, pushing in front of Zak, picking up the tape measure and busying herself with a fence board.

"I know you don't," Zak said.

"Don't stay by me. Leave me alone."

"Hey, listen," Zak said, moving to take the tape out of Rose's hand. "Why don't y'all hand me some fancy tapestry and tell me to sew you a dress?"

"It's not a dress." Rose glared at her. "It's a fence."

"Fine. You want to see me make a hee-hawing ass out of

myself?" Zak said. "Okay. Let me try. Sophie said you're the boss."

"To hell with Sophie. She ain't my friend. You, too. Leave me alone," Rose said.

"She is your friend. I'm supposed to do it. You leave me alone."

"Leave me alone," Rose said louder, moving toward the child.

"Leave me alone," Zak threw back just as loud.

"Leave me alone." Rose bellowed, fixing her eyes on Zak's.

"You leave me alone," she yelled back. But her eyes flickered away. She squinted.

Rose narrowed her eyes, intensifying her look. Zak, tough, but out of her league, was so nervous she smiled.

Rose took her time. What a weird kid. What do you do with a kid like this? Then she stuck out her tongue. Zak's eyebrows shot up.

"Okay," said Rose.

"Okay?" Zak asked.

"I said okay, can't you hear?"

A jay let out a long line of racket behind them.

Zak spent most of the afternoon trying to cut boards and pin them up with nails. Every now and then, she cussed under her breath.

"*Co?* What happened?"

"I smashed my pointing finger, damn it. Leave me alone."

Rose turned away. She heard her again and again but shut up. Maybe the kid liked to be private when she was mad at herself. Rose got that. She was streetwise in a more turbulent way than Rose needed to be. She didn't like to talk much, and when Rose insisted they rest, she would pull out a pad of paper and make drawings.

Except for the watering. Jesus, did that girl like to water!

Finally, Zak was finished with pounding. She looked around, stretched her arms above her head, and kicked at some green in the dirt.

"After I finish, do you want me to help you get rid of the crapgrass over here?" Zak asked. A chill ran down Rose's spine.

"What did you say? What?"

"The crapgrass," Zak said, her brows knit, staring at the stuff her toe was nudging.

Grace called it that one time, as earnestly as Zak did now. Rose had laughed until Grace caught the laugh if not the joke and they both had tears running down their cheeks and their laughter had nothing to do with anything but the laughing. Rose finally told her it was called crabgrass. But the new name explained it with such emotional accuracy for a gardener that they'd called it that forever after.

She didn't laugh this time. It was a secret thrill to hear it again. "Yeah, sure," she said. As the child knelt to finish the fence, "Crapgrass," Rose repeated to herself, fat with sudden joy. She opened a book on annuals, not looking at it, sitting near the garage, savoring the memory.

After going at it for a while, the child approached. "It's okay?" Zak held her head crooked, as though she were a dog being asked if he wanted to go for a walk. She was turned slightly toward the new fence.

Rose looked up from her book, perhaps the first time she looked directly at Zak. She was a big little girl. For the first time in a hundred years, Rose's arms ached for the soft curl of little Grace against her chest. She forced her eyes away to the fence. "It's good," she said. She meant it. The verticals were atilt, the spacing off balance. Rustic, maybe. "You're pretty good."

"You don't have to buck me up," Zak said without a grin.

And Rose turned back to her book. Rose was a bit tired today. It was a good space for planning the new garden.

After a bit, Zak was watering a new bed for the third time. She stopped whenever Rose hollered at her, but Rose would turn around and there'd she be again, with the hose in her hand. "You're going to drown them flowers," Rose said. It came out like a complaint from someone in an old married couple.

But Zak smiled back. "It feels good, smells good. It's a purity."

Rose had put the book aside, but kept refuge from the heat of the day in the shade near the garage. Even as she sat, she saw where to transplant the larkspur, how the cosmos could grace that corner. Sun-sodden birds darted beneath the arching spray. Zak turned the hose a few degrees and a mist fell over Rose.

"Watch it," Rose said, warning Zak that her aim was off.

But Zak was not off. "Don't panic," she said. She sprayed Rose clearly and intentionally, with just the edge of the fan of spray, more gently than a sun shower, cooling her, bringing relief from the parch of the day. "We used to do this back home. It'll cool you down."

Zak was watering as if she were the rain itself. Rose felt the mist land like rosewater. A sparrow fluttered at the corner of the spray above her.

It lasted only a moment.

Zak was all right.

It might sound minor—even dismissive—but in Rose's world, it was an accolade, a Pulitzer, the Nobel Prize of liking.

Rose was surprised to hear herself say, "You come again?" She examined that at arm's length. In her head she'd already held a conversation with the girl.

"Maybe. I mean, yeah, man, I'll be here."

CHAPTER NINE

Rose
Heart of the Matter

Rose was seething. How the hell did she get involved here? Goddammit.

All of a sudden, it had been two, then three weeks since Zak had showed up, her stringy body and mouth full of funny sayings.

Rose came most days. On every one of those days, Zak showed up and Rose got in a little deeper. It was like those old cowboy movies, where the fellow falls into quicksand and the more he squirms, the deeper he's sunk. Zak never mentioned the in-between days, when Rose was so mad at herself for caring, she went off. She'd been there, though, Rose could see it in the work.

For those weeks, when Rose needed lunch and independence, she'd been going to St. Stan's Kostka (not the nearby Stan's B&M, they didn't have any lunches), which was around Polish Broadway. This day, she needed her old life, her old bleak sense of home, and took the time to make her way to Martin's, located in the vein of the heart of the city. The people there were different. It wasn't so "churchy."

She liked to take the El at the foot of Fullerton. Sometimes, she'd transfer twice, just to have a ride over the streets, too. It was a nice-looking city near the Lake. She used to get off in different places to walk to Martin's. Now, since that stupid toe, walking was hard and sometimes slow. Still, it gave her a sense of possessing the city.

This time, she popped up from underground and walked west.

The buildings facing her were huge and endless. Door upon door, must be thirty same doors to a floor; floor upon floor, maybe thirty same floors to a building; building upon building upon building, feeling like fifty thousand buildings making up the area, the life, known as "the projects"—Cabrini-Green. Upright caverns, created to house the bone poor, and immediately abandoned by maintenance. Dominoes made of despair. Plywood in some high windows; others, jagged-edged, broken at random; others, framed in the same yellow brick sooted by ancient fire.

Guys and guys and more guys hung out on every sleazy corner. She felt their eyes on her.

"You in the wrong neighborhood?" one of them murmured with an unpleasant smile.

"Kissmyass." To hell with that, it was her city, too.

Mere blocks to the east and north was the Gold Coast. Chic days, Rush Street was the setting for galleries, clothing salons, interior designers. Rose had walked there, too. Why not? Fuck them, she lived here. Rush Street, alive at glittering night with the rich, with the young who passed as Fortune's babes for the moment, looking over beauties like themselves. They would turn their eyes from her. She could be out at night, too. She would grin inside.

Both sides of the imaginary and invisible tracks were the hustlers. Bloodless greed on the rich side. On this, the projects side, a person had to pray and dodge the bullets. It was a matter of style.

Because Rose read the papers, especially the little two-inch stories, she knew the biggest scam of all was the land beneath Cabrini-Green, which was the shoulder of downtown. It was rumored that it was leased to the city, owned by a real-estate magnate. It was no secret either. One day, the lease would be up and it would revert to the magnate just about when downtown needed to expand. She was sure that info would disappear like a knife in the water. Nothing illegal, as Americans are fond of saying.

Hustlers on both sides were smalltime chumps. They didn't know a thing about a scam.

Finally, Rose was facing the first sign that she was home, in turquoise-blue scrawl: "St. Martin De Porres - Welcome."

The second sign was the Walker.

The man had looked the same, more or less, every day she ever saw him. He wore his straight hair as it must have been styled many years before, though probably a lot shaggier now, parted on the left side, plastered by habit and without flair against an unyielding skull. His face was the color of fish belly. He was uniformed in gray- or brown-cotton Sears workpants just fit to his spare, tall frame. A polyester shirt was buttoned to the neck, almost always without pattern, but now and then with a crest over the pocket, an uninteresting embellishment that became almost jaunty on him, simply by contrast. His spring and fall windbreaker of unremarkable blue graduated in winter to a cheap, dark, navy, hooded parka. He was thin, as an animal on a veldt is. Bare bone, nothing to spare. He often performed certain personal rituals, seemingly meaningless gestures.

The Walker seemed never in a hurry. His face was composed. He was steadfast, indomitable. He walked with imperceptible head movement, arms barely swinging from the shoulder, one foot directly before the other, eyes forward, shoulders straight. Lady Bird's china could be balanced across those shoulders without a cup getting chipped against another; a carpenter could strike a level against them. He didn't look, even in heavy traffic, to the right or left. He just walked and walked and walked.

On the ground, inches from the light pole, the Walker had placed his briefcase. He touched the knob on the main door with the middle finger of his right hand, his index finger poised for running along the edge of the window seal that ran the width of the storefront. At the end, he used the same finger to dot the center of the second sea-blue ceramic tile from the end of the window. Suddenly, all motion stopped.

He went back, picked up his briefcase, and set it down in the exact same place. He touched the knob on the door with the middle finger of his right hand. He repeated what he'd just done, performing his touching tasks like an altar boy. Finished, silent, he stood, respectfully distant, facing the door at easy attention. A voiceless, aching man with a yen for touching goal.

The building was a dilapidated thing, two stories high, the upstairs windows filthy with years of street dirt where they weren't broken out. The storefront itself was painted cerulean blue. Rose loved that name of a color, if she was saying it right. Seroolian. Spotless windows shone like a chrome bumper in a junkyard.

It was all men waiting, except for Rose and a lost woman with two kids under four. Tired army fatigues, blue jeans, and work clothes were the uniform of the day. Some hippies coming for convention were here already—boisterous, proud of themselves for being broke. A few men stayed on the edges, scowling to themselves, enmeshed in one-man wars. She moved toward the side of the building, leaned against the hot bricks, and felt more warmth move into her shoulder.

Within a few minutes, Jake, a man of medium height, dressed in a black T-shirt, jeans, and with sandals on, opened the front door.

"Good morning, Wendell," the man said.

He had a name then. Wendell did not meet his eye, staring just past his left ear, a quirk that might have challenged a differently adjusted man.

"We'd like to invite you to stay for lunch." Jake gave the

impression overall of a middle-aged St. Francis of Assisi, with some brilliant flash that suggested a patch over one eye and a bandana across his thinning hair. His voice was medium range and his tone a cross between a song and a laugh. "It's no surprise, I'm afraid. Turkey soup." As he stepped back, he winked toward Rose's general direction and made a welcoming sweep with his arm. See? She was home.

A big, dirty, blond guy held his hand out to the chest of a staggering drunk who tried to swerve in the door before Wendell.

"Excuse me, friend," said the blond. "I think he was here first."

The drunk looked stupefied. He tried unsuccessfully to nod his head in greasy agreement.

The Walker made no eye contact, spoke no word, and moved in.

The heavy soup pots were in place, big stainless steel bowls filled with good cut bread standing at each of three stations. There were little squares of a dark cake lined up on a hundred white paper plates behind the glass.

Rose swept in and settled next to a couple of guys who looked like they'd ridden the rough side of life. She headed toward the line.

"Hey, Rose," said an intense-looking woman with a ladle in her hand, "haven't seen you in a while."

"Ya. I ain't been around," Rose said gruffly. Then she added, as if they'd seen each other only yesterday: " Boody. *Tsaw*? You PG?"

"That's right," she answered, looking surprised. There wasn't any puff or swell to indicate. But Rose could tell a pregnant woman when she saw one.

"You got to take care," Rose said, stepping in the space between the two lines to get out of the way. "Eat extra meat or your hair will get stringy."

"Thanks. How's by you?"

"*Dobrze*. I started to work on a lady's garden. I stay by her place sometimes."

"That's great," said Boody. Silently, they summed up the evidence of each other's recent good luck.

Rose growled at the two men who were sitting too close to her bags, slammed down her soup, and each of them moved a little farther away.

She took a mouthful of the hearty soup. Not much in the spice department. Chicago demanded nothing much in its food. It was okay with her.

The convention kids were noisy. Arrogant. They acted like they were "ripping off" somebody, having lunch here. But who? People who gave their time to make soup? That's when she noticed Stan, the neighbor. He was in the back part of the kitchen. Her mind twisted a little, bringing life around Sophie's crashing into her soup kitchen. And with that came Zak. Rose had to do something. She walked back up to where Boody was so she could get a better look in the kitchen.

"You got vegetable ends left over?"

"Ends? Sure. Carrots, potatoes, cabbage, whatever goes in the meals. The meat doesn't stretch far."

"I need stuff for the garden," Rose said. "Not meat."

Boody clearly had no idea what Rose was talking about.

"I don't get it."

"Just scraps you don't use. Things that rot."

"Sure," Boody said, perplexed yet helpful, "we must throw away a lot of that."

"I need it to be separate, for, such-a..." Rose started to say. She had to think of the word in English again. "For a compost," she said, triumphant.

"Okay, kiddo. I don't know about a compost," Boody said. "But talk to Jake after dinner, okay?"

Jake was bringing the last pot of soup out with that Stan. She didn't acknowledge Stan. He showed a hint of surprise before he looked away. "Hiya, Rose," Jake said, seeming to have overheard

Boody's last comment. Steam settled among the nest of his beard, along his eyebrows, his face sweated with it. "We can talk later on. Can you stay after?"

Rose grunted a yes. It was that Stan all right. It made her think of Zak and that started a chain she stopped right there. She went and sat tight and looked around.

Wendell was a table away, holding his soup spoon in his right hand, his napkin tucked into his collar to protect his shirt. He took equal portions each time and brought them to his mouth. His arm was rigid, as though there were only one right way to eat. He never took a random bone in his hand to put his teeth to it. He swallowed carrot and potato, held a piece of bread in his left hand, and took a bite after every seven spoonfuls of soup. She counted, of course. Every now and then, all would stop and Wendell would first slowly but then with blinding speed touch his thumb to each finger on his right hand three times in quick succession. His chocolate cake was placed on the precise meridian of his world.

Rose admired his mathematical certainty. She finished her meal and moved toward the front.

Jake stood inside at the partially opened door, two police officers outside like centurions in the vestibule between the door and the sidewalk. "No, we never do allow it," Jake was saying, stepping aside to let Rose pass and then he was outside and firmly closing the door behind him. Rose bumped out between them. "It's not right for you to bother our guests while they're dining."

Rose waited on the sidewalk and listened.

"Maybe you don't understand," the young cop said. "The guy we're looking for is a felon, a two-time loser; he killed a guy."

"If the man you want is in here," Jake said pleasantly, "he'll have to come out the front door when he's through and you can visit with him then."

The cops bulged a little. "Look, jagoff," the young one continued. "You got a lot of lowlife in there," he nudged his nose
toward the storefront. "You might need some muscle one day,
maybe call us. Maybe we won't hear that call."

Jake looked amiable. "I don't think so, really. We don't like
business of any kind to be conducted on the premises. And we're
full of hippies. I think you'd make them nervous."

The older cop took over. "We'll just make a pass through," he
said reasonably, moving his shoulders more than his body toward
the door. "If the guy's not here, no problem."

Jake acted as if he mistook that slight movement toward him
as a request for intimacy. He lowered his voice like Rose imagined any good maitre d' would. "I'm glad you understand," he
said, his hand at chest level, his fingers curled so the forefinger
would brush the sky-blue uniform shirt if the officer moved an
inch more toward him. "You can imagine it's hard to digest prop-
erly if people are wandering around looking for you."

The silence was profound. The cops shifted on their heavy-
shod soles. Finally, the older one took a backward step onto the
sidewalk. His partner followed.

"Wanna go get something to eat?" the older cop said to the
young one. The younger guy looked unbelieving. "Let's go,"
said the older guy. "Hell, why not have a little peace ourselves
for half an hour?"

Jake stood in the doorway, not victorious, not snotty, just
unperturbed. His quiet stance made him approachable, yet he
ignored Rose in a profoundly decent way.

"Goddam. That was rich," Rose said as soon as the cops were
out of earshot.

Jake immediately went from quiet absence to being right there.
"If somebody's hungry, he can eat here. No one's ever been murdered here." He spoke in that slow way he had. "You know

Edith?" Rose shook her head no. "She says, though I can't hope to approximate her cigarette growl, 'We sure as hell need something if we're coming here.' I also don't approach her conviction or style."

"You don't mind that somebody in there might be a murderer?" Rose threw in. She liked having her gun not too far away. Punks think you're old and wonky. She'd love to see the look in their eye when she'd turn toward them with that little bit of metal. You never know.

"No one should have to gulp down his food like an animal with a predator breathing down his neck, even if he murdered someone," Jake said. "It's just not civilized, don't you think?"

Rose laughed out loud. "How come you invited that one," her chin pointed toward Wendell, "to come in?"

"Wendell needs to be invited in. At least, I think he does," Jake said.

"How come?"

Jake breathed out. "I don't actually know. The first time he was our guest, he was carried in feet first. He stood out here and everyone came in and then he leaned against the post and finally he fainted. A fellow who was from his neighborhood when they were kids thought maybe he was waiting to be asked in, that he remembered something from when they were kids about Wendell always waiting to be asked in."

"You tell him what's for lunch?"

"Oh, I just throw that in when I have time. In case it's a deciding factor. Now. Let's talk about compost. It's so hippie," he said gaily.

Rose didn't laugh. No meat, only vegetable or fruit, rotten stuff okay. Then it occurred to her. "That Stan. He works here. Maybe he can bring this in a car to his house?"

Jake didn't ask how that was relevant. "Let me go ask him," he said.

Stan came out. " *Pani*," he said. "*Jak sie masz ?*"

Rose explained to him. She didn't ask what the hell he was doing at her Martin's. Maybe because Jake was there. She could speak in Polish, so she didn't sound as awkward. He agreed and said he'd bring stuff from Sparky's, his restaurant, too. Well, the more the merrier, she thought.

As soon as she started back toward the subway, she began to fume again.

Mad had kept her alive when she was new on homeless soil, eating cardboard food and with no one—just her DP self. The streets paved with gold? Not my gold, Papa. The streets were paved with Polish blood that came from scrapes on white knuckles torn red by the hod, from cuts imbedded with the clay of bricks slammed against stiff fingers, from detergent splits on the hands of the wives who scrubbed and aired their men's work clothes to rid them of the stench of the streets. The streets were paved by Dumb Polacks, and the foremen never let them forget that they were stupid not to have been born with English on their tongues. But she couldn't go back to Poland because it would be home no more. You can make a family, a home, but it can disappear and you are always a traveler.

A woman has no home but her mother.

Mad had kept her alive when she had to get married to a man nearly three times her age with children almost as old as she was because she was a teenager fat with child.

What did she care about the damn yard? It wasn't hers.

It struck her like a bolt. It wasn't the yard that was making her go off.

The only person Rose had been close to in thirty years was her sister. Once little Grace was gone, her sister was all that tethered her to this world. That was her belief.

At the end, Grace said no more words. She would touch her taloned hand to the spit in her mouth, as if she were dipping into the holy water font, and she would throw her hand in jerking motions, spraying her silent words. They would land like a blessing.

No matter how long Grace dipped and jerked, Rose could not find these words. What did she mean to say?

She had a horrible intensity about her. Did words seep into her brain and fill her head? Was she desperate to get them out in spittle sprays before she drowned in them? Or were the words an avalanche of split and shining rock, lost at her peripheries, pebbles over a cliff, and Grace, reaching before they fell, was left empty-handed with only her urgency. Displayed as a pathetic sprinkling. Dipping, jerking.

What happened to her words? For years, Rose looked for them in the folds of her clothes. She wondered: What could I do differently if I were to find out what she wanted to say?

When Grace went out of her life this way, this definite way, Rose knew what loneliness was.

Yes, she'd lost her daughter.

All those years, she couldn't allow herself to feel. A hole that couldn't be filled. Rose had been reaching absentmindedly into it, her fingers flailing to find some edge, her long, moaning cries waiting for an echo. No wall, no bottom. Only cold. Only dark. Only the ache, the stretch into it. Empty. Little Grace left her forever and the hole arrived at the same time, as if she'd dragged it behind on a long rope as she went away. She let go. This hole was her home, what Rose had from her. It was nothing. It was worse than nothing.

Frantic with loneliness. Nervous, fretting, impatient. Life was bitter, busy. Her brain jumping from task to task. Pointless, nothing accomplished, but busy. Rose could not imagine that the leaves dared still turn, that the idiotic sun would try to warm her bones. How did she not die? She cut herself off, lived in the hole of nothing.

Only her job making decals at American Spirit; only vague cousins at holidays; only her garden, behind the little two-flat, her beautiful, glorious garden, that one pleasure.

Then came her sister, her twin. For a time, there was life again. There was laughter and the closest friend.

Grace described when the first package Rose ever sent back home arrived. Excitement of Easter. They wondered at these good clothes. What didn't fit, Mama chose for certain neighbors she wanted to thank—as if she'd gone to Saks Fifth Avenue to buy them. Then the letter came separately. Papa, sonorous, read about the red wagon Rose pulled her package with, to the little store with a sign that said "*Pola do Polska.*" It was run by a man who lived only 100 kilometers from their farm. They stopped and talked about where it was, went to look at a map. Every detail so important. When Papa read about the money Rose had sewn into the hems, they all looked at each other. A minute passed. And Mama, laughing, ran to her new dress and began to feel for the crinkle. There it was. With what delight she started to tear the hem out. Rose must be in Paradise, so much she could afford to throw away to them! They even tore out the hem of the beaver coat she sent. Of course Rose would never put money in it—what was the likelihood they'd ever see a fancy coat after the inspectors opened it? Oh, they laughed about that. It got through unscathed and they ripped it. But Mama could sew it back better than new.

Rose had saved every penny, after paying her rent to her aunt and for the little food she ate at home. She came to share her bed with another boarder who worked nights and lessened her own costs (long negotiations with *Ciotka*) a bit with that. As much as she could, she sent, thinking they would come. Stupid Rusia. These stories, Rose's stories about being new here and such a greenhorn, a hundred tiny blessings made them knit together.

With her sister, love had entered her life again.

Love. What was that?

Rose remembered her one romantic love, her only chance and regret in that department.

Francis. A funny, joking fellow only a year her elder—a magician who could make coins appear at will, trick everyone with cards, and play the piano, sing in falsetto. They talked and argued until they were exhausted in laughter. There was that day, his silky chest, his rough hands, their bodies hot and later cool in contrast. Delicate veins, a map of life, the swell, the flush of his face, his full lips. Never did she forget that face, the mouth swollen with love, the eyes turned in and bringing her in at the same time. It was too late already when their moment came. Her loneliness and terrible coincidence had concocted her mistake only a few weeks before that. She was swelling already. And still, knowing it couldn't be him, Francis said they would run away. They didn't know that once they'd loved, it would be impossible to let go. But how? They didn't have ten cents between them. Ridiculous, that they both got across an ocean, but could not find their way to Milwaukee. His father kept him in the flat. Francis lost his job because of it. Francis struggled against fate, but his father saved him from Rose. Rose had to go on with her life that was meant to be.

Love. Little Grace. Who can explain that love? Beyond love. Not like a lover, but more. The smell, the touch, the breath of that girl. Her whining cry and her giggle. The feeling of her little hand right there, patting Mama's shoulder. Even her fits were as familiar as her mother's own cells. Rose and little Grace grew those cells together—she grew those fits. The little girl getting bigger and more. Until that stopped.

Rose had to stand and get her breath. Lord, could this breathing just stop? How much more, Rose thought, do you have to do to have this end? She had not let these thoughts surface in a hundred years.

Walter, her husband. Sad, sad man. Sometimes she thought he was so angry it had to come out as irreparable sadness. It was true for a lot of them, these immigrant men who came here and things didn't turn out the way they expected. Who expects to start a job with no respect? Who comes to America to be treated like dirt? Who expects that love will fly in and light and fly out? Children think, every one of them, that when they grow up, things will be all right. Immigrants, too. Walter, Walter. He tried to hang himself twice, once in the attic above their apartment, but his favorite daughter, Eleanor, still a child, found him and cried out and ran to him. She led him down the stairs, he sobbing, she serious, like a priest.

Another time, only Rose around, he in the closet, groping above for a hook. Rose was not the same audience as his little girl. She took the rope from him and she shamed him. He cried.

"Life is too hard," he'd said. "Too hard."

"What else is there?" she said to him. "Don't be crazy."

She didn't know why she thought that if she said it, he would stop being crazy.

A few years later, he outsmarted them. Rose wasn't there, but this is what his dearest girl, Eleanor, who had his nature, told her.

On August 15th, the feast of the Assumption of Our Blessed Virgin Mary, a holy day of obligation, and as beautiful a day as Chicago allows in August, he stood at the window before church, dressed in his suit. He called to her. As she came into the room, he said, "Good-bye, Norca." He toppled out of the low-silled window. She dashed forward, her arms stretched, her small hand catching only his shoed foot. The weight pulled her, slammed her against the sash of the window. She hung there, her body anchored by his 200 pounds against the opening, her insufficient little hand holding her father's flesh from the fall. Until the muscles gave out and he slipped from her grasp. Later, we found out her nose had been broken and her pelvis, too, was fractured. He landed on his head and neck. A woman screamed. The men nearby gathered his writhing body, carried him upstairs to the couch. No hospitals for the poor. For hours, he died there. When death was inevitable, the ambulance took him to Cook County.

Poor Norca. She survived the flu that would take her sister and Rose's child, but with this knowledge—that she let him go—out of her size, her pain, out of the weight of him, out of the weight of his despair. She still lived, but was an unhappy woman. She did not stay in touch with Rose.

He fell out the window by accident, Rose said. Eleanor would never go against that. So he could be buried in St. Adalbert's. No suicides allowed in a Catholic cemetery. His life insurance, since no one could say different, was paid. Rose bought her flats.

So, these were the loves in her life.

Grace. The very first and last other part of Rose. Everything good that ever was in her had been reflected from, magnified by, those eyes. Rose searched as Grace slipped away, staring into them to see the person Grace had made her. As Grace lost her understanding, Rose, too, was lost. She thought: Who will explain me to myself? Who will know the best in me?

She did not know where to look. Her mirror was shattered.

Without thinking about maps and buses, Rose found that she was in front of Sophie's. She shrugged and walked in.

CHAPTER TEN

Sophie
What's to Move?

The tide was receding and thank God, it was taking the stuff with it. Tentatively, she had started to put things away. They seemed able to stay put.

This accomplishment wouldn't have been one a few years ago. You brought some thing out for a dinner, whatever, and it gets put back away again after you use it. That's the everyday of life.

Who knows how things get out of control? One stumbling misstep and another, one more off balance, and you're atilt in your world. Until stupid dullness makes the world itself lopsided.

It was Saturday afternoon, her every-other-week day off. So, she was reading in the kitchen when she heard Rose.

"*Pani*," she said. Rose nodded. Sophie tried to not register her surprise. She was not indifferent to Rose's life. Her own, well that's another story. What? she argued. I've been living. I go to work, I come home, I go to a movie, play cards, see friends. I laugh, I even cry.

"I need to sit."

So, she sat.

"You look tired."

"Ya. I can't do so much. That kid here today?"

Sophie shook her head no.

"She comes, she don't come. Why should I care?"

"Maybe you do, though?"

"That gets my ass tired," Rose said. With that, Sophie knew she hit a nerve.

"I got to run do an errand," Sophie said. "You okay to stay here?"

Rose began to get up. "I can do something for you. Dishes? Something?"

"Sit down and sit," Sophie said.

No sooner was Sophie gone than there was a knock on the door.

She could see it was the neighbor, Stan.

"What?" she opened the door.

"I brought the compost stuff."

She wasn't going to look a gift horse in the mouth. "*Djiekuje.*"

"Don't mention it."

"What're you doing there?"

"I just help out."

"There," Rose said. "Martin's. "

"Oh, *Pani*. I met Zelda—Boody, you know—a long while ago. She used to stop at Sparky's, my restaurant, you know? And she asked if we could contribute, so I asked the owner, he's a friend from church, and he has me over-order. Then I started taking the stuff there when their truck broke, and now sometimes I help out."

"I don't get there so much anymore. I never saw you there."

Stan looked embarrassed. "I saw you there a couple weeks ago, but I didn't say nothing. I was out back. I'll just drop a can off when it's full. You want me to throw it in that box?"

"No. You don't throw new stuff on top or it won't get done. I got a system."

"Okay, *Pani*. See you."

As he left, the phone rang, which confused her. She reached for it before she thought not to.

"Ya," she answered.

"Hey, it's Zak. That you, Rose? You answering the phone?

What? You live there?"

  Rose was frozen.

  "Did you move in?"

  "What's to move? Everything I got in my bags."

  "Yeah, what's to move? Cool."

  "You okay?" Rose asked.

  "Yeah. I'm good."

  "It's good you're okay."

  "Can I talk to Sophie?"

  "No."

  "Why not?"

  "Cause she's not here."

  "Oh."

  "What do you want?" It wasn't what she meant to say.

  "I don't know. I guess I want to know if it's okay to keep coming to work, even if I miss sometimes."

  "Yeah."

  "Yeah, it's okay? Or yeah, you understand?"

  "What do you think, I'm stupid? Yeah, I understand and yeah, it's okay."

  "Groovy. I'll see you tomorrow."

  "Ya," Rose said. She hung up.

  She put the phone on its cradle on the doily on its own little table where the phone books were neatly packed into the opening beneath. She realized that she didn't even know enough about Zak to get bad news about her. If she'd never called, she could have evaporated. What was she talking about? Same with her. She'd be at Cook County Hospital or Jail and nobody would know.

  She opened her book on math and read.

  Sophie came back with a pile of kraut pierogi and chrusciki. "Surprise! My girlfriend was making pierogi today, so I told her I'd come and help. This is some for us. Then I stopped at the bakery." She was grinning. "You'll stay?"

"My foot is throbbing. I walked too far today."

"Yes, then. Sit on your ass," Sophie said. Somehow, Rose made her talk that way. "Rose, maybe you want to stay here tonight? Don't jump on me."

Rose grunted.

Sophie wasn't going to push her luck. She went on making dinner. She was in a cheery mood.

"Zak called," Rose said.

"You answered?"

"I didn't think about it. I just picked it up."

"So, what did she want?"

"She wanted to know if she could come to work more. I told her yeah." Rose said the last part into her chest, as if she didn't have the right to have done it.

"Good," Sophie said. "I wonder if she has any family living? She seems awfully on her own. You know, how she stays for dinner when we ask her to."

"Lots of kids don't have anybody. Maybe yeah." Rose shrugged. "Maybe I'll stay here tonight."

"What?" Sophie looked like you could have knocked her over with a thought. "Want to see the room?"

"Okay."

Sophie led her up the stairs to the low-ceilinged bedroom where she'd been sleeping. She was a nomad in her own house. But lately she couldn't stay in the room where Barbara had died. "This used to be our room. And later Barbara had a nephew, Alex, who used to come and stay in this room in the summer," she told Rose as she opened the windows for airing. "Then we'd go down." Sophie's hands remembered opening windows just a bit during a rainy evening, letting in the spray of the storm with the fresh, electrified air.

"He stopped coming after she died?"

Sophie grunted a sad laugh. "Well before that," she said. "Barbara's sister, Harriet, wouldn't allow him to visit after a while. It was after Barbara had gone to visit in February, a few years before she became ill, maybe around '62, or was it '63?"

"So, why?"

Sophie got busy, checking sills as she opened the windows, removing bed linens. "I don't know what was said. Barbara kept to herself about her family. I think it had something to do with us."

"She, the sister I mean, didn't want him to spend his summertime with just women?"

"Oh, nothing like that. Harriet was raising the boy alone. Her husband was a truck driver who left on a long haul and never came back. I mean," Sophie struggled with her words, "with me and Barbara, with our being together."

Rose looked blank.

"Maybe I need to tell you this," Sophie said in collapse, sitting on the edge of the window seat. "I don't know the words for it."

Rose held her tongue.

"Barbara and I were like a couple." She took a deep breath. "A married couple. We were intimate with each other." Sophie flushed fully. "Like a man and a woman."

I am a lesbian. There, she'd said it, if only to herself. She didn't think she'd ever known one. They didn't wear a decal to say. Though people in the neighborhood used to say behind her back about that lady, Johnnie, who owned the tavern on Marshfield, that she was a "L." No one ever said the word if they knew it. They just sort of snickered it. She's a "L." They still drank there and asked her to run a tab.

"You don't have to stay here if you don't want."

"Are you crazy? You said stay. You don't want me to stay?" Rose asked.

"Yes," Sophie said. "I mean to invite you. I just thought that maybe you wouldn't want to be here."

Sophie sat, rigid, looking straight ahead, as if she were on a train, as if she were waiting to give her ticket. The silence was thick in the room.

"I'll stay."

"You don't mind that I'm that way?"

"I don't care."

Sophie was relieved, anyone could see it.

Rose didn't want any of that. "You don't need to look so happy. I just don't care."

"That's something to be happy about," Sophie said. "Some people..."

"Such a little bit makes you happy? It's crumbs," Rose answered.

"Crumbs." Sophie glazed over. "You don't know how slippery love is then. You think you're in something and find happiness seeping out under the door." She absentmindedly handed fresh sheets to Rose. She didn't know where this was coming from. "You can see the pain in that, can't you?" she asked. But Sophie wasn't really talking to her.

"I can't stay here," Rose said.

"It's hard enough to weather the outside when your love is a little—unusual—but when the storm is inside, too, well, there's no shelter, is there?" Sophie looked drained. "OK," Sophie said. Defeated.

Rose put her hand on the handrail—the same one Barbara had used, that Sophie had used, that the boy barely touched as he dashed up two steps at a time—that went unused after some-one, who was supposed to be family, found out something she didn't understand.

As if I do.

Sophie was exhausted. "You're not going to stay?"

"JesusMaria, are we going to argue about it? I'm ready to stay." said Rose. She nearly glared. "I can't stay inside. I'll sleep in the yard. I like that."

"If that's what you want, fine. You know where the bathroom is. Just make yourself at home."

"I'm going to head upstairs, then." Suddenly, she wanted to be in that room again. "Good night, Rose," Sophie said gently.

"Good night."

CHAPTER ELEVEN

Zak
Home Again

Zak and Linda Lee were down at the Lincoln Park Conservatory. They breathed in the warm humidity.

"It's like being in the tropics, isn't it?" Linda Lee said.

"I don't know. I never been there. Been to Georgia, though. Feels like that."

"Me neither, silly, the tropics. But can't you just imagine the tall, cool drinks and we're sitting next to a swimming pool? Or walking along a white beach with the water glinting diamonds at us?"

Yes, she could. Zak could imagine almost anything with her right now.

They had managed to get to the Park even though the CTA strike was going strong. Linda Lee stood out with her thumb pointing. After a car stopped and she thought the guy was okay, Zak hurried out from the shadow of the building at the bus stop. That was some disappointed look on the driver's face when he saw this scrawny thing was with her, Zak laughed. But they were a team now, that was clear.

Zak had her new sketch book with her, the one Linda Lee got with a mess of colored pencils and acrylic crayons so Zak could get together more stuff for her class at the Art Institute for "gifted teens." It was just these few weeks, but what they called intensive, meaning three days each week, seven hours each day, ending August 25th with the show. It was the nicest stuff Zak ever had. And she liked hanging around with other people who saw weird and had to get it on paper.

After she and Linda Lee left the white-glassed conservatory, they went to sit a while at the lagoon.

"Draw me a picture what you see," Linda Lee said. And Zak took in the birds and the few people around except for the hippies, plenty of them. And of course, there were starting to be cops. Porky cops, rolling back on their heels without a clue what to do but look redneck. Zak started in to draw a scene without any of the last two bunches.

"Hey, man, do you think the convention's going to happen?"

"I don't know, why not?"

"There's that strike with the phone people, Mama. Don't you even look at the papers?" Zak liked to push Linda Lee's buttons a bit. "I think it ain't going to happen."

"Yes, I do read the paper. But Richard J. Daley, Mayor, is not going to let it pass. Sometimes, you got to read in between the lines, Pearl. He'll have his convention. He couldn't show his face if he don't."

Zak had lived through another setback with her mother only a few weeks before. Zak called their number sometimes, thinking, what if someone Zak didn't even know took her away so she would never see her again? One tiny part of Zak was convinced her mother wouldn't leave her, but other parts said sure, she would, if something better came along. Maybe she'd never left where she got on a train, but.... Besides, Zak had left Linda Lee, hadn't she? Her mother was not the patient type. Maybe she'd got mad enough and lonely enough to move on. She wasn't such a much that Linda Lee ever chose her even over some sad little bottle of pills or a open beer. If you were a guy with those to offer, forget about it, she could be gone six ways to Sunday.

So she had dialed the number now and again. I just want to hear her voice, she'd tell herself. And when it occurred to her that she wouldn't know what to say, she'd hang up before anyone answered. Until, one obsessive day, ten attempts, ten tosses of the coin later, Linda Lee answered on the first ring. Her heart filled her chest, made speech impossible for a second.

"Mama?"

"Hey, girl. That you?"

"Uh-huh."

"What're you doing?"

"Nothing."

"Why don't you come see me?"

"Now?"

"Sure."

Zak heard her covering the phone and talking to someone. It made her heart hurt. "I don't know. Not nothing, exactly. I got to go to my job."

"You come over and tell me about it," Linda Lee said.

"When?"

"Now."

"I'm supposed to go to my job," Zak said again, mourning rising, her resolve to go to Sophie's softening. Linda Lee covered the phone again and she couldn't hear the words. But she could hear anger in the man's voice behind the hand.

"Zak, honey, you come over. I got to get off. We're waiting on an important call."

Zak's blood turned to ice. Important call, my colossal ass. And some ape yelling at her to free up the phone.

"Somebody sick, Mama? Somebody dying? You got to call Peoples Gas about a leak?"

"Don't talk that way, Zak. My friend told somebody to call around now. It's important."

"Shit, Linda Lee, I thought maybe you'd think this call was important."

"Listen to the tone of your voice. I hate when you treat me this way, Zak. I really want to talk to you. That's why you should come over."

"I can't now." The voice in the background got louder.

"You come by," she said. "I'd love to see you."

The line went dead.

"I'd love to see you," Zak heard. Like she was some old pal.

Zak shoved aside the rest. How filthy everything was the last time. If she were there, she could keep the place clean. How Linda Lee loved, loved, loved her but any raggedy man with a sweet mouth for a minute could keep her from doing anything with Zak. How Linda Lee took a little alcohol or a few tokes or any damn pill to ease her unease with life. If she were there, Linda Lee would have something else to think about, maybe she'd take up some hobby or get a job and they'd spend the evening together after school like she did with the old gals. Dinner and cleaning up and pools of yellow light in the living room illuminating a book, a crossword puzzle, the radio on with the Beatles playing, her making pictures.

She had not spent five days like that in her life before she met Suzee and then Sophie and Rose.

She didn't have no home with Linda Lee. The thought had made her fall apart. She'd sobbed. She didn't have no home with Linda Lee.

She gave up on work after that call and had sat her skinny butt on the bus on Diversey, which she liked in spite of its being a two-lane street. She was in no hurry to do nothing.

The bus headed east and she let her agitation take over. Eddie. That sonovabitch. Was he staying by Mama? She liked to think of Linda Lee as Mama lately. Didn't sound like him, though, she could remember. Zak almost jumped the bus to grab the Kedzie line, but as much as she wanted to see Mama, she did not want to see him. She watched the neighborhood change to better-kept houses, maroon brick, some back from the street a little, with green buffer to the street. That block and line of color brought a relief.

She thrilled to the turn onto Stockton Drive with its beautiful little sandstone buildings and bronze sculptures of hard-muscled men in front, the statue of Goethe, green dripping down him, in the delta opening into the park. As they moved south through Lincoln Park, Zak thought maybe she'd walk along the water. In the lake-forsaken part of the city, the concrete and asphalt gave off heat and took away air. By LaSalle Street, she was off the bus, heading to the wide open blue on the other side of Lake Shore Drive. There was North Avenue Bath House, a long building with smokestacks, made to look like a boat. It tickled her.

Lake Michigan was inviting, the waves winking in the sun. The air was nearly cool. There was practically a breeze. Her hair almost moved. She walked south, the lake on her left, the sand before her. A million indentations from shoes and feet had nicked the sand. In the mornings, the sun's angle made them into dark pockets, giving the beach a lively pattern. At this time of day, they held no tricks.

Damn, damn, and damn. She was a mess inside and it was only this motion, this walking, walking that would keep her from imploding. Why in hell and heaven was it so tough to be home?

She'd just have to keep going to work and staying with Macy and Suzee or something.

All that day and the next and the next after, the wanting ate at Zak like bone-penetrating Chicago cold, like the sun pounding on you until there was nothing to do but lie down. Maybe the guy would be gone, maybe Linda Lee didn't take any drug or such and she'd talk to Zak, maybe. All she wanted was Linda Lee's laugh and the smell of lilacs and a few damn sweet moments. Home was all those things wrapped up together. She wanted to be home.

So she went.

Lo and behold, Linda Lee was there. The apartment was cleaned up some. And Zak presented her case.

"Let's start again, Mama," she said. She was ready for the storm, for the you-don't-understand and the you-don't-care. But , with Linda Lee, you never knew.

"Baby girl, I am so happy to have you here," she said.

"But?"

"No but, child. You are the most important thing to me in the world."

A glow started somewhere deep. Zak didn't want to fan it with even a breath of hope.

"We need to get out of here and move. You and me. I am done with looking myself in the eye and wondering who I am. And where you are."

Two parts doubt, one part wish. The ratio began to change against every grain of experience Zak had accumulated. "You had somebody here when I called," Zak said, trying not to sound angry.

"You called?" Linda Lee said.

"Three damn days ago, I talked to you and you said I should come by."

"Great God, sugar, I thought I dreamed that." Linda Lee looked clean and sweet. The flat didn't smell bad or anything. "I don't remember it except as a dream. It was another mistake, that man. I don't want to tell you what all has got into me. I think I got it, though. I am done, Zak. I want to stay clean of the life I been dragging around. Can you help me, though?"

"What?" Zak was immediately on her guard.

"You don't need to be that way. I mean, I want you to help me figure out how to start again. We got to move. Too many assholes have the key to this place." She looked abashed, if that was the word, like humble and just a bit embarrassed.

Linda Lee opened her arms. And Zak fell into them and felt the short breaths that meant she was trying not to cry. That was good, that she wasn't getting all dramatic. This whole conversation was unusual. Zak liked to think of it as a turn of events. "Okay, Mama."

They had found a place near Logan Square, where a lot more of the Polish still lived. It was nearly a boardinghouse, some of the people there, just in rooms. But they had three rooms to themselves with a kitchen and whatnot, just like an apartment in a big old building probably used to be one whole mansion of a house.

And today, they had an outing.

After hanging around the lagoon for a while, they walked West in Fullerton.

"I'm getting hungry," Linda Lee said. "How about I treat us to lunch?"

"That disability you started on getting can handle lunch out?" Zak was used to their never having an extra dime.

"Yes, sweet. Your mother can pop for a bite to eat."

"How come you got disability, Ma?"

"Cause I'm disabled, child. Didn't you notice?" She bumped her hip against Zak and knocked her a little off balance.

"You're going to make me disabled," Zak laughed. "The government just decided like that?"

"Is this the most boring conversation you've had in your life? Ever? 'Cause it is for me."

So, that was that. At the six corners created by Fullerton, Lincoln, and Halsted, they walked into Sparky's and settled into the air-conditioning.

Linda Lee looked at the menu. "All meals include lettuce and tomato, salad, OR soup, choice of potatoes (French fries, mashed, boiled, baked, choose one), Jell-O, and coffee." She laughed and pointed out to Zak that next to the spaghetti it said: "Potatoes are not included with this meal." "I swear," she said, "when a Chicagoan eats, he expects a potato with everything, meat cooked plain, and salad full of iceberg lettuce."

"I like the lettuce," Zak said.

"Then you have become a Chicagoan. You want a potato with your pasta, too?"

They were laughing about that when the man came up. He brought the water and a small mountain of butters.

"Hi. Hey, aren't you the girl who works at Sophie's?" It was Sophie's neighbor.

"No," Zak said straight up. "I don't know anybody of that name."

"Sure you do. Zosia, maybe? Do you call her that?"

"I don't call her nothing. I don't know nobody like that."

Stan gave her a look a bit askance. "Hmm. My mistake, maybe. Okay. Jaz, the best waitress on the North Side of Chicago, will be with you in a minute."

"That's a sweet name," Linda Lee said.

"Short for Jaszczurowski," Stan said and smiled before he walked off.

"Shoulda' guessed," Linda Lee said.

The restaurant was filled with all kinds of people. Two booths of cops sat stirring their iced tea waiting for their orders. Regular people all over the place.

Then some hippies from the park came in.

As they passed the boys in blue, looks passed. One cop couldn't keep his mouth shut. "Hey," he said as one long-haired boy passed, "I heard your free-love girlfriend is giving out freebies back of the Historical Society." It was where the cops were getting headquartered to keep the park clear. He looked around the table for the gang to back him up. "We're going to check it out when we get back."

The kid stopped for a second. Zak waited for the hippie to call the cop a pig, something the TV said they did. The kid just looked at him. He reached in his pocket and the cop planted his feet as if to get up. The kid put a quarter on the table and addressed Jaz instead of the cop. "Let me buy this guy a dough-nut," the kid said, loud enough for a couple of tables to hear him. "He needs to get in a better mood." The kid kept moving to a table with his pals, all of them wearing jeans with the bot-toms frayed and colorful shirts like he had on. Zak felt a grin crack across her face. The cops looked kind of mad, but one of them said something must have been funny to the rest and their food was just coming, so nothing developed. It had been tense for a minute there.

The waitress was unfazed and hopped right over. "What do you gals want? We got salads today. These convention kids are…" and she mouthed the words like a secret "…a lot of them, veg-etarian. We got lots of that on special."

They just ordered burgers. Linda Lee looked Zak right in the eye and said, "Who's this Sophie?"

"He got me wrong. I don't know who."

"When you tell a whopper, your eyes bug out just a little, don't you know that?"

Zak was speechless. "My eyes?"

"Uh-huh. You need to start letting me know who these peo-ple are you spend time with. You don't have to work no more, honey. Like you don't need to stay with your little colored friend. We're solid."

"Mama, nobody says 'colored' no more."

"Negra?"

"Negro. She calls herself black anyway."

"That sounds plain rude."

"It's what she calls herself and wants to be called."

"Nevermind that, tell me about Sophie."

Zak started to get a little mad. She had to make her some money, had had to offer something to Suzee for her keep. And when she did, Suzee said each word slow: "Child, since when do you think," and she hesitated a long time right there, "that you have got to pay a grown-up to take care of you?"

Zak knew precious little but being small, scrounging around for returnable bottles and going through the purse and the sofa cushions for enough money to eat, or later to get new clothes when the nun said she was a mess and should be ashamed. Her old ones had been put on her new and left to about fall off. If she had a few dollars, surely she should offer some, keeping her quiet two twenties safe apart. It cost money to raise a kid.

Suzee hadn't left any time for Zak to answer, but had said, "You think you're needing to pay your way?" And Zak insisted three times, like Linda Lee told her you have to do if you want someone to take something for true.

Suzee had taken it then with a shake of her head and she had put her hand by Zak's cheek just as she walked out the room.

"Nothing to tell," Zak said. She felt confused. All of a sudden, she wasn't supposed to watch out for herself? Much as she loved Linda Lee, this sudden mother thing was annoying. "I got to go to the bathroom." She had "her time" and was all on edge now.

"I'll come, too, Pearl."

"Stop it, Linda Lee." The light shown pretty in her eyes, though.

"You can tell me when you get back, then."

Zak didn't know why she wouldn't just let it go. So, she was glad to see the food got there when she got back. They talked about how good it was and Zak started to make her laugh with a story about a boy she'd met, acting him out for her audience of one. She was happy just to be with her.

But, when they left, with Stan waving her off like an old friend, Linda Lee started again. "So, is this Sophie one of your school-mate's mothers? Is it that Macy's mother?"

Zak was messed up in her head, anxious for no reason and irritable. "She's just a lady who hired me to do some work," Zak said. "I met her at a library."

"Which one?"

"Huh?"

"What library?"

"What do you care?"

"I just want to know where you're hanging out. People can be dangerous, you know."

"Tell me," Zak said, thinking of, well, just about everything she'd rather not. "It's too damn bad you weren't there to tell me that when I met her."

"Where?"

"The Rogers Park Library. Up by Northwestern."

"She got a last name?"

"Not that I know of," Zak said, making sure her eyes did not bug out. It was useful to know things about yourself that maybe only your mother would notice. And was fool enough to tell you so you could keep an eye on them. Some things were not her mama's business.

"Maybe I can meet her sometime. If you think you want to keep making pocket change. You don't need to, little Pearl. We're okay now."

Zak decided to let this go. They didn't need the money? That was new. How the hell much was she getting on disability? Was it that much better than welfare? Or her jobs, one after another? Anyhow, they had either a hell of a long walk or they had to get started on hitching a ride to get home. She wanted to work on a picture she'd started for class tomorrow. All this interest in her little life was new to her. Maybe that's what it's like to have a mother, she thought, with a sudden warmth. Maybe they just irritate you half to death because they want to know all about you.

It gave a lilt to her step.

CHAPTER TWELVE

Rose
After the Garden

Rose woke in the yard in her own sweat. She had grown comfortable staying outside at Sophie's instead of all that running around. She ambled inside to find Zak at the table, fumbling with colored pencils. Seeing her was like drinking a glass of cool water.

"Hi," Rose said, lifting her chin an inch.

"Hey," said Zak.

"You just get here?"

"Yeah. Sophie said it was cool to hang out. You want me to start?"

"Too damn hot out," Rose said, feeling no complaint in it.

"What we doing today?" She kept her eyes on her paper.

Rose made a dismissive sound. There'd been plenty of dog days that July that had forced them inside. Today was just another. No need to knock themselves out.

"Maybe move that dirt you got?" While she sat, the perspiration was standing on her face.

"Go jump in the lake," Rose said.

"I wouldn't mind."

"Ya, maybe we should," Rose said. Then she remembered what was going on down there, all the kids and the cops, no place for a smartass and an old lady. "Maybe Riis Park. It's got a pool to swim in. How about that?" There was a moment's delay.

"I think I kind of need the work," Zak said. "I got to buy all these colors and such. I need them. I'm in this thing at the Art Institute."

"Art Institute. Oh. What?"

"It's for kids who can draw. My mother got me in." It was the first time she'd mentioned either.

"That's good, right?"

"It is way beyond cool. I'm copying on the paintings and learning techniques. And I like the other kids and the teachers are really groovy. They dress like me."

"Oh, that's too bad," Rose said. She saw the hesitation before Zak got it as a joke. "You're good at this. You study."

"There's going to be a show at the end, all our stuff. Last Sunday in August. You guys can come if you don't have nothing to do."

"Ya, maybe we will," Rose answered. "Listen, we'll pay you to work today, but you don't have to." She had money of her own, she could pay her. "It's too damn hot."

"Cool," Zak said.

They took the Fullerton bus west to Central. Zak could have gone alone, but then what would Rose be doing?

"You coming in?" Zak asked.

If she was a grandma for someone, maybe, she'd go. But she wasn't. "I'll wait here."

While Zak chattered in with the crowd, Rose moved under the shade of the elms. She spread a thin, pastel-plaid blanket and opened *World of Mathematics* by James R. Newman. She was astounded and amused by it. She'd come to think that numbers are the basis of all life—music, nature, art—which would make the "music of the spheres" more than a whimsical metaphor. Rose relaxed against the rough bark and looked up into the canopy of serrated leaves. Elms adapt with a freely flowing branching, their small leaves filling every inch of the structure they've created, reaching every inch of sun and rain they could that way. A mathematical wonder, every tree. The sunlight traveled through when a breeze moved a series of leaves. She felt a light sweat descend between her breasts and she sunk into quiet. The canicular summer was made bearable by concord of light and heat and torpor.

Zak didn't exactly confide in Rose, so her even mentioning the Art Institute was surprising. She was bubbling over. Sophie told her that Zak was living with her mother now which, of course, hadn't seemed to be true before. Who knew if it was true now?

She remembered the night Sophie asked her to stay for dinner back toward the beginning. Zak said, "Sure." Then Sophie'd said, "Don't you think we better call your mother?"

"She's kind of busy tonight," Zak had said.

"Call her, won't you?" Sophie looked at her as if they had an understanding. Zak dialed the number and stretched the coiled phone cord from the wall around the corner to the relative privacy of the hallway. She lowered her voice, but they could still hear her clearly. She was doodling something on a paper on the telephone table, talking away.

"Hey, what's happening?" A few seconds passed. "Cool. Hey, I got a gig for tonight. I'm gonna stay up north to eat." A full minute passed. "You got it all worked out, Einstein. It's a old lady." And she giggled in a way they hadn't heard from her. They talked a bit more, Zak's voice low but cheerful. "Okay, man, you tell Suzee?" And then, "See you when I see you." She hung the phone up and presented herself back in the kitchen with a grin. The cord hung three times longer than it had, the coils loose, the wire stretched beyond itself. "It's cool," she said. "I'll set the table."

"If that was an adult, I'm a nun," Rose had said under her breath. She held her tongue through dinner, the cleaning up. When Zak had taken her last cigarette and left, Rose spoke.

"Who the hell's she calling? She's a mystery, that one. How is she so free to work all day, to stay for dinner?" Zak was a straw in the wind. "Who the hell was she talking to?"

"Maybe we should just ask her," Sophie said.

"JesusMaria. We'd see her tail before the question was out. You might get something out of her. She likes you." Rose waved her hands. "All these Yippies and flippies. She'd run off with them—split, she'd say. I ask her anything, she'll end up in San Francisco." A hothead herself, she knew better than to give word to certain things.

When Zak came out of the pool, she had the look of a happy kid, not her usual look by any means. Her skin was taut over high cheekbones, her fingertips were wrinkled and the smell of chlorine splashed before her. Rose remembered how that felt after you'd been in water for hours. She felt it with Zak.

They decided to walk back to Sophie's. They could always hop on the bus if it got to be too much. Her foot had healed pretty well. This weather was good to her arthritis and she needed to move around or she'd be in a wheelchair soon. The long cement-shimmering walk reflected the heat until the soles of their feet were burning.

"Did you meet anybody in there?" She didn't know what she meant, maybe potential friends. The girl was alone too much. At least it seemed so.

"This one boy, Arnold? He's about this tall," Zak showed a line at her shoulders, "and he's a bully. All the time, he's pushing the little kids in the water when nobody's looking. But I'm looking, the other kids are looking, just not the lifeguards or anybody. He's gawky looking, and his eyes are blank, like nobody home." She shows her eyes going off in different directions. Acting him out, she looks a foot shorter. "So I wait until he's going to the low board and I dare him to the high dive. He's chickenshit, right?" She shows him looking a fretful bully. "But I did it in front of a bunch of guys that didn't think much of him. Wouldn't give him a handful of hay if he was a donkey in a cement pasture. So we both get up there and I can see he's getting up the nerve. I'm behind him. He's at the edge and the lifeguard turns to yell at some little kids and flippin' run out and I shove his rabbit asshole self off." She gives a profound impression of him swimming in midair. "He hits the water half-standing and half-laying like a hen." Zak crouched to the sidewalk with one leg spread to the side. She had a ludicrous look on her face, something between surprise and despair. "Man, he didn't bother nobody after that. I bet he ain't riding his bike home."

Rose knew she should be scolding her, like Sophie would. But Zak's story made Rose laugh until she needed to pee.

Fortunately, there was Benny's hot-dog stand, a crazy yellow and red with blue print, the color of every Vienna Franks in the city. She could use their toilet, they knew her.

"You want a hot dog?" Rose said because she did and was sure Zak's answer was yes.

"Sure."

The dogs came on a poppy seed-topped hot-dog bun, with hot peppers, onions, relish, mustard, cucumbers, tomatoes, everything but ketchup. They had a sign up said: "Don't even THINK of asking for ketchup." Italian Beef came sliced super-thin, laid out on a half-foot chunk of Italian bread with cooked sweet peppers on request with absolutely nothing else, except if you requested extra juice. Good, greasy fries. They were the cheapest meals in town outside of St. Martin's. They together had kept Rose alive.

They walked out with their dogs in a few minutes. There wasn't another park along Fullerton until Logan Square. So they sat on a bus bench across from Benny's, their backs blocking out an ad for Casey Kozlowski's Funeral Home.

"I love that yellow," Zak said, looking across four lanes of traffic. "It's unreal."

"Ya," Rose said, tapping her forehead to release information. "I saw today in this book an interesting thing for you. I think, maybe you, too, that yellow is yellow, green, blue, that everyone would recognize these colors…"

"Is this a trick? Like a color-blind guy can't."

"That, too," Rose said. "But listen to this. The Greeks and some Natchez Indians had one word for yellow and green. They didn't separate them. That would make it hard to paint them, no? I know I could ask you."

"Not to paint them," Zak said. "I mess with colors all the time. It's almost that there is no real-life color, just mix a little yellow in the green to make it stand out or like for a bud on a flower, more blue mixed in to fade it back."

Rose saw her old garden, the one from years ago. She'd explained it to Grace, why she put the cranesbills, veronicas, the campanulas, the catmints, at the back of the lot. They were all blues. It added depth to the garden to plant them in the distance.

"But there is no green," Rose said.

"Yeah, no green. Just, like, something we start with called green."

"So, a rainbow has no colors, just such-a changing."

Zak looked perplexed, maybe for how to explain what she meant. "It's not like there ain't colors but, you know, when I do something white, it's not white, it's blue and violet and yellow, but it looks white."

"The colors are—" then said a word in Polish and paused to pull it into English, "—slippery," Rose said dreamily in English. "Infinite."

"I don't know about that," Zak said. "I just mix them to show what I see."

Rose smiled. "Maybe I need goggles."

The bus came just as they finished crushing their white wrappers into the grease-splotched brown bag. They decided to hop on. Once the momentum of walking had worn off, it was too hot to keep on.

Rose put her token in and began to follow Zak back. The bus was practically empty. Two seats back from the driver, Zak turned around. In spite of the tan she'd started on, she looked pale and wide-eyed, a bunny caught in headlights.

"Go ahead," Rose said, facing the back, pointing her hand toward the back.

"I got to get off," Zak mumbled, facing her.

"What the hell?"

Zak pushed right past Rose to the front of the bus. "Next stop," she said sweetly, lowering herself down to the first stair.

Rose had turned back front to follow Zak with her eyes. She was directly in line between the man seated a few rows back and Zak. Rose had been looking forward to the ride home. "I don't want to get off," Rose said as she moved a step toward Zak.

"Then don't," said Zak quietly, looking at her with intent. "See you later," she added as the bus stopped and she darted out the door. Rose was stuck where she stood, staring at the vacated doorway. Zak was gone too quickly for Rose to think of following her.

"*Psie krew*," Rose said, as she lowered into the first seat, straining out the windows to see if she could see her, but Zak was nowhere.

"JesusMaria," she said under her breath. Rose turned to look at the other passengers to see what Zak might have seen. There sat a lady, in her thirties, who smiled in the way Midwest women do to say I'm-okay-don't-blame-me-whatever-it-is. Rose hated that smile and refused to return it. The boys on the back seat were engaged in foul-mouthed ill-humored teasing. The man was still staring out the window. She studied each of them. It was something with one of them or Zak was a nutcase.

Either was possible.

She got herself up and moved toward the middle of the bus. She sat near the open window, but turned her body toward the aisle so she could look around.

The woman was dressed respectably and with no flare whatsoever. Rose didn't pay attention to what she herself wore but this woman did, and came up with an outfit that any grandmother might wear to go on the avenue. The woman turned her head and smiled again. Rose looked away.

The boys were in their early teens, maybe even fifteen, in blue jeans and tired-looking shirts. Their hair touched their shoulders. One didn't seem to be in a very good mood at the moment. He looked like he spent most of his waking hours trying to be worse than he was. The other was awkwardly nonchalant. They were inarticulate to the point of its being painful, even for Rose, whose standards were not rigorous. "Fuck" was the major component of their conversation, as an adverb, adjective, any way at all. She didn't take offense, but she couldn't make out what they were talking about. Their hair was to their shoulders, one light and stringy and the other dark and sleek. The stringy-haired one was slight the way only teenagers can be, his chest and shoulders childlike. He had a rooster's attentive nerves. The other boy looked like he'd rather be smoking or spitting. Neither one of them paid any attention to her by lowering their voices or altering their manners. That was fine with her. Why should they?

She looked to the staring man who was opposite her, one seat back. He had brown hair that maybe used to be blond. It had the look of hair that had changed, gotten worn out. He was sharp-featured, with tiny eyes that darted as he kept his gaze out the window. His face at rest had a sour, lost look. Tight, like he expected to be cheated. By his complexion, he was either a farmer or just hard-living. She looked at his hands. They were not the hands of a farmer, more like an alley gambler. He must have felt her stare because he turned from the window all of a sudden, all neck movement like a bird. Rose knew the value of her years and the street. She kept staring until he turned his eyes back out the window.

"Next stop," she said out loud, with her eye still on the man. She pulled herself from the seat, sticky with the heat, and made her way to the front door. Just as she was about to step down, she looked back. Their eyes met. Though she showed no sign of it, she shivered.

When she got to Sophie's, she poured a glass of lemonade. Zak would come when she came. The Möbius strip of her mind turned again.

Rose became estranged from the world when little Grace disappeared from it. Nothing could catch her for thirty years, just moving, working, just nothing.

Then big Grace came to the United States after so many years apart. Her twin. And my God, how they talked and talked, all the books they'd read, philosophizing and wondering. It was almost life again.

So when her sister died, she was alone as only a twin could be. Not a half of her was gone, but someone that in unexplained ways *was* her. Of course, it reopened the biggest, saddest, loneliest loss. Little Grace. The only reason that didn't finish her at the time was because she had to care for the others. Then they went. Ai, ai, she said inside. Damn it, Zak. She was mad at herself. Zak.

She opened the *World of Mathematics* and sat to read.

Orphaned Josef Von Fraunhofer was given a tremendous opportunity when the Prince Elect (who would become Maximilian

I Joseph) took an interest in him, providing the youngster with time and education to pursue his abilities. Fraunhofer observed and studied the dark lines in a spectrum. They were determined to accurately reflect measures of certain chemicals in the star. What seemed nonsense to the eye became a tool.

Her mind wandered from the page and she reread and reread the same thing. It occupied her.

The phone rang maybe an hour later.

"Hey," Zak said.

"What happened?"

"It's none of your fuckin' business," Zak said.

"Ya."

"Did anybody follow you?"

"No."

"You sure?"

"Pretty sure."

"What the hell does that mean? He either followed you or he didn't."

It was the man, then. Not the kids? Rose wanted to yell at her, to say something so hurtful, Zak would yell back. This was her way. She shut up.

"You don't give a shit, do you." It wasn't a question, just a statement.

"Ya," Rose said. "I do." Where was she going? When was she coming back? Oh, God, was she coming back? Rose didn't have the right to any of those answers. Her heart was filled with liquid sorrow at the idea. Oh, for Chrissake, no more going away, Rose wailed inside. "You don't need me to, what you say, 'bug' you, right?"

"Right."

"I…," Rose didn't know if she could say it. "I…," and she failed, "…give a shit."

"I'm gone," Zak said, and hung up.

Rose covered her forehead and her eyes with one hand. She rubbed her forehead with her extended fingers, pressed her left eye with the fleshy part beneath her thumb, the right with the middle part of her fingers. She wanted to not care whether Zak meant "gone" for an hour or tonight or forever. Rose began the slide into her litany of loss.

From all these whispers of happiness faded in my life, oh Lord, deliver me.

From the death of my dear girl, oh Lord, deliver me.

From the senselessness I live in, oh, Lord, deliver me.

From caring about life when it cares not for me, oh Lord, deliver me.

She went on. Because the list didn't seem to end.

She would sink and sink. Why not give in? Discontent took a hold of her and restlessness was in her bones. Rose tried to open a book. She went out to the harsh sun, but its warmth mocked the coldness that was settling into her organs, her bones. The brightness threw every plant, every insect into cruel lurid light. She stumbled back inside. She closed the shades.

She was an atom, in constant motion. Picking up a newspaper, putting it down, starting to wash a dish but leaving it in the sink without rinsing, moving her book to the living room then going back into the kitchen to get a glass of water before she read a word. Forget the water, start to make coffee, abandon that in mid-scoop. Where was her little Gracie?

Stop, she told herself, just stop now.

Rose forced herself to the kitchen table. She needed to be still. Her life depended on it. For the first time in a long while, she might need to hold on to it. Zak might need her.

She placed her hands on her knees and closed her eyes. I know I can breathe, she thought to herself. One must continue to breathe. Her eyes blinked behind closed lids. A habit of body. She listened to her breath, wondered at its persistence all these years. Why hadn't it simply stopped? It did for others, whose hearts had been only half as beaten. She tried to remain calm and quiet, no more thinking of anything. She was running, maybe, but running inside and to dead center. Her muscles spasmed to go water the garden; her thirst was suddenly fierce; her back ached from sitting under the tree that morning. Anything but sitting still. Inside, no movement. Her cirrhotic heart gave the blood no place to flow. She was a contradiction of full tilt and stone. She tried to empty her mind, to let her body rest just this once. A green light came to her closed vision and her busy mind raced to figure out what was that, sunlight twice-filtered? Something wrong with her eyes? They hurt, as if she were trying to see writing too small, a distant star. Straining to see nothing. Stretching to see space, by which she was surrounded, which was in her. There is nothing in the world, she remembered reading, except curved space. All the things are manifestations of that space: geometry is made gravity, undulations pull space into electromagnetic waves. She pulled her brain back to neutral. "Help," she heard herself. No word had escaped. This was an inside moan, a prayer. "Help." She breathed. The color turned toward blue. The conversation about color flashed through her mind, tempting her to its path. She continued, as all living things do, to breathe. The thought of all that respiration wanted to make her laugh. Vapors, steam, the ghost of breath in the cold air, the humidity of plants taking her waste and turning it into oxygen. The turquoise moved to her heart and pulsed and squeezed through the rock-hard structure, began to open a narrow path, to pump through. All she needed was to trust that it was not her fate to lose and lose and lose. She felt a tear well into her eye. JesusMaria. She breathed deeply to the depth of her lungs. She strained against her unquiet brain which was ready again to catalogue what had been given and then taken, what had happened, her personal litany of sorrow. She breathed out—fed-up, hurt, and pissed—and breathed in forgiveness, trust, and something quite, quite shy of belief. Rose sat, trying to, and nearly succeeding in, doing nothing.

For how long she sat, she couldn't say, maybe long minutes, perhaps hours.

By the time Sophie came home, Rose was there.

"*Jak sie masz*?" Sophie said.

Rose wanted to be careful what she said, even what she thought. "Not too great."

Sophie had come in with groceries, juggling bags onto the tabletop. One sat at a tilt. Sophie saw it. "What's wrong?"

"Zak's gone."

Sophie immediately understood not why or how, but simple fact. For a moment she looked startled. Her eyebrows straightened, relaxed into the reality.

"I don't know what. We got on the bus and she jumped off and then she was in a terrible mood on the phone. She called. I think she's really gone."

"Oh, my." Sophie stood with her feet apart as if to receive a blow.

"Ya," Rose said. "Oh, my."

"Is she coming back?" Sophie asked.

"How the hell would I know?" Rose shot back in a clipped voice meant to insult Sophie for asking the question she couldn't answer. Rose had lived many years in a habit of internal rant. Something outside her seemed responsible for taking everything, the aimlessness of her days; she who had the nature of a peony, to root and remain undisturbed. It had been such a long time since she'd had a friend.

Sophie was a trooper. Bruised, but a trooper. "It's a good question, though. How the hell would you know? Unless she told you something, which is what I was hoping."

Rose nodded. Of course that's why Sophie asked. Information. She was a librarian. "No, she didn't tell me something."

Sophie started to put the groceries away, arrange what they needed for a dinner neither of them was much interested in. Rose was a lump. Sophie laid a bright yellow tablecloth on the table before Rose, she poured iced tea. Sophie made a light meal, a tuna salad with canned peas aside. She was silent during the preparations with only light tinkles, scrapes, and mixing sounds accompanying.

Sophie sat across the table. She did not lift the shade that kept the dusky sunlight, the most beautiful color of the day, out.

CHAPTER THIRTEEN

Rose
Heating Up

Rose woke that morning as she had for the past four weeks. She was eager every day to get up and plant herself near the phone. She was grateful now to live in this house, to be in one place where she could be found. Yes, she had finally gone inside and already she couldn't remember why she wanted to sleep outside. She was a puzzle to herself.

Still. No Zak. No Zak.

This had been her news for the twenty-nine days since that bus ride, since the light had dimmed. Waiting gave her the only reason to awake.

Every day was filled with ancient moments. Gracie's first smile when she was too young too know what it was, the joy of being alive bubbling out; the belly laugh when you said "Boo!" to her, over and over until she lost her breath. She fell asleep in her peas. Her first steps; the first time she threw a ball, of course, at her feet; later, the "why?" about everything in an infinite stream. She would pat her mama on the shoulder, as far as her arm could reach. Words, gestures, wide-eyed clumsiness, unexpected grace. Rose grew angry with herself now for every impatience, every cross word she'd ever delivered, every time she was in a rush and treated her as if she would be there forever. Gone is forever. Gracie is not here.

Grace was hers alone.

She had a father, but she'd never know him.

How Grace started. It was impossible to think about Grace without that fact.

Rose had sat on the stoop with Paul, on the Friday night of her mistake and her blessing. They were drinking beer from the tin bucket he'd bought on his way home from the shop, where he was learning to make cabinets. He lived upstairs from where she lived with her aunt and uncle and four cousins. All those people in three little rooms, sharing a bathroom with the apartment behind, so if you didn't lock both doors, someone might walk in on you. Everyone crowded together all the time. And the same with his family. So, the stoop was private.

It was a hot night as Chicago gets hot, slow hot and breezeless, humid, almost airless. He was ruddy and broad and had some slowness, like an animal, in him. She liked that. Eventually, they went for a walk on the steaming night sidewalks, full even so late, at ten o'clock, of running, flushed kids twisting their bodies to avoid the tag of "It," sidewalks packed with joshing, sweaty adults who all seemed to be making racy jokes at the expense of no one in particular, foreplay to the slippery embraces that would come later. There was sex in the air, but did she know it? She was restless, but she didn't know that kind of restless. She was hot, but didn't know that kind of hot.

She was tired of being the cousin from across. Her sister kidded her in letters, called her "favorite." What did she know? No one paid any attention to her but to collect her rent.

When Paul gave her his attention that night, she walked with him until they were almost out of the neighborhood. Most of the signs weren't Polish anymore. They stopped in front of one that said: "Carpentry, Fine Woodworking by Old World Craftsmen," with the white eagle on its red shield balancing the middle. Paul said, "See, this is my shop." She nodded, laughed. "Do you want to see inside?" he grinned his cat's grin, pulling out a key on a ring like a jailer's. It felt like something they shouldn't do without the boss there, but the beer made her bold. "Let's go," she said, shrugging her shoulders so he shouldn't know it was a big thing to her. He was twenty-two, a full grown man. She was in the middle of fifteen and he had asked her to walk with him. She didn't want to look scared, like a D.P., displaced person it meant, even with a curl of the lip, to their own people; "Dumb Polack" it meant, to others; in truth, even amongst themselves.

Inside, as soon as she heard the door click behind, he groped at her in the dark. She got scared. His paws pulled at her dress. Something was happening. "Don't be stupid," he was saying. "You know you want it."

"Want what?" She asked out loud, lightly slapping him away. He laughed.

"Don't pretend you're a saint," he said, his body right back against her. He was breathing hard. He smelled of beer and tobacco and the day's sweat. His strong broad chest was against her breasts. No one had ever touched her chest before, not even she, really, just to wash. She was afraid, but she could feel a heat starting down there.

"What the hell are you trying to do?" she said, as mean as she could.

"What I want. What you want, too," he said. He said it as though it were a game. It sounded like a secret she was being let in on that she didn't want to know. It had something to do with filth. She felt different than she'd ever felt. He was all over her. His huge arms first pulled her toward him, wrapped around her shoulders, then his hands, moving to her backside, pushed her from behind against the hardness below his belt. Her back was up against an old barfront stored there. She remembered thinking: This place used to be a tavern. She'd never been in one before.

She made a noise like a laugh and said, "That's all, Paul, I got to go."

She slipped a little from his arms and saw the two reflected in the backbar mirror. Her eyes caught her reflection, her and her, conspirators in this. Mirrored Rose looked more scared than Rose felt. She could see the two of them, too; his eyes fixed on her, his head down. His face red, sweat beaded on his brow. There was a layer of sawdust over the mirror. She wanted to touch his face right then, but he couldn't know that.

At the precise moment of her near tenderness, he moved her, shoved her against the wall. He was not talking, he was unbuttoning his pants, he was pulling up her dress. She was pushing at him, but not hard enough. Pushing at a wall, the earth. He moved his hips strong and rhythmic, and she felt his stiffness pushing toward her through the cloth. It hit her right at the front of where her lips down there started and that motion and the knowledge of what it was that was coming toward her made them swell. She wanted it to stop, but she was fascinated that this was happening to her. My God, she could be a ruined woman. When she thought that, she tried to slap him, hard. He let out a chilly laugh as he grabbed her wrist in his monkey fingers, stretched her held arm up above her head against the wall and shoved his lower half hard against her again. It made her moan in spite of herself. She could feel that her crotch was wet. She still wanted him to stop, but she wanted, dear Lord, to feel this. She was a curious person. Him, muttering, grunting, making noises. She far away, watching. Watching with a wet crotch and an eagerness and a dread. She couldn't make him stop now.

She was a little flattered. She was all he could focus on. Rose. She was fifteen.

That ends the part where she was curious. Right there. Not even when he put his thing in her, because that hurt. Sure, her body on its own was wanting, but the whole of herself didn't want that, and she let him know. But would he stop? He was stupid and rough and she knew by then he didn't care a thing for her. He made animal noises and he spit when he finished.

When they walked back, he didn't talk to her. He was grumpy. Why did he do it if he was going to be mad about it? She felt lightheaded, shaky. She felt stupid. Dumb Polack. There wasn't a living soul she could tell this to.

"Don't try to pin nothing on me," he said when they were about a block away from the house. He looked like he could hit her.

"I didn't need nothing from you yesterday. I don't need nothing now." English, of course. He was the enemy, it was clear.

"We'll see, little whore," he said. "I'll swear I had nothing to do with you and no one will believe you. They'll just think you been around."

"You know I ain't," she added in English.

"You ain't gonna grab me for your old man. You're too ugly for me to get stuck with."

Who needed to hear that in her own language? "Who the hell wants you?" she told him in English again. "Kissmyass." And she meant it just as mean as it had ever been said to her.

So that was how she got married. To nice, steady Walter. He seemed kind. He needed a wife. He acted blind to her swollen belly. She ignored that he was old enough to be her father.

Later, after he married that *szlacta*, Sabina, Rose started in secret to have sex with Paul. It was a small neighborhood and tight quarters. He lived in the same building as Walter and the girls and they passed each other in the hall. That was stupid, too. She hadn't made the best choices. She didn't have so many. There he was, mellowed with a few years, with the connection that came from that time he forced her.

From that first time, came Grace, her blessing.

Then she was gone, her curse.

Rose heaved a huge sigh. All this she had buried. Deep. She never thought about it. She lived her life step-by-step, expecting nothing and getting exactly that. It came roaring out of its grave. The grave where she had buried every tenderness, every hope, with her life, her little Grace.

Where was that Zak? The phone was her enemy. The girl had the number, that was good. Rose was not used to fretting over anyone. She had no right to care.

When Sophie came home, she found Rose poring over a book. Sophie peeked over her shoulder.

"Latin, Rose? You planning a trip?"

Rose didn't get it. "My father, he had us study. He said it would help us with words. I can't keep anything in my head."

"Brushing up, then. I noticed you speak in English more now. It's healthy, keeps the mind agile."

"From 'agere: to do,'" Rose said, her heart not in it.

Stan came to the door, having delivered more leftovers for the yard.

"Just throw that in the box," Rose asked.

"Sure, *Pani*," he said, easy-going about her change. "Hey, things are really heating up down by the restaurant. I went for a walk at Lincoln Park just to see, you know? The cops are all pumped up. It looked like a scene from the Wizard of Oz, where the soldiers are marching over a bridge, one way, while another gang is marching across the opposite way."

"Are there kids there yet?"

" Oh, yes. The hippies are all over and regular kids, too, probably come down to see what's going on, just laying in the grass. There was a girl, maybe nineteen, with her black lab goofing on a little hill. A cop on a motorcycle drove over the grass and yelled 'Get that eff-ing dog out of the park.'" And when the girl who was with the dog looked through him, Stan said, like she couldn't believe her eyes, he aimed his gun right at the dog. "He didn't shoot."

"He'll get a medal for that," Rose said.

"She was shocked, you could see it. Just a girl, not a line of worry in her face. She was saying, 'They can't do this.' But she leashed the dog and ran away. Right in front of God and everybody, he did this. It could be bad. The Yippies and hippies just laugh."

"They have no respect," Sophie said.

Rose thought of the girl. Smartmouth.

"They're rude," Rose said and both Stan and Sophie turned to her as if she were a talking bird. "I'm no fan of cops, but you got to be careful. They're not just any cops. They are Chicago cops."

"These young people could behave better," Stan suggested.

"If you can get shot for being a dog in the park, manners isn't what they want." She didn't care if Stan agreed or not.

"It's kind of tense down there," he said.

Rose made her dismissive sound and stopped listening. Sophie walked him to the door and stood outside with him a while. Rose looked over at the phone. She hated it.

Rose pulled out a deck of cards. She would try different events with cards. It was not chaos. It was a mathematical exercise. A setup. Count, shuffle, try again. In this way, she came up with the Keystone card trick and any number of what would be astounding tricks if you were not attentive to the mathematics of the world. Busying herself this way kept the nonsense numbers out of her head, the old phone numbers that went with people long unseen, the license plates she'd passed in the street weeks ago. No, no, no. She shuffled the cards again.

When Sophie came back in, she stood at the door for a minute. Rose could feel her there. Finally, she laid a mimeograph sheet on the table, then, firmly, a photo of a fresh-faced Zak.

Rose could see "Reward" across the top and without glasses, she saw it was Zak in the photo, she wasn't that blind. She wanted to see it with true eyes, read the fine print. She shuffled to the back door and pawed at her purse hanging on the knob. She got her glasses. She stopped at the sink and rinsed them, wiped them with the soft flour sack dish cloth until they were clearer than her own eyes. She came back to hover. "*Ço to jest?*"

"Missing girl," she read. "Information of advantage to her." A phone number in Chicago.

"*JesusMariaMatkaBozku.* We'll call, no?"

"No," Sophie answered. "Not yet."

"Wait!" Rose spit, and dashed past Sophie to the yard. She grabbed Stan by his shoulder at the back gate. "Come."

She brought him to the door. Stan stood like a statue, hands crossed modestly over his crotch. "I thought you should see it," he said.

"She's not in any trouble?" Sophie said.

He shook his head slightly as if to say, don't explain.

"Where did you get this?" Rose demanded. He hesitated. "Did someone give it to you? Was it stuck up somewhere? What?" Rose was losing her temper at the entire situation.

Sophie stepped in, motioning Stan back into the kitchen. "Good questions, Rose." This slight intervention gave Rose a minute to calm herself.

"Martin's," he said. "A guy."

"What's he look like?"

"He hopped from one foot to the other. He wore straight tight bluejeans and a bluejean jacket, too. In this heat. He looked like a windup cricket."

"What did he say?"

"He had a Southern accent. He said he's looking for his little girl." It was all he had to say. He turned to leave again and Rose didn't barricade him with more questions. She saw the door close behind him.

It was the father. The man on the bus. She hadn't heard a damn thing about him. The kind who drops his quarter in the slot and leaves, that's what she thought. Zak sure got a pair in those two. What does he want now?

"Now," Sophie said, "we talk."

Rose glared at her.

"I'm not the enemy," Sophie added. "You may as well be mad at the sink."

"She's gone," Rose said.

"No."

"Well she ain't here."

"She has a life, Rose. To whatever extent."

"So, this," Rose shook the paper away from her as if it were contagious.

"Maybe you should call him. Or I can. But I think it should be you."

Rose was flattered without knowing why. "And what?"

"See what he has to say. Find out what this is about."

"I think it's the man from the bus. Remember?"

Rose walked over to the phone off the kitchen hall. She leaned over and dialed the first three numbers, an Uptown exchange, she was pretty sure, then she felt bile come up but she calmed down. Her body was not going to boss her. Let the fear run, but she was still in charge. It rang three times and she was feeling some relief at the emptiness on the other end when he answered.

"Y'ello."

She hated him already.

"Ya," she decided to go with her heaviest accent. It was convenient sometimes.

"Your dime," he said.

Rose took a silent breath. "I saw your paper."

"Hey, hello Missus," a new tone came in. Sophie was standing next to her and Rose held the earpiece so they could both hear. Her presence gave Rose the strength to shut up. "You know my daughter, Zakaria?"

Rose was not great at thinking on her feet. She had learned a thing or two about reticence, though, dealing with social workers trying to save money from you and cops trying to humiliate you. When she was the only one at stake, she might blow up, but now, now there was Zak to think of. She stuck to her path. "What is this?"

"You know her? You know my little girl?" Rose tracked her eyes to Sophie and stayed mum. "I'm her father," he went on. "I got to find her pretty quick." Rose hated his accent. Zak had a little bit of it, but his had a heaviness, a syrup in his voice, the kind that brought up pictures from the newspapers, of hoses being turned on Negroes. She never liked the South after all that mess started for all the world to witness. It was arrogant, ignorant. There was some attitude in it worse than anything she could think of to say.

"Tell me," Rose said. And Sophie broke into a little smile, nodding her head.

"I can see you ain't much for jawing," he said. "So's I will tell you. Now listen up, 'cause this is important. There is a great uncle of hers, name of Zachariah Stone. He was a mean son of a bitch, God rest him, and he wasn't all there, you get me? A bead off plumb. So, besides the fact that he wrote up a huge philosophy and set aside more money than you and me seen in our lives to make a church of some type to preach it, the most he's gone and left to his namesake, which is Zak. He never even met her. Just, it's his namesake."

Rose forgot herself for a minute. "So why don't they give it to her?"

"On account of he was nuts. The will's got all kinds of things in it. Like she got to agree to keep her name and name her first child the same and how's she's to get educated. But mostly, first thing, she got to show up by September or it all goes to his crackpot what they're calling a church."

"I got to think about it," Rose said, admitting in this way that she knew Zak. "I'll call you another time," Rose said and could still hear him talking as she rested the phone in its cradle.

"Did Zak ever mention him to you?" Rose asked.

"Not that I remember."

"So. We know nothing until she comes." The fact that she might not come back lay there like a three-day-old fish.

"I think we should meet him. There got to be some papers, something."

"It couldn't hurt. You would be the one to go. He's talked to you."

"I can meet him at Martin's, it's the soup kitchen. That's where he gave out the paper."

"That's good," Sophie said.

"Rose." Sophie took a minute after she had her attention. "We don't know much about her. We don't know if she'll even show up again."

Rose wanted to smack her—it, the fact of that. She began staring at the phone again before she redealt the cards.

CHAPTER FOURTEEN

Sophie
Secrets

Sophie was surprised to find how much she cared whether they ever heard from Zak again. Zak was becoming necessary to Rose in a way she, who never had known what good she was to anyone really, would never be. Sometimes Zak came and just "hung out." The money Sophie left was never touched those days.

Just before the "bus" incident, she'd been thinking about how much Rose seemed to look for the girl any more. Sophie thought of the million times she'd just let things go in her own life. And the one time, when she met Barbara and every day Barbara lived after that, when that wasn't enough for her.

Rose couldn't do it, but Sophie had decided to talk to Zak about school, something Rose had mentioned a few times already. Did that talk have something to do with her not coming back?

She had gone to the yard through the basement and placed herself as if casually, at the foot of the steps where Zak was reading.

Zak looked up. "Hey," she said.

"Hi. Can we talk for a minute?" Zak showed that she was not committed to this conversation by looking toward Sophie's face, but keeping her book open. Sophie was out of patience at the start. "Zak, it's mid-July. When does school start?"

"I don't know. You want me to find out?"

"No, I can get that information at work, really. What I really want to know is, are you enrolled in a school?" Sophie asked.

"Not at the moment," Zak said, a little haughtily.

"You were last year? Or not?"

"You know that guy up at your library? The one who lays out all the holy cards and then starts stacking them?"

Sophie already knew this part, where Zak deflected any real conversation with a story—usually so entertainingly you let the thing at hand get carried away. It was something Barbara had valued and perfected in a more subtle form, the precisely correct droll story as a diversion from a matter of importance.

It made her remember that awful night she'd waited hours without any word, ate dinner alone, went to bed alone. And then Barbara had finally come in.

"Where were you?" Sophie'd asked.

"I met my cousin after work," she'd started.

"Couldn't you call?"

"She's my cousin," Barbara said, looking as if Sophie had tried to suggest she was with a Vegas showgirl. "She told the greatest story about her brother, Bobby. Listen," she said, "we still call him Bobby, and he's a District Attorney…" She went on with a story that was clever and wry and made Sophie laugh until she'd almost forgotten the hours, the sadness, the waiting. Until it would've been gloomy to bring them up and dishonest not to. As became the norm in their relationship, she chose the latter.

"I don't want to talk about him," Sophie stopped Zak. "I'm asking about the school issue."

Zak shrugged her shoulders. She went back to reading Ellery Queen. Sophie wasn't crazy about detective novels. She caught herself—the girl's young, what's the difference if she reads pulp, as long as she's reading.

"Zak," Sophie had said, gently, tentatively reaching her spread-fingered hand to the page. It landed like a glider. "I never asked you where you used to go to school when you first started coming here," and raised her hand, still perpendicular to, but an inch above the page, adding, before Zak had time to get bent out of shape, "I'm not asking you now. I'm sure you have a plan to complete your secondary education. You don't strike me as a difficult child."

"I'm a freak, man, don't you know?"

"A freak. I don't really see that."

As if to make her point, Zak closed her book, marking her place, and fumbled for her cigarettes. Her hand trembled as she lit one. Sophie took a step back to avoid the smoke. She was careful not to grimace. Zak created the distance she might have been looking for.

"What do you care, anyhow?"

"Frankly, because Rose mentioned it. Rose cares."

"That's weird," Zak said. "Who's she to you?"

"I don't know," Sophie answered. She was not a lover interest, she knew that of course, but she didn't know exactly why or how she wanted Rose in her life. She just knew her life was different, more present, since Rose was in it. "That's my concern." She saw the beginnings of Zak-attitude coming along. "I'll be happy to help in any way I can," Sophie said, knowing it sounded as if someone had died and she was offering to polish the family's shoes for the funeral.

"Okay, man," Zak answered, opening her book back to her place. She blew a light trail of smoke away from where Sophie was standing.

Sophie took this as a sign of consideration. At least the subject of school, which was coming up soon, had been broached. It probably seemed eons away to the girl. Isn't that how kids are? Sophie tried to offer her hand without requiring the girl be connected to any place in particular. Still, it might have pushed her away.

With Rose, talking was a repetition of surfaces, topics, a distancing, skimming, a diving; neither was afraid as they delved into something. Zak reminded her of Barbara. Talking to Zak made her crazy. It was a stroll among land mines. Zak was a liar, a teller of tales, insouciant—always leaving— ambivalent, funny, elusive. No wonder, Sophie smiled at herself, I'm starting to care.

And now, this flyer. The girl has secrets.

So did Sophie.

It was a burden to her that she had killed her father.

Not literally.

That, she had saved for her mother. Her mother in great pain, no hope, really, of a cure. Sophie couldn't relive the grotesqueness of the disease even in her own mind. Mother had begged for relief, not morphine, she'd said pointedly, relief. If you're hell-bent, and perhaps by this act, she literally was, it was not so hard to find the something that stops the heart. You do what you need to. Your morality, your ethics, fly out the doors when someone you love begs you to stop the pain, when she gives you the look that says you-know-what-I-mean. Sophie was a matricide. But she didn't know it would kill her heartbroken father. She hadn't thought of that. You never know where your actions lead.

Sophie slipped out while Rose sat dealing cards over and over. She wanted to talk to someone else this time, not make another monumental mistake if she could help it.

She went around the front, because the visit felt formal. Chicagoans always answer the back door, but the front door reserves their right to be not home, even when you know they are.

"Hi, Stasz, mind if I come in?"

"You better," he said moving aside to allow her in. "I can't afford to cool off the whole city." The air-conditioning was a relief.

"The girl. That paper you brought," she said.

"Yes."

"You met the man?" She knew he did, but she didn't know how to start. He hmm-ed agreement. "How did he seem?"

"Nervous Norvus," Stan said. "He's some other American, southern or from Texas, not from here. 'Sir this and sir that.' To tell you the truth, I didn't really look at that mimeograph 'til I got home. I kind of showed it to Jake, he works there, and he said, like I thought he was going to, 'We don't help with that kind of thing.' So, I shoved it in my apron pocket. I didn't see it until I unfolded the apron to put it in the wash at home. The picture, too."

"Did the man say anything?"

Stan thought. "He said it's in her best interest, she'll be on easy street. I remember thinking, all the guys who come to Martin's, if everybody looking to get there gets there, it'll be one hell of a crowded place. You ladies going to do anything about it?"

"I don't know. She just comes to help Rose sometimes. Rose has developed an affection for her."

"How are you involved?"

Sophie laughed. "I guess I have an affection for Rose. The child does seem to be without an anchor."

"So you going to call the guy?"

Sophie hedged. "I'm afraid not to." There was no need to tell him they just did. "The question is, what would be the next step? Do we talk to the girl about it, if she ever shows up again? We don't even know if she will. How is it any of our business, even if she does? The truth is, she seems to be a straw in the wind. And we have no position with her."

"I don't like the looks of the guy. He was up to something. I mean, on two minutes meeting."

"That's good information. But what if it is in her best interest? Is she old enough to judge that? I wish we could talk to her mother."

Stan let out a low whistle. "You don't know the mother?"

This was unheard of, even in modern times. Letting a perfect stranger child in your house and yard and you don't know her family. It broke every old-neighborhood rule. You might not distinguish a Jew from you, who were Catholic and Polish; you might let a crazy gardener touch your roses, but a kid without a family contact?

"No."

"Why don't you call her? Or have her over for coffee-and?"

Sophie was in deep now. "I can't reach her. I don't have a number."

"Just the guy's."

Sophie heard it ring. "Yes, just the father's."

"Well, there's the Hand-of-God for you. There's not much you can do."

"If she comes around again, do you think I should mention it?"

"You got me," Stan said, honestly perplexed. Then he got an idea. "I'll pray on it."

Oh, Lord, Sophie thought. Well, better than nothing.

"I'm going to the cemetery tomorrow again, you know, it's the Assumption. So, maybe I'll get an answer."

"The cemetery?"

"Yeah. St. Adalbert's, out on Milwaukee—it's in Niles."

"That's where Mother Mary appears? A cemetery?"

"Yeah. That's where Chester saw her."

"Does the Virgin actually speak?" Sophie couldn't help it.

"Not so I can hear her. Chester understands her. She speaks to him. Some people hear a buzzing sound when she comes." Stan looked disappointed. "I don't even hear that."

"But you believe she's there?"

"Yes. I'm not worthy, I guess. I try to pray beforehand and say the prayer he taught us."

"But you don't see her?"

"Oh, nobody but Chester sees her. Other people, well, they had their rosary change colors or see the sun get big. No miracles for me, though."

Their rosaries change color? Was that a miracle? Well, it was a miracle that you walk through life and find the beauty in it enough to get up every next morning. She'd heard about the sun falling, as at Lourdes. You couldn't know as many Polish Catholics as she did and not pick up all that.

Stan went on to tell her things the Virgin said. "She talks about the Communists, the roving bands of homosexuals, the Grand Masters of the Evil One—who she says are many of the bishops and cardinals." Stan looked shocked that he was saying it, but seemed unable to stop. Sophie got a little stuck on the "homosexuals." Bands of them? Us? She hadn't heard.

"Chester says she says Moscow and Cuba are terrible threats. Maybe it's because she appears here, but she has an interest in the United States. Submarines, she says, are around the shores of the U.S. of A., full of destructive weapons and ammunition, put there by the Brown Bear. That's Russia. Children are drained of their blood for satanic rituals. Something about the Black Pope and International Bankers, I don't get any of that." (Sophie thought she knew what International Bankers meant. Her people, she assumed.) "She condemns someone called Black Muslims, the B'hai Temple. What she calls 'the Civil Rights' are a plot, African drumbeats are the beat of the devil. The way Chester tells it, it's evil, not good, organized by people in high places in the Church. And somehow they are connected to Russia, to Satan."

Sophie didn't know what to say. This was the man she was asking for advice? At the same time, she knew she couldn't ask her girlfriends. They thought the whole Rose thing was odd enough. They'd have her put away if she brought Zak into it.

"Do you believe these things?" Sophie asked. They were madness, of course.

"I don't know. It sounds mean. I don't know that the Mother of Jesus is mean. I think Ches hears this, though. You should see how he looks, like in a trance. And, if the Blessed Virgin's not saying it to him, who is?"

Sophie decided to go home.

"I'll pray on it. It's worth a shot," Stan said as she left.

It's worth a shot, Sophie repeated in her mind. On the other hand, maybe it was not better than nothing.

When she got back, Rose was reading on the front porch, so she saw her coming from Stan's. Damn. Sophie took a page from Barbara's book, from Zak's, and told her some of the things she'd just heard as a way of deflecting what she might have been doing there.

Rose wasn't happy with the leaflet nor with Stan for bringing it. She listened. "He's a jagoff," she said at the end. "His Virgin talks crap."

CHAPTER FIFTEEN

Zak
Weiners and Whitey

Zak wrapped up her bedroll and headed to the kitchen. What these guys ate for food was foreign, but when you're hungry, a tofu scramble didn't look so bad. No way. Better yet, it was "communal living," which meant somebody else made food most of the time. Zak's turn had come and gone.

"All I know to make is hot dogs and beans from a can," she told the others.

"We don't eat meat, baby," said TreeFrog, one handsome though, she wouldn't mind saying, proudly smelly, guy.

"Beans ain't meat," she showed him the can. He laughed.

"They're pork and beans. Pork is meat."

"Oh, hell, I never thought of them as two things, just like porkandbeans, like a kind of beans." This turned out great, 'cause she didn't have enough to buy more than one package of weiners and two cans of Boston baked beans for the lot of them.

"The girls will show you," he said and glanced over to Daisy. She was gaga over him. So, she took her cans of beans and weiners back to the A &P and bought a ton of broccoli with the same money. They steamed it, which was a new one on Zak. They had a big bag of brown rice at the apartment, which they ate all the time, every day. And they put some kind of brown sauce, salty, over it. That didn't hardly cost a thing and it fed the lot of them.

It hadn't taken long after seeing him, like ten minutes, soon as the shock wore off, to figure out that if Eddie was on the bus and in town, Linda Lee knew it. Zak suspected that he was the "disability" Linda Lee had come into so easy. Her new hippie friends, some of them were on it. SSI. It took them a year and more to go to all the meetings and appointments and such. It didn't take Linda Lee but a minute. So, the source of their new-found money, unlikely as it ever might be, was Edward Jefferson Stone, for sure in Zak's mind.

It almost made her stop going to the Art Institute, but she wasn't going to let him take that away from her. They thought she had something worth working on. And, a couple blocks away, in Grant Park was where she met some of these cool people she was living with. She was cautious coming and going from the Art Institute lest someone (meaning Eddie) was lying in wait. They didn't let just anybody walk in where the classes were and she kept on alert whenever she got outside. He could say he was her father 'til doomsday, but they would want to see some paper before they let him in, that she knew for sure. There was a boy there, well, she liked his work an awful lot and him, too. After the class, she hung with him inside and copied paintings and drawings, hoping that if Eddie'd come by outside, he would lose interest if too much time passed after the rest of the kids left. Just in case he figured it out.

The nights right after she saw him on the bus, she'd gone on back to Suzee's. Suzee was great about not asking no questions. She was like what you dream about when you think of somebody to take care of you, not that Zak needed taking care of. First, Zak had stopped at Logan Square and went up to their "apart-ment rooms" at the top floor. She heard voices through the door. Unless Linda Lee was starting something all new again, it had to be Eddie. She couldn't make out, just that it was Mama and a guy. If it was somebody new, it still wasn't so great. Damn it.

She packed herself right down to the South Side, stopping only to make the call. Things were kind of tense, her being a white kidney bean in a pot of black peas. With the Disciples and the Rangers and the Panthers doing for black kids and, let's face it, hating whitey, well, it was a mite uncomfortable. Macy was getting into it. The other thing was, there wasn't a dime to be made out that way. She still had to get her some job.

You simply can't walk around with no money, even if you do stay with a bunch of hippies. A lot of them seemed to have some cash, not to flash around, but they weren't hungry or without a roof over their head. She was afraid when the convention time was over, they'd all go back to wherever they were coming from and she'd be a toad in a desert. One sweet little old gal taught her to make bracelets from leather strips and try to sell them, but she sat on the sidewalk all day and only ended with a couple bucks, half a dozen joints, and a lot of offers for what sounded like shelter, but she was pretty sure that's not all the boys were offering. The joints might could have been useful, but everyone expected you to share them, so they weren't exactly coin, just friendly and got you in with people. Mostly boys. The old gals were her best bet. She'd have to go back round to see them, get some cash.

She was learning not to miss Linda Lee so much. Her theory went: If your heart's broke too many times, there comes a point you can't get all the pieces together to present to anybody, including Linda Lee. There was a sadness in that she didn't want to visit. She was doing all right for herself. This hippie thing might work out great.

CHAPTER SIXTEEN

Rose
The Assumption

So, on August 15, the feast of the Assumption, Rose didn't go to church. She went hunting. She didn't know where to go, but she was tired of sitting around and trying to fill her mind with something other than what was at its forefront. Her foot was better and she'd lost a little weight from doing all that gardening and eating homemade food instead of whatever came along. She felt like she could get around.

But where to? Sophie was at the library most days, so if Zak showed up there, she'd see her. She had to admit she didn't know any other place. Then she remembered the Art Institute. She knew where it was, but hadn't been there. So, she checked her purse for some money and her gun, grabbed an apple to munch on and got on the Fullerton bus. At least she was doing something. She left a note at the house saying: "Zak. Stay here or call tonight. Important."

At least they hadn't set a curfew in Chicago, not like Miami, though that was only for the Negroes. She knew her own tendency to get obsessed with things and that's what this was about, she lied to herself. She always thought it interesting that she had conversations with herself like this. Who was she talking to? Who was the I and who was the you?

She remembered Grace, in the last weeks, how she couldn't speak, couldn't recognize the details of her own life. She didn't know her own age or who this old lady, her twin, was. Though they looked the same, except that Grace was skin and bones, Grace's sister was no old woman, but a girl. Grace didn't recognize photographs of their father or mother when they were older. She knew Hauczaw, where they came from, but not Kelvyn Park where they walked every day. She didn't remember their cousin, who stayed with them when she was sick. She would see him and wave Rose over and whisper: "There's a man in the kitchen."

Who am I when I don't recognize the details of my own life? Who am I if I forget campanula? It's some idea, she thought, what is real, what is not real. It's not so clear as some people think.

The only place Rose could check was the Art Institute. Zak's face lit up when she talked about what they were doing in her classes. It was the only place to try.

Rose knew she might just toddle off again if Zak were nowhere to be found. Why not?

On the way, she would stop by Mozart Street, her old two-flat. She'd forgotten to get her social security check. The cousins knew she didn't keep to a schedule, it should still be there.

Rose had tried to live in her house after Grace was gone. The emptiness caused a vacuum, sucking details in. Bills came and they hovered in a pile; red-outlined ones came and lay abandoned. There was food to buy and clothes to wash and dry and put away. Inside was cold, inside was empty, inside was sharp. Inside was heart's blood dripping over everything—the floors, the walls, the tables slick with heartbreak. She was disgusted by the work needed to keep a life. She hated garbage day and folding a paper bag and washing a dish. She didn't want to go anywhere, but she could not stay there. She could not lock a door. If she were ever going to shit again, she would have to buy toilet paper.

She couldn't stand it. She'd packed a bag, one of the ones they'd bought for their trip. She'd looked back at the bloody swamp that was left of her life. She walked out of that house. The relatives did something with it, took it over. They could do what they wanted.

It was after Grace died that the madness crept out.

In a neighborhood where people punched in and were on the line by six a.m., as she herself had been for years, where even retired men and housewives were dressed by six for Mass or shopping or just as if they had some place to go, it would often be ten in the morning before Rose got herself out to the garden. This alone made neighbors raise their brows. It was a sign of how far she was drifting, they must have talked among themselves. Later, when nothing changed but for the worse, no one made a joke with her about it any more. They were not the type to talk about an obscenity.

Over that terrible summer, the summer of Grace's death, overlooked weedlike Trees of Heaven shot up. Each a sprout, soon a shrub and not much later, a tree, was popular among the kids in the neighborhood; made of long feathery branches, which, when stripped of leaves to its solitary center stem, made a whip that left a wicked welt against each other's tender summer-shorted legs. Such an easy and irresistible cruelty. These trees started everywhere, in the cracks of the sidewalk, over an uncared for back fence. In Rose's paradise. She was blind to them.

With Grace gone, Rose began to come out every day and turn soil. She would start at the deepest shade of the yard, up near the house, and till toward the fence. She pitched and turned sightlessly until every living thing was uprooted, except, along edges, in cracks, the strengthening weedy trees. They persisted against every indignity. She continued the gestures of gardening with all joy and beauty, discrimination and wholeness gone. The wild softwood weed forest began to canopy over her constant tamper and turn. Bowered in safe shadow, she opened the manhole cover over the sewer access, which was placed in every yard in the old days, and she dipped her roped bucket in and sloshed the rotten water over the dirt.

"Sewer Lady," cried the kids, who could have been raised better, taunting her from the alley and the gangway, making crazy faces until she would pick up her old broom, its straw half-gone, eaten away by the steady brush-brush-brush against the brick path, and she would shake it after them. She threatened nothing real, they well knew. As the soil slopped back over the path with her next bucketful, so would the children be back, pulling at the few four-o'clocks left along the fence. She would yell for them to get away and then turn and mutter to herself, busy, busy with the work of turning over constantly disturbed soil. They would catcall. Finally they threw clods of dirt that landed like overripe strawberries on the sopping mud that once supported her garden. She remained bent over her work, her back to them. Her ire was up, the moment they were waiting for. She flicked her skirt, showing tired gray drawers and said as one word, "Kissmyass, you sonofabitch." They squealed with mean delight.

These empty motions went on for two summers before she left her house.

By the time Rose got off the Fullerton bus and steered herself down Mozart toward her old house, she was exhausted. She stopped a few doors away from her old place to catch her breath.

Julie Czarnowski, all dressed up, was getting out of her car, coming from church, probably. Rose should have gone, but if she felt like going, okay, she didn't make herself go. The husband, Flory, who didn't open his window but gestured a half-assed wave with his driving hand, was dropping her off out front and would probably circle round to the alley to park in the garage. They spoke a kind of Polish, but it was idiosyncratic, so mixed up with German that outside of clichés, when they spoke to other Poles it had to be mostly in English or nobody would understand.

"Rose," she hailed. Her and Flory both, they hollered and laughed at the top of their lungs, even to say hello. It made them seem enthusiastic. It also gave you a headache. "*Ço ty robicz?* Whatsa matter? You ain't got a dime? You can't call? I thought you was dead."

"I'm still kicking," Rose said.

"I see that," Julie yelled.

Flory was vocalizing from inside the car. Julie turned to him. "*Ço to jest?* What are you hollering?" Then she turned back, laughing out loud. "Flor says you got to come over." She turned back to the running car. "Go, then for cripe's sake. Get your ass in gear." Then to Rose, "Come on in, we'll have something to eat." He pulled away.

"I got to check the mail."

"Okay, for Chrissake, check it. Then get your ass over here. Flory brought some good kielbasa from the shop." Flory was a butcher. His place was on Polish Broadway, Milwaukee and Ashland. "You ain't had no kielbas good as this. I got good rye from Rosen's , too. I'll make a nice sandwich for you."

"I don't have nothing to bring," Rose said. She remembered the rules.

"Don't be silly," Julie screamed. "Flory," she yelled to the backyard. "Flory! *Cholera*," she said to Rose, "where is that son-of-a-bitch? Flory!"

"Yeah, what?" his voice roared from the back of the gangway.

"Rose is gonna come for kielbas," Julie pealed back. "C'mon, Rose. We got blood sausage, too. Everything. It's like a holiday, you here."

"Yeah, okay. Let me go by my house. I got to get my check."

She eased her way down the sidewalk, turned a right angle, held the rail, put one testing foot on stair after stair until she was up on the porch. There was regular mail in the box, nothing special—the social security, of course, on the nail at the side, a life insurance flyer, an offer to buy a perpetual Mass from the Servants of Mary.

By the time she got to their front door, Flory was there, dressed as usual in a striped polo shirt, like little kids wore. And a belt. And suspenders that pulled his pants above his waist, exposing quite a lot of socks. His thinning hair was combed flat with a cowlick at the back of his part.

Julie was at the top of the stairs. Her chubby hand held a bag of candy for the candy dish on the hall table. Her full body stressed her taffeta turquoise dress. Beneath the hall table were nearly-matching blue-green pumps she'd abandoned for stretchy powder blue slippers. The blues didn't match, but they were all one color, which was the important thing when one's dressed up.

Rose remembered to make conversation. "Your house looks nice," she said as she got to the top of the stairs.

"Ach," Julie said. "Same old shit. We ain't got nothing new around here in twenny years, ain't it, Flor?" The frontroom was done in plastic-covered floral.

"We can afford it, you want anything," he shrilled. "Anything you want, not diamonds, I'll get for you."

"What do I want with diamonds?" she screeched.

"Not diamonds, anything NOT diamonds. See what I got to put up with?" he yelled to Rose.

Julie was fussing at the table as they approached. Bread. Dill pickles. Meat and more meat. Preserved beets, marinated herring, homemade horseradish with the egg. Even fresh corn from the garden. Flory insisted the water boil before he would go pick it.

"How's the kids?" Rose asked as the dishes were passed.

"Our Danny, he got his own business," Julie bellowed.

"You bet," boomed Flory. "He's his own boss. Like me. He's like his old man, Julie, don't say he ain't. But he don't like blood on his hands." Flory was aggressive about being a butcher. He brought up blood and fat and pigs every chance he had. "He's in a office. A appraiser, got a nice shop."

Rose ate what they put out, careful not to eat every bit of one thing or, she knew, a new scoopful would land on her plate.

"His shop's on six corners, Diversey Avenue. His name is on the window 'Daniel Czarnowski, Appraiser.' You can see it when you drive by. Then it says, 'Sean T. Kelly, Abrograbo.' Something that means lawyer in Spanish. He's in a office with a LAWYER," she said it in capital letters. "Not a Jew, he's Irish, for Chrissake. I don't know where the Spanish come in." Her smile was broad.

They bragged at the top of their voices about Flory Junior, who they called Flo and what he was doing, though they didn't really seem to know. He lived down by Diversey and Clark and did something with insurance but worked as a bartender, too. Here, with the babka, came good strong Eight-O'Clock coffee, half-and-half.

"I was going to get kolazcky," Julie screamed. "Why didn't I get the kolaczky, Flor?"

"How'd you know we had a guest? Service," Flory howled, "that's where the money is. We didn't raise no dummies."

Rose wanted to go. She didn't want to seem ungrateful, but she needed to get going. "I ain't feeling so good," Rose said, "so I got to go."

"Oh, no," screamed Julie. "It ain't the kielbas, is it? Honest to God, it's the best there is, the best. Flory makes it hisself." Flory looked appropriately modest. "Something didn't agree with you? You like it, but it don't like you?"

"It's okay. It's good," Rose said. "I just got to go."

"Where you living?" Flory said. "You want a ride? I'll drive you. It's no trouble," he said, going toward the back door.

"No thank you." Rose thundered to stop his forward motion. When she tried to match their pitch, hers came out too high, too angry, too something. It was too much for her, people.

"You don't hafta yell," Flory screamed. "You don't hafta take a ride. I don't mind keeping my feet planted in my slippers. I like the air-conditioning. The whole apartment, one in every room."

Julie bawled confidentially, "You okay, then, Rose? 'Cause you know, you used to be kinda oofty. Though your cousins said you got okay and you sure don't seem off now. But, you okay? You living someplace now? You don't want a ride?"

"Ya. No," Rose breathed. "I'm over by St. Gen's." She never went there, but it was the closest to Sophie's. "It was good, the lunch. I'm glad your boys are good. I got to go. I got to go to the Loop."

"Flory," Julie whooped. "She don't want a ride. She's going downtown, anyway. All that craziness, those rotten kids." Rose wanted to defend them—her.

"No skin off my nose," he said, cementing his grin, settling into a beat up armchair.

Julie had to mention it. "JezusMaria. When we gonna get rid of that piece of shit?"

"When I'm pushing up daisies," he said. "First thing you do. Before I'm laid out."

"He loves that thing. Stuck with him, stuck with it." She shrugged her shoulders as if to say, what are you gonna do? She saw Rose down the stairs.

At the door, Julie almost whispered to her. "They don't take care of the place like you used to." She nodded a few times.

"It's not my house no more," Rose said.

"You think I don't know that? I know that. It's your cousins'es. It's all their married kids, now, living there, with their little ones. That one, it's a mixed marriage, you know."

"Mixed?"

"Yeah," she screamed confidentially. "He's not Catholic."

"Oh, ya. I don't see them so much." Which was more then true. She hadn't been to the weddings, the baptisms, nothing. "I got to go."

"You better come ring the bell next time you get the mail," she said opening the door for Rose to leave. "We'll have coffee-and."

Flory yelled down, "Don't be a stranger."

They roared their happy good-byes at her and she did her best to be nice to them. They were nice, bellowing people. What could she say? I am off on a wild goose chase, looking for a girl who is not my daughter. I don't know why or if. And if I don't find her, I might lose my goddam mind.

She walked back toward Fullerton. It would be easier to take the L down near the lake than the one from Logan Square. Less walking. She was more tired than she would admit.

One transfer, up the stairs at State Street, a couple blocks east and bingo, there she was. She passed the limestone and granite library with its Tiffany dome at Michigan, crossed the crazy six lanes of Michigan Avenue and she stood in front of the lions at the entrance. She went in the front door and they sent her back outside, around the back for another couple blocks, to where the school was. When she went to that entrance, they wouldn't let her in.

"I'm looking for a girl, she's in the school for teenagers," Rose said.

"Sorry, if you're not on the list, we can't let you in." She gave them Zak Stone's name.

"So, she's here?"

"I can't say. The class gets out at 3:30, but I don't know if any-body's here. They don't tell me about it."

"Is this the only way out?"

"Yeah. Well, if she comes straight out from the class, but she could go out through the museum."

Rose sunk.

"There's some art show at the end, next week Sunday, ain't it? You know when that starts?"

He looked around his desk and pulled out a paper. "Yeah. Three o'clock."

She waited outside, on a bench under the trees, eyes glued to the exit. It was muggy. When the temperature got up in the 90's and the humidity didn't allow you to sweat, there was nothing to do but sit. She felt the library pulling at her, but she stayed. She turned on her transistor radio and listened to the Cubs game. They were losing 6-0 to the Cardinals.

About half an hour later, there was the man from the bus, Zak's father, if he was to be believed. He stood around the exit, too. She studied him. He didn't look like much, sort of like beef jerky. His muscles were tight and he was skinny. She could see Zak in him. It made her wonder how her Gracie would have looked, though she'd had big bones, not smaller like Rose. She thought of marching right up to him, but she didn't. What could she say? "I hope I find her, too?"

By four o'clock, the man threw down his fifth Lucky and marched off. Rose waited a few minutes more until she was sure the Cubs had lost. They were close to the pennant, but this game did them in, in her opinion, which differed from most Cubs fans'. She heard Leo Durocher say "It's not over yet." After an 8-0 loss. That was the Cubs.

She knew how the players must feel. She was batting .100 herself.

She headed back toward Sophie's. She had no idea what she was doing anymore. If the girl didn't come soon, she should move on. This pretense of living regular was getting her down. She patted her old bag, feeling the heft of that little handgun. She always carried, maybe everyone did, the possibility of no longer being.

Rose always assumed she understood the world, but that she didn't have much use for it. Lately, she knew that she didn't understand anything.

CHAPTER SEVENTEEN

Rose
The Art Institute

The following Sunday, Rose went to Stan's B & M. She sat at the back of the church and studied the ladies in the parish for how to look.

On Monday, she went on the avenue with Sophie to get new things at Theresa's Tots to Teens, which, as the old clientele grew up, the proprietor had handwritten on the sign "and Mrs." No one under forty shopped there. Rose bought a print dress popular among the "babkas." She preferred mickey dresses with slacks at home. Home, she thought, isn't that odd.

The following Saturday, she had her hair, which had settled down a little in the past few months, washed and set at the "Unisex Beauty Shoppe" on Diversey. It was like being in a different world. Everybody was talking about the invasion of Czechoslovakia by the Soviets, though they just called them the Russians. The spoke about the rumor that Dubcek was killed as if a relative were murdered. The Rumanians had got into the act, too. The second possible CTA strike was big talk, but not a word about the convention, which Rose had become glued to once she realized that Zak might get caught up in it. It was as if they ignored it, it would have no place to land. It opened tomorrow. Sophie started bringing the *Trib* home every day so Rose could get more information. It might be Republican, but it gave a thorough story unlike *Sun-Times,* which had shorter stories without the meat. You needed to keep the Colonel's point of view in mind.

When she got home, Stan was there, filling Sophie in. He was telling her about the "snake dances" he'd seen the Yippies and flower children practicing in Lincoln Park.

"It's not dancing, though. It's from China or someplace. A way to go up against the police." Rose thought of the barricades they'd put up at the Amphitheater, where the convention was—far from anything downtown or from the Park; the LSD the cops said the unsavory outsiders were going to put in the water; the National Guard troops that were standing by. Did they think they could dance that away? Richard J. Daley was not going to be embarrassed by a bunch of radicals. Any Chicagoan could tell you that.

"They didn't get a permit," she said. "The judge said no, who used to be Daley's partners with him in law."

"Judge William Lynch," Sophie added.

"They going to have a parade anyway?" Rose continued.

"They don't care about permission. I think they did that for the newspapers," Stan said.

This was Rose cutting him short. "There's supposed to be an Indian boy killed in Old Town last night. The cops chased them down the street. Shot him dead."

"Yeah, yeah. I walked a ways up there. There were garbage cans knocked down. These kids are out of control."

Rose hadn't forgiven Stan for bringing that mimeograph. "It's the cops that are out of control."

"These kids are ill-mannered. Self-righteous," Sophie said. "They have no respect."

"Those Blackstone Rangers want to assassinate candidates," Stan added. Rose held her tongue for some reason. "LSD, too, those peaceniks."

Sophie jumped in. "The city has to be careful. Conlins? I can't remember his name. James Conlers? He's with the police. He said that the eyes of the nation and the world will be on Chicago and that the police should never permit 'personal feelings or animosities to influence their actions.' It was in the *Sun-Times* Friday."

"Pfff. 'Outside agitators?' 'Shoot to kill?'" Rose said. "That's Hizzoner in April and he'd say it now, if he could get away with it. For Daley, this is a personal insult." That ended the discussion.

Stan left, unconvinced that maybe Daley would overreact.

She didn't pick up the conversation with Sophie, whom, she assumed was all for law and order. Rose would be, too maybe, if it applied to her. It had not for these many years. Hell quietly breaks over you if you step outside the norm, because you are showing a lack of respect for hard work, you are challenging someone's rules, whether you gave it a thought or not.

Rose broke her own gardener's rules all week. It was late in the season. There was no time to plant from seed. If she wanted bright beauty, she had to buy plants. And buy she did. Creating a glory for Zak to see was more important than the sum in her savings account. She even paid a man to bring the plants to Sophie's. She could hardly lug them on the bus. If it was breathtaking, Zak would see it. So, the delphiniums and hollyhocks went in. No marigolds, though. No, never marigolds. Some special trilliums, just at the shade of the garage. Delicate, enticing color. Yes.

Finally, it was the last Sunday in August.

When the time came, Rose started to put on makeup. What was she dressing up? A face that had drooped, eyes that had folded, lips that had always been too thin. She didn't have that much illusion in her mirror. She blotted her lips and stopped.

"I'm ready," she said to Sophie. "*Jedzie* boat." Rose was surprised to hear herself say it. Her newly American uncle would say it when she was a girl to mean "Let's get going." When she asked him, he said it meant "Let's go, the boat." She didn't know if anybody else said it, if it was a phrase of his or some Polish/ American cliche.

She was nervous in a way she didn't remember being.

Sophie parked beneath Michigan in the Grant Park garage.

They made their way to the back of the Art Institute. When they got to the well-lit rooms with all the students' paintings and drawings, it didn't take a minute to pick out Zak's. The exhibit was bigger than either of them might have expected, going on for three rooms. Standing across the room from her work, like a critic, was Zak.

"Hey, you guys," she hurried over to them. "You came."

Rose wanted to shake her and hug her at the same time. "Of course," she said in her flat way.

Sophie saved the moment. "We wouldn't miss this. It's impor- tant, Zak. The prestige of the school means you are on your way to becoming a professional."

"I didn't get paid nothing," Zak said. "Isn't that what makes a professional?" She looked dingier than she did even when she was working in the yard. Her clothes were a bit dirtier, her hair too long and messier.

"Anything. It can take a long while before an artist is paid. That doesn't make her less an artist." Sophie turned to the paintings, one of Sophie's yard, but as if everything Rose had planned had come to pass. "This is luminous, Zak. It looks better than the yard will."

"Ya," said Rose.

"And look, you got a prize."

Zak smiled, kind of shy. "Everybody got a prize. They're going to speak them out later. Hey, man, there's free stuff to eat in the other room. TreeFrog and them were here, but they had to get going to the protest. I wished I knew about these places

when I was a little kid. You can just fill your pie hole for nothing. Come on."

People stood in small groups chatting. There weren't so many
there—just the kids from class and their folks. Zak introduced
them to the teachers, who looked just like the students, with long
hair and jeans, except older. Saul and Elsbeth and Thor. They
went by first names. Odd first names.

"The whole class is some kind of talented," Zak said. As the
prizes were awarded, each student would tell something about
his work. Zak just said: "I paint what I see."

Zak introduced them to another student, John Henry, and
Rose could tell she liked him something special.

When it was his turn, he talked about the ephemeral nature
of his materials, the "being" of his work, the "now" of paint.

Zak looked a bit lovesick. "I love the way he talks," she said.
"He's not a representational artist. I found out I am. It never
occurred to me to try anything else, nor that there was anything else to try."

"That's what going to school for this is about," Sophie said.
"You find out what else is possible."

Afterwards, there was another light go at refreshments. It was
fun with nobody but parents and friends, not stuffy. No suits.

Which is why the sudden approach of the man in the dark
suit stood out.

Zak went all red. She pulled on Sophie's arm. "Let's go, man."

Sophie was talking to John Henry's mother.

The man was at her side in a breath. "Let's see," he said, "you
created such a, shall we say, glorious spray of columbine. You've
won an award."

Zak looked numb and mute.

"Zakaria Stone. Your mother would have been proud," the
man said.

Sophie, who was mostly still talking to John Henry's mother, smiled at him. It was quizzical.

"Let's leave now," Zak said quietly to her.

"Why don't you, let's see, stay and chat for a while?" the man said with a smile, which seemed to take Sophie in. "Introduce me to your friends?" Rose was standing about ten feet away, talking to no one, just watching, listening.

"We got to leave," Zak said weakly. Her body was half turned away, her neck stretched forward, head cernuous.

Sophie started to say something to the man, but Rose was already there, taking them both by their elbows. "I don't feel so good," she said. "Maybe I got to throw up. We got to go." Whatever was bothering Zak, it was urgent.

They huddled out, their rush leaving John Henry's mother wondering. Sophie looked startled and a little irritated. A fatuous Cheshire cat grin hung from the man's face. Just before they got out the door, Rose looked back. He winked.

Outside, Sophie was discombobulated. Rose was determined. Zak walked like a zombie on speed.

"What was that about?" Sophie asked.

"We need to get to the car," Rose said in a tone that left no room for discussion. "We'll talk there."

They receded underground into a cavern of cars in the Grant Park garage. Zak looked behind her a few times.

"It's okay," Rose reassured her, "he's not going to follow us."

"Who?" asked Sophie. Rose didn't answer but gave a light shrug. Zak didn't respond.

When they got in the car, Zak relaxed a little, but now her face was white. The car was tense as if they all three were on an asteroid heading into a black hole.

Sophie went north on Michigan until she could enter Lake Shore Drive.

"What the hell was that about?" she said uncharacteristically. Rose continued to say nothing.

Zak took a breath, what looked like her first since she saw the man. "That was a guy named Emerson. He used to be the social worker for me and my mother."

"Oh," Sophie said. "Was he a parent?"

"Shit, I don't know. I don't think so. I think he was there for me."

"Why?"

"He went to my old school, to Trinity, where I used to go? Don't tell anyone where I went to school, okay?" Sophie and Rose nodded. Who would we tell, Rose wondered. "He was looking for me at Trinity just before the end of school. Macy said." The lake was dark and noisy, noisier in a persistent way than the cars whizzing by on their left. "I think it's because I ran away." Silence filled the car.

Then Sophie: "Why does he care?"

"Just 'cause. It's what they're supposed to do, ain't it? When you're underage?" The women looked at each other for the briefest moment.

"He winked at me," Rose mumbled.

Sophie let out a breath. "Maybe he just does that. Maybe he's friendly."

"My ass," Zak said. "He's a prick."

"Don't be vulgar, Zak."

Zak was wrought up.

"Like he always tells long stories and always talks like to make you wait, throws in words he doesn't even need just to slow it down. Like one time we told him that we needed some extra money on account of the landlord was bugging us to pay our share to Peoples Gas, 'cause there were two apartments on one meter and he would bill us for half. Then this Emerson, he'd say, and she began to imitate him, "'Let's see, you say the landlord wants you to pay for his gas?' See, he would get it wrong, too, so he could turn you down or catch you in a lie. Or he'd all the time start a story about how somebody tried to rip off the welfare." She took on his cadence again. "One time he said, 'There was a young woman, let's see, who used to come in here who had four kids and let's see, every time she came, at least one of the four was different.' He would say it formal, like a speech, slow, like your time belonged to him. He'd say stuff to try to scare you, you know? He said that the woman must have thought he wouldn't notice, but that he had a photogenic memory."

"Photographic?" Sophie corrected.

"He can remember what he sees like it was a photograph."

Rose asked in Polish and Sophie explained back. Rose made a disgusted sound.

"Any idea why he was here?" Sophie was the one to ask.

"I don't know. Fuck."

"I can't converse with you if you're going to say hateful things."

Rose interfered. "This man knows your mother? Your father?"

"If they get me I'm going to get chopped up like tobacco. They'll send me somewhere. I gotta split, man."

"Zak," Sophie said. "Don't panic."

They were at the Fullerton exit, where Sophie turned to go home.

"Come with us. We can talk this out," Sophie said.

"No way. I got to think." Silence as they progressed west, now at Clark, passing the stately houses.

"We can help you," Sophie suggested. "It sounds like you have a lot going on."

"No," Zak said big and shook her head. "This is for me to think on. I got to go home."

They were stopped at Halsted, Zak with her hand on the door handle.

"Promise me," Rose said. "Promise me that you'll come to the house, that you'll call and let us know. I will help."

"If we can," Sophie added. Rose heard that "we."

"I don't know."

"I spoke to your father," Rose said. Sophie startled. "I didn't tell him anything. What do I know? But there's a will…"

"I know all about that. What the fuck, you talking to Eddie? How did you meet that punk? Did he find you, did he follow you off that bus?"

"He didn't find me. I told you he never followed me. Do you think I'm stupid?"

Zak's hand was still on the handle. The light had turned twice and cars were going around them, drivers signaling the finger.

"He's full of it. Anyway, that's got to be the biggest lie, this will or what they call it. There ain't nobody got two dimes to rub together in the whole bunch, 'cept Linda Lee's people, Linda Lee, she's my mother, they got the glass shop. You talked to that jag?"

Sophie couldn't seem to help herself. "Language, Zak."

"I called him. There was a paper with your picture. Come with us, I'll explain."

"I can end up in some group home."

"NO." Rose was explosive with it. "I won't let that happen." Zak had opened the door and the dome light shone. "If you won't come with us now, promise me you'll call. I'm waiting at Sophie's house. I'm waiting for you," Rose said.

"Maybe," Zak said.

"Be careful out there. It starts tomorrow. They beat up newsmen. It's dangerous with the cops. It's not a game," Rose said. "Today's Sunday. You call tomorrow?"

"Man. I. Don't. Know."

"This week," Rose said, "just this week. Will you?"

"Yeah."

"Promise?"

"Fuck. Yeah."

Zak was gone.

Again.

If she didn't keep her promise, Rose didn't know what she would do.

"Talk to me," Sophie said.

"She promised."

"She's fourteen."

"And she lies. That doesn't make me feel better."

"I think we better check with the father," Sophie said. "I know you don't like him and she wants to avoid him, but we better look into it. If we're going to try to help."

"Maybe." She said it, hearing that she sounded just like the girl. Then she corrected it. "Yes."

The Democratic Convention
Chicago
August 26, 1968

CHAPTER EIGHTEEN

Sophie
Sophie's Choices

On Sunday, they'd come into the house without words. Rose hung her purse on the kitchen doorknob. She changed out of her new good clothes. She landed in the chair in the front room. The lighting was dull. She neither turned on a lamp nor opened a curtain.

Sophie didn't change her clothes. She'd pulled some ham slices out of the fridge and started them frying. She filled a small pot with water. She peeled three potatoes, sliced them, started the water boiling. She found a can of peas and opened it, poured them into a small saucepan. The meat sizzled lightly. The potatoes plopped into the pot. The water came back to a boil. After they were cooked, she drained them and watched the steam come up from the colander. In the serving plate, the pad of butter melted over the potatoes, each slice releasing its moisture, the oil melting around the tiny droplets.

"Come eat," she said. Rose moved to the table.

The light outside was fading. The shadows lessened. Twilight. They ate out of habit. No words. Fine.

Sophie picked up the plates, settled them on to the worn, clean porcelain of the sink. She shot liquid detergent into the plastic washpan and let the water fill. She wiped her hands on the clean dishcloth and picked up the piece of paper that had Eddie's number on it. She brought it, its corner carelessly folded over, slightly dimpled just from being moved around the kitchen, to the cleared table, not yet wiped. There was a stain on it, a light rusty arc, as though from a teapot.

"So, this," Rose shook the paper away from her as if it were something contagious.

The Uptown exchange told a lot of the story. It's where new people who hadn't gotten to a neighborhood came to live in passing.

"We know more about her now. She has a mother, Linda Lee. She has a father."

"A jagoff."

"Maybe. We can call him again, meet with him."

"Not now. I don't know about now," Rose said. She stood up, got her balance.

"I'll clean up in a while," Sophie said. "Why don't you go turn on the Philco? Let's see about the convention."

In between talking about Humphrey and how many votes he had tied up, the newsmen talked about Daley and about Chicago, which was the same thing. Eric Sevareid, a reporter on CBS, had seconded Chicago to Prague as "the world's least attractive tourist attraction." The newscasters found that Daley's agreement with Bell Telephone, with the union, to install equipment only at the Amphitheater, had disabled their coverage at the delegates' hotels and the candidates' headquarters. Then, after tightening restrictions on cameras on rooftops and from windows, Daley forbade mobile trucks, where the news people were taping action to send over to places that were able to show them, to go on the air. That would stop their broadcasting of anything outside of the Amphitheater. Smart, that Daley, Sophie had to admire him, gruff and crude as he was. The broadcast news' campaign against this de facto censorship had started on Friday. They were still airing their grievances.

"He's got everyone under his thumb," Rose had said.

"Not the peaceniks," Sophie said. "They say the convention is not a democratic process, and they will stop it. They show no respect."

"Peaceniks. That's a *Trib* name for them," Rose said. "They call themselves protestors or Yippies, hippies. He'll try to stop them...."

"It might get ugly. They can't get permits."

"Permits. Who should need a permit to make a protest? The people giving out permits are the people you're protesting against. You disobey a wrong law. You must."

Sophie couldn't think about it. She knew there were times—extraordinary times—when you had to challenge the law. She herself was law-abiding. She liked to see herself that way.

"You see the cops. They took off their badges, their name tags. The reporter just said, "Billy clubs flying."

"It's happening all over the world now. France, Prague, the Negroes here. Protests against injustice, war. I don't agree with how they are doing it. They have to expect to get arrested, even to get hurt in other countries."

"Oh, not here? This is Chicago. Remember when that King walked here? They wanted to lasso him with their rosaries. Remember when he was killed in that horrid place in the South? The riots? They will be hurt. Daley will win. That's how it is."

The news had switched to Vietnam: fresh faces smeared with mud. Soldier boys the same age as the kids in the park, waste-high in fetid water, surrounded by a dream turned nightmare of lushness, a jungle of tropical plants, with the underneath—leeches, whatever. The TV showed how many of ours died, how many of theirs.

"More 'them' than 'us.' I guess we win today," Rose mumbled. "What is this place?"

"Vietnam. Who knows?" Sophie said. "It was just a place on a globe. I never heard of it before all this."

"Them, either." Rose nodded at the startled faces of the boys, the newly become men fighting out of their league. They were clearly in shock. "People don't want it."

"It's us, Rose. It's us, as in U.S., fighting over that little country. We've dropped more bombs there than were dropped in all of World War II."

"This is not World War II."

"No."

They had gone to bed without talking about Zak. Sophie wanted sleep.

★   ★   ★

On Monday, Rose started in before the coffee had percolated.

"I should meet this 'father,' right?"

"We could check it for her. If she comes to talk to us."

"She'll call. She said she'd call." Sophie said nothing. "I don't know if we should interfere, but we must find out. It could mean her future. Her parents aren't such a bargain. If we know something, we could maybe help her."

Sophie was without patience today. She didn't know why. "If she'll take any help from us. Or anyone. Do you understand what's being offered?"

"No, do you?" Rose said. "I need to know if it's legit. The parameters."

Sophie laughed. Rose used language like a glutton used food. Latin to street talk. It made Sophie appreciate her at that moment. "It's a good idea. Do you think he'll show you papers?"

"He'd show me his bare ass if he could get her. He's crazy to get her. There's something in it for him."

"Then, I think you'd better see his butt."

So, after coffee and a slice of apple pie for breakfast; after they both looked at the paper and saw that late last night, the police beat up on the hippies, a *Sun-Times* reporter and an American Broadcasting Company newsman, Rose called the number.

Sophie got ready to go to work. She came back into the solemn kitchen.

"I'm going to meet him at Martin's, at the soup kitchen," Rose reported. "That's where he gave out this." She was staring at the photo of Zak. "She's still got baby fat here."

"Martin's sounds good," Sophie said. "Are you safe there?" She felt better to know Stan worked there some days. She would call him on the sneak and see if today might be one of those days.

"Ya. I practically lived there before. They know me. I'm okay at Martin's. Boody and Jake will keep an eye on me. In case he turns out nutty. I don't like the looks of him."

"What?" this was the first she heard that Rose had seen him.

"I went down to the Art Institute, remember I told you?" Sophie nodded. "He was there. The same man from the bus when Zak went away. That's got to be him."

"You talked to him?"

"What for? You think I'm stupid?"

"Of course not, Rose. Stop that."

"He was waiting for her. Like me. I only saw him. It must have been him. He looks something like her." There was a long silence. "A little. I'm not sure I should talk to him now. She don't know."

"She's a child. We're not meddling. Yet. Think of it as fact-finding. This is an adult thing, not something for a child to pick through."

"When I was her age I had to be on my own. You said, 'We.' You in this?" Sophie nodded.

Yes, I guess I am, she surprised herself. I seem to be. For now. She nodded.

Rose continued, slipping into Polish. "Einstein told Max Born:

'You believe in the dice-playing god, and I in the perfect rule of law.'" Sophie stood suddenly still. "It is of great importance if things happen for a reason or by accident. Whether we have free will or not depends on one's view."

Sophie nodded again, acknowledging the great debate of Western scientists in the 20th century to date. It was so like Rose to go from 'you think I'm stupid' to this. Careless of context, the luxury of the unschooled. Sophie envied that freedom. She found her mood was changing with the course of this odd talk.

"Of course, it's foolish to believe in unrestricted chance because there are many regularities in the world. On the other hand, unrestricted causality would make us automatons." Rose stopped, rubbed her discalced feet. "The only conclusion is that laws of cause and chance apply in a certain mixture."

"Cause or chance. But, what? His being here, our meeting her? Is that what you're wondering?"

"All night," Rose said.

"You won't figure it out now, old girl. Now you go meet him, you come back with information. We'll look at it. Together." Then, stating the obvious, "We're not necessarily going to be listened to."

"That's for sure."

"If we ever see her again."

We'll see her," Rose's voice raised.

"At least we'll have real information. One point for causation. Not so much left to chance."

Rose laughed.

Sophie felt an archeologist's delight. The layers in this woman were like a dig, though not nearly as orderly. Whether by earthquake or flash flood or eruption, everything showed up everywhere, striations be damned. The tumult of what might come out was intriguing, if befuddling.

Sophie let an impulse guide her as she snatched a scrap of paper off the telephone table. She made her way to work. As soon as she'd checked her responsibilities, she found she would have to stay for an evening presentation: "You and Your Finances." She was impatient with it. She wanted the library to be about erudite, enduring things, not everyday workings. She called Stan. Yes, he was going to be at Martin's around lunch and yes, he would have an eye out for Rose. He had to go back to Sparky's, of course, but he'd watch out. Sophie was pleased that she didn't need to tell him why or what Rose was doing. Since his wife left for Montana so many years ago, he had become less a busybody, more solid and elastic at the same time. People have their reasons, he'd said at different times, in quite a few more circumstances than Sophie would have. People do what people do.

So why had she palmed the doodled telephone number of Zak's that was lying next to the telephone? Why did she bring it with her to work? This *was* meddling. She didn't believe she was doing it, but she dialed the number. She had no idea what she was going to say. A soft voice answered.

"My name is Sophie Warshawsky," she started. "Do you know Zak?"

"Who are you?" The woman was Negro. There was no mistaking the inflection.

"I'm...," and she hesitated, because who was she? "I don't know how to explain this, but I am a person Zak has worked for—at my house—in the garden. Are you her mother?"

"No."

"You're somebody, because this a number she called from my house once. I think you care about her. She's in a pickle." That sounded friendly enough, if not her language. She had to caution herself not to try too hard to sound colloquial. Was it because the woman was not white? To sound less like some authority figure? "We're trying to help her, though she hasn't asked us to." This was pathetic. "Do you know anything about her father?"

"A bit."

"Me, too, just a bit. She doesn't want anything to do with him. He has flyers out and…" This conversation was deteriorating. "There's some inheritance."

"I don't know about it. How exactly did you get my number?"

Sophie was losing her. Any explanation was going worsen her credibility. "She wrote it, probably not thinking, a couple weeks ago and it was on the telephone table and I took it to work and I called you." She had ten seconds before the woman hung up, she could feel it. "Don't hang up. I want to meet with you." Lord, why did she say that? "Zak's in trouble. There's a man, Emerson, and this flyer and I think you've helped her. She called you. I think you care about her."

"How do I know you do?"

Sophie felt defeated, but she hadn't hung up yet. "You don't," she said, deflating. "Look, I could come to where you are, I get some time off this afternoon because I have to work late. I think Zak is in trouble. I don't think she gets any help from her mother and, as I said, she absolutely doesn't want anything to do with her father. She's only a kid."

"Did she ask for your help?"

Sophie was sunk. "No."

"Then you definitely know her. She wouldn't ask for the time of day if there was a time bomb attached to her."

"She would not be happy that I'm trying to reach you or anyone. Frankly, I don't know what to do. Nor why I'm doing it." There was a long pause.

"I happen to be off today and Lord knows, I have nothing to do." The woman laughed. "I have got to be back before the kids get home from school."

"I think I know who you are. Are you Macy's mother?"

"That's right."

"I can come there, I don't mind. Where is 'there?'" She realized it could be anywhere, well, realistically the South side or the West side. If it was the West Side, it would take her all afternoon.

"I'm willing to meet you, but not by my house." The heavy truth of race and class and everything else hung. "Are you anywhere near the 95th Street 'L'? I'm down around Comiskey Park."

Sophie told her yes, though on the North side they called it the "Howard 'L.'" They arranged to meet downtown at the State/Lake stop, hopefully far enough north to avoid the convention conflict. They didn't need to ask how they'd recognize each other on the corner. Not that many white ladies looking to meet Negro ladies and vice versa. The El still ran like a champ. As long as they just hopped off and met, they could both get back in time.

So, while Rose was off meeting Eddie, Sophie met Suzee. She only hoped they'd have a chance to present Zak with all the information they were gathering. Who knew? Where is the Dewey Decimal system where you need it most, with people?

The first words out of Suzee's mouth convinced Sophie that she was right to call.

"What's the trouble Zak is in?"

Sophie explained the little she knew and Suzee seemed to completely understand about the mother, about Zak's independence. Nothing about the "inheritance." She said she didn't expect to see her any more, although she would welcome her back. Sophie tried to not jump all over the place, but she only had bits and pieces, so it's all she could present.

"Whew," Suzee said. "Not too many good ways for her to go."

Sophie agreed. "My friend is looking into the money thing and the father today. I thought if we could talk, I might have a broad-stroked picture. If she comes back by us. And you, too, if she comes back by you."

Suzee waited until the end to explain that she had something for Zak. It was the money Zak gave her periodically while she was working, probably the whole time at Sophie's house.

"I didn't want to take it, but I thought I would just save it up for her and give it to her later. I don't know that she'll come back." And she brightened. "Is she staying by you?"

"No. God alone can help her if she stays wherever she is, probably with a bunch of hippies."

Suzee made a face. "It's not the worst…"

"She had us drop her off after the Art Institute show. Halsted and Fullerton. 800 west and 2400 north."

"The Art Institute? She never mentioned it. She has not been down by us in a while. Where you think she staying?"

"I don't know, I just don't." Sophie wanted to get back to work. "I've got to go soon. What about this money for her?"

There was an awkward gap.

Sophie realized that the woman was not going to hand over a pile of money to a stranger—a white lady at that. Trust was not running high among their races these days. Was it ever in Chicago? Suzee also wouldn't have been naive enough to carry the amount of cash she was talking about. Sophie suggested that if Zak appeared, she would front the money and Suzee could send it to her after it was delivered, though God knows how she would believe it was. Zak could tell her, of course. That could be a part of her getting it, to call Suzee right then in front of Sophie. Somewhere in here, depending on how things went, they would have to trust each other. In the meantime, Sophie could afford to trust she'd be paid back more than Suzee could hand over three hundred dollars. What if Zak never showed up again? The one thing they agreed upon is that Zak owed Suzee or Sophie nothing and that was where trust must begin. They left, each believing the other meant the child well.

On the way back the sometimes pretty trip on the El, she wondered how Rose was faring.

More than anything, Sophie was happy to get back to her library. She was loving the orderly shelves. Everyday people. Quiet, studious in their way, sometimes lonely. All in the context of order. Yes.

CHAPTER NINETEEN

Zak
Like a Rolling Stone

Zak wasn't thinking so clearly. When she got to the pad last night, first thing, she called Macy. Who the hell else could she call? She was the only one who knew the whole entire story.

"Can you come up here?" Zak said. In Chicago, "up" meant north. "There's a lot going on."

"It's not my convention," Macy had said.

"What convention?" Zak was genuinely confused. "Shit. This is not about the war and shit, Macy. It's about ME. Emerson was at my art thing. And so were the old gals."

"Emerson. Oh-oh. You afraid of the ladies?"

Zak wanted to yell, but all the fight went out of her, until she whispered it. "No. But that Rose one talked to Eddie."

That seemed to get her attention.

"What!? You in a mess."

"Yeah. As usual, you going to say?"

Macy laughed. "Not like you did it yourself."

"It's like a flood. I can make it worse, you know? I don't know should I keep staying with the gang here or find my old man, who is probably with Linda Lee anyhow, not a mind twister—or what. I need you, Macy." The baldness of that made her want to cry.

"Okay."

"Tonight?"

"You *are* messed up. At night to the North side? With my mother? Tomorrow, I can."

"Anytime. Any place."

"There going to be anybody else my color around?"

"Yeah, at the pad. Not like your neighborhood, but yeah, there's 'protestors' and stuff black around here. They may be out on the streets tomorrow. What's with that? It's not like there were a million of y'all at school."

"Just want to know there's a brotha or sistah around. I'll come."

"You'd come anyhow, right?" Zak knew she was practically begging. Lame.

"That's right."

By 10 in the morning Monday, Zak was waiting at the El at Fullerton.

Macy had an Afro that made her head look like she was wearing a halo, like a holy picture of a saint. "Cool hair," Zak said.

She was wearing a marvelous, colorful, flowing top. Zak couldn't take her eyes off it.

"It's called a dashiki," Macy said, seeing the question.

Zak was too nervous to take her to the flat. They put their white and black butts back on the El and headed south, toward downtown. They liked to go to the Loop sometimes and have tea and toast at a burger shop called Plato's. It was like no man's land. Not so many blacks there either, but in the middle of their worlds and smack in the middle of adult world.

They spent the next few hours going over signs and signals in the world of Zak. Emerson appearing meant something. Eddie and Rose talking was another. A man's voice at Linda Lee's. Rose and Sophie showing up at the Art Institute. Linda Lee not showing. The hippies she was living with and their offers to go to San Francisco.

"Are those old women safe?"

"I think so. Yeah," Zak said, pretty sure as she heard herself say it. They didn't mean her any harm. And they weren't stupid enough to do it accidental. She hoped.

"Eddie?"

"Never meant me any good before. But what the hell was Emerson doing there?"

Macy shrugged. "He creeped me out." They both nodded amen to that.

The conversation diverted as Zak asked her what all she'd been doing since school ended anyhow. They'd be coming back to what's up with Zak all day. Macy seemed reluctant to say. Something about breakfasts for kids in her neighborhood, because there were no pay jobs, of course, she said. Otherwise, she'd be working.

"You going to be a Devils' Disciple now?" Zak said, snickering.

But Macy didn't crack a grin back. "Do you mean am I going to help my people like the Blackstone Rangers do?"

Oh-oh, Zak backed off. "I know, I read in the *Times*, they are doing stuff with kids and all. You doing that, too?"

"That's who I'm doing it with," Macy said.

"Jeez. You go up to Woodlawn? Aren't you scared?"

"No."

"Aren't they military? With guns?"

Macy took a breath. "Militant. Did you get that from the papers? Or did you give that up? You know what happened in Harvey?"

"Where those cops were shot?"

"After that cracker pig shot a young brotha and was 'exonerated.' And did you see what they did in Miami to the black folks? Hundred and fifty put in jail—a black 'riot.' All because they were having a rally—mostly to protest a damn curfew because of the other convention down there. It's occupied territory. Hit a man in the head with a rifle butt because he want to sit on his own damn porch. Did you read about all that?"

"Yeah. It's in the papers. I read."

"Little Rock, Cincinnati, St. Petersburg, Owensboro, Kentucky. All over."

"Bourgeois!" She'd learned to say that for "bullshit" from her new friends. "It's the Negroes rioting, Macy."

"No reason at all, right? Fool. Except, a kid is shot because his hand moves toward his pocket—oh, it's a Negro, could be a gun—something bogus."

"Are you militant?"

"No, not yet. Never probably. But I am getting blacker by the minute." She seemed to remember just then that they were friends. "Can't you tell?"

"I don't get it much. I saw with my eyes, though, people are really poor your way."

"Not like you debutantes on the North side."

"My deah," Zak said and put her paw out with a limp wrist.

"Why'd you call me? What you going to do? What are you thinking?"

Zak appreciated her changing the subject. "Who else would I call?"

"Mmmmm-hmmm."

"I like where I'm staying. All these people, they don't bother with how old I am or what I wear...."

"I can see that," Macy said. She always had worn right things, always looked fresh. Even her big hair was all neat, not lopsided, like you'd expect. Zak never was that way much, so it didn't hurt her feelings.

"I'm trying to figure something out here, Macy. I need to live someplace, and not with my mother and Eddie."

"You are too young to stay with a bunch of hippies," Macy said flat out, sounding so much like Suzee, Zak stopped short. She hoped her apple fell farther from her sweet and crazy tree. "Why don't you come back? Stay with us?"

"Oh, man. Nobody wants my white ass down there." She seemed to be trying the idea out loud. "I like these hippies or whatever. I might leave town when they do. Haight -Ashbury, summer of luv," she tried to say it like Marvin Gaye. "Why not?"

"Just quit school forever? Not going to learn a damn thing? You better not let my Mama hear that."

"These guys, they say drop out, tune in, something."

"Turn on. That's drugs, stupid. And drop out from what?"

Zak started in laughing and then Macy, too. Sure didn't have one thing to drop out from. She turned on, though, so she thought. She had toked, she fessed up to Macy. "It was funny. Once you get past that you're coughing like you ate a hot pepper. Everything kind of mellow and wah-wah-wah and everything looks special, all bright colors and lights are way interesting and you just want to eat stuff, stuff tastes so good. I liked it." She had a big grin on.

"How cool is that?" Macy said. Her tone undercut the words. "You want to get started like Linda Lee?"

That landed. Zak's smile stopped dead.

Macy saw it. "And fat to boot…," Macy threw in, to lighten it up. "For real, is the scene safe? I'd be scared without my Moms. Just between us. I think I'd like to try some, if I got my Mama to come home to."

Zak got a flat face. "I don't have much of a Mama."

"No, you sure don't. No offense. What about the boys?"

"I don't know I should tell you this. There was a black guy, I'll bet he was twenty-two, an old guy. I see your face, Macy, getting cold and stiff. You want to hear this or not?" Macy nodded. "He was wanting me to lay down with him and I was laughing, 'cause it puts you in a good mood, you know? Then he started on saying I didn't want to because he was black. It made me mad. I told him, no, stupid, you're not black, I'm jailbait. I'm 14, for chrissake. He left me alone, then, but..."

"That the only guy? The black guy?"

"No. Yes. That way. They are all touchers, always giving you a shoulder rub or asking for a back massage, tired from protesting."

They were both quiet.

"I don't like it," Macy said.

"Aren't there guys like that down your way?"

"It don't come up over breakfast with kids," Macy said. "I am so not ready for that. I like them looking, they talk a talk makes me feel superfine, but I am not ready for a touch."

"Me, too. I don't want to end up like Linda Lee, a wee baby and then just a little bit of alcohol, a little bit of this, help you get through. I don't want to gotta calm down. I just want to BE calm. I had enough running around all my life."

"Listen to you, sistah," Macy said. "Sound like you've been all through woe and back."

"Close enough to see it. Once you're in it, you don't even know you're there."

Long pauses seemed to be most of the conversation now.

"I don't think I can come stay with y'all," she said finally.

"I see your point. I'm all about being Black with a capital B. Lot of us are."

"So, I fit in exactly nowhere. Truth to tell, I'm worried you and I can't be friends anymore. I am not black at all and sooner or later, I'm not going to be someone you hang out with."

Macy shrugged. "You could still stay by us. You know my Mama is fierce to protect her children, if you want to be one. This Emerson thing, though, what is that about? That's what started this set of worry."

"Fuck if I know. Makes me nervous as a hen on a hot roof. He's official. They put me in some "home" and I am dead and drowned. And Eddie's here somewhere and looking for me. The old lady, Rose, the Polack, she talked to him on the phone."

"Don't say Polack. It's like saying other nasty words."

"Oh, like... Hey, I didn't think of that."

"That's the damn problem. You don't think."

"Shit, all I do is think. I'm not good at it, but that's all I do. For instance, I think my ass is done for. School's a trap, Linda Lee is a trap, Eddie is a trap, your place not that, but still." She was thinking about bringing trouble to Suzee, like her friend Renee had said. If Emerson and Social Services was looking for her, if she was truant.... "The hippies might could work for me."

Macy's eyes were big. "Shit, if that's your best choice. 'I'm goin' down'" she sang the old blues song "down, down, down, down...."

It should have been funny. But it wasn't.

Outside the window, there were swarms of young people all of a sudden. They were moving quickly and Zak saw TreeFrog, from her pad, with his arm around the neck of a girl couldn't be much older than Zak. The girl was walking all crooked, like a cripple, from the way he had her pinned, but seemed happy enough. Zak almost ran out, like an iron filing to a magnet, then stopped because she already was where she wanted to be. There were a lot of kids out there.

"Oh-oh," Zak said. "Something must be happening down at the park."

"That mess," Macy said like an old lady.

"I know that guy," Zak said, "the one with his hair in a ponytail."

"Dragging that girl?"

Zak laughed. "Yeah. Real respectful. Actually, they treat all of us like that. They always have meetings about what's going to happen and "tactics" and what not. If I try to say anything, they ignore me. Or sometimes, I say something and twenty minutes later one of them says the same damn thing and everyone thinks it's suddenly such a smart idea. None of the other girls even say."

"Well, that one was listening."

"You don't get no credit. Just 'Make coffee' or 'How about some cookies?' They did ask me to make coffee once. I made it terrible, accidentally-on-purpose and they never asked again."

"Now that is a good idea," Macy said, pointing to her temple. "I'm going to remember that one. It happens with us, too. The black man needs respect from the black woman."

"Around here, it's a one-way street. I don't count for much."

Macy folded her haughty self. "Same here" she said.

Then they both, at the same time, said: "I don't know...." That made them laugh again.

"Okay," Macy started, ignoring the irrelevance outside. "Eddie is no place to be."

"There's supposed to be some money left to me. Linda Lee started in about it."

"Money? Left? Huh?"

"From a dead guy, some uncle."

"That doesn't sound real. Nobody ever left anybody I know money." Then Macy said, "You're a kid. Ain't nobody giving you money."

"Not direct. I'd have to go with Eddie."

"May as well throw it in the lake. Won't be anything left by the time he gets through."

"See? That's what I say. If there is money, which I doubt, that fathead will take it all someway. I don't know why Linda Lee doesn't know that if I do."

"And Linda Lee wants you to...?"

"Come home. Man, I fell for it, too, you know. I was staying with her and she got me in this art school and I thought we were going to be okay. She had a story about getting on the dole, but I think it was Eddie brought the money, 'cause all of a sudden he's in the picture. It's not..."

"I don't think Eddie is trustworthy," Macy said. "Is your Mama?"

"What you think, Macy? Of course not. 'Come home,' whatever that is, and then we'll all be together like 'Leave it to Beaver.'" Macy looked blank. Zak saw that Macy had no idea what she meant. "It's a TV show about this family, this white family," she threw in, "all helpful and no fun at all. Oh, forget it."

Somehow that little bit made the gap between them look like the Grand Canyon suddenly. She wondered how many times that happened for Macy with her. Different references all together.

"It's not good. He's more than no father to you. He's a danger, ain't he?"

"Used to be. So, I guess yeah." The noise outside from all the hippies and protestors was fairly loud, not like they were being chased, like some times, but they were loud and hanging together. She saw TreeFrog again. That little gal had got out of his grip. He saw her the same minute and they were coming through the door soon as he could get to it. "Here comes that guy I live with." She wasn't crazy about the way that sounded.

"Hey, baby," he said as he pushed his skinny butt next to hers. She moved farther into the booth. "I'm TreeFrog. This is Raven. Who's the fine girlfriend?"

Macy introduced herself, a chill in her voice.

"You girls coming down to Grant Park? It's kind of whacked out, with the pigs."

"We were having a conversation," Macy said. Zak had never seen this side of her. She was ice-see.

"We could use some R& R," he said, reaching over and swallowing Zak's toast. "What are we talking about?"

"It's a private conversation," Macy said.

"Oh. Women's Lib? I'm into that."

Zak thought she better stop this. "We ain't seen each other in a while, so we need to rap."

"Privately," Macy added. He was reaching over to her plate toward the fries. She picked her fork up and put it in front of her plate, tines facing down like a gate.

"All right. I can dig it," he said. "We're moving on, anyhow. March going down to 11th and State. You guys can come if you want to. Otherwise," he reached his arm around Zak, "I'll see you at home, baby." Raven looked as sullen as she was silent.

"If you don't get arrested, I guess I'll see you there," Zak said. He licked her neck good-bye. She was grossed out but didn't say a thing.

"Keep the peace, sister," he said to Macy. She looked out the window.

As soon as he walked away, Macy said it. "Asshole." Zak wanted to defend him, but what the hell? She was wiping that spot he licked with her paper napkin.

"Tell me he is not one of the people you would be going with."

"He's not so bad," Zak said.

"Oh, shit."

"He never did that kind of thing before." Zak said, rubbing her neck again with the napkin.

"First time for everything."

"Bummer. Should I talk to Suzee? She's smart about stuff."

"You know what she's going to say."

"For sure, you think? Could she put me up, just 'til I get out of high school? I could get some kind of job, help out. I could drop out, in a year and some."

"She would not let you drop out. I don't know if she has money for you to go to Trinity. But, what about Emerson? He found you this time. If he's so good at it, he can make you go by your parents."

"Shit, Shit. Shit. I can't go to Trinity. Maybe I could use a different name, go to some other high school."

"I don't know. You should come talk to my Mama. She knows how to work it."

"Okay. I think I'm going to go see Linda Lee tomorrow or the next day. I miss her like the sun."

"I understand. Then you'll call my Mama?"

"Yeah. I'll figure out some more stuff, if I can and then I'll come see her, if she'll do that."

"You know she will."

"I think I need to get some dough. I'll go see the old ladies. They always have a job for me."

"Wish I knew them. What are the chances they'd hire me?"

"Oh, I don't know..." Zak started to say, but she saw that Macy was being sarcastic. "Oh. You didn't mean it."

"No, little white girl, I didn't mean it. Ain't no white ladies on the North side going to hire me. You know I ain't lying."

"They're not that way."

And here was the new distance. Macy looked even and hard. "What the hell do you think you know about what way white people are with people like me? You don't, and you better pay attention, know shit about it."

"Fuck off."

"Your own self." Macy hoisted her bag over her arm. "We done? 'Cause I got to be going."

"Yeah."

When they got outside, they headed for the same subway stop, but they would be parting. Macy was going to the South side. And Zak was going to the North side. The way it had always been if one of you was white and one of you wasn't. Zak caught herself thinking exactly that. No wonder Macy got mad. Zak's own mind could only see white and not-white. How could that be true, and her an artist?

So, just before they split, Zak said: "Thanks. You're still my best friend."

"You're welcome," Macy said. There was nothing else coming from her eyes.

The times they were a-changing.

CHAPTER TWENTY

Rose
In the Name of the Uncle

The last thing Sophie said to her Monday morning was, "Good luck. Call me, okay?"

"Ya," Rose said.

The ride over on the bus and the El was noisy outside and in her head. Chance. Probability. It's how life happened, even when she thought she was planning it. Maybe Zak was just a moment. Rose tried not to take herself far from the moment.

When she got to Martin's, there were not too many men. She went in and stood like a mountain. The stream divided around her and subsided. Everyone was getting his place, going to the line. She stood.

The door creaked opened. Coming in with the summer sun was that man in his jean jacket, weather notwithstanding. He pushed the door closed with his foot behind him. "Shit," he said to no one and anyone, "hot as snatch in this damn town."

This endeared him to Rose right away. He wanted to see hot, he should meet her temper. It wouldn't disappoint.

It was the man from the bus last summer, the man at the Art Institute a couple weeks ago. She would bet money on it. She saw Zak's odd smile in the line of his mouth. Zak had disappeared rather than have him see her.

There was no other woman in the room except for Boody, who had smiled at Rose when she came in, but kept busy serving lunch.

Jake was back there, too. They watched her without being dramatic about it. They had a sixth sense about trouble. Rose didn't want to talk to anybody except this father of Zak. It was a good thing she had always been so moody. No one approached her. It took him a good five minutes to look through the room and finally put two and two together, finally notice the one woman standing not fifteen feet away. It gave her time to concentrate her wits, her strengths, her edgy bit of certainty. It was far from her. She pulled her heavy purse to her side and stood as tall as her small frame allowed.

"Missus," he said, coming over to her with his hand out to shake, "Eddie Stone."

Rose didn't take it, of course. She moved to a table far away from where everyone else was. He followed her like a puppy.

Rose sat with distinction, a judge. He scampered to a place across from her. She said nothing again. She knew that he would become uncomfortable, because there was nothing Americans liked more than to have the room filled with their own voices. They also seemed to think that because you could not speak English in the careless way they did, that you were maybe simpleminded. That meant he would not expect an ulterior motive. She sat in her confidence of at least that, like a stone.

"I know y'all want to check me out," he said, pleasantly, without a hint of malice.

"Ya," Rose said. "You are not a good father." That would be a good start, put him on the defensive without any details.

He looked forlorn. "Them days are gone," he said. "I mean to make it up to her. But I can't get this rig on the road without you give it a little push."

"You don't need my push," Rose said.

"Hell if I don't," he said. "I wasn't born a lucky man. I'm willing to do what I need to do now to bring luck to my own. If you're in touch with her, you can push Zak toward coming with me. I ain't lucky, but I ain't stupid neither. If it's up to you and if there's any way I can aid you to decide, you let me know."

She turned her chipped mug of burned coffee around and around, slowly, as he talked.

She felt like a bird looking down at them. He thought she had some influence. Fat chance.

"You'll want to see the papers from the lawyers," he said, opening a flimsy vinyl briefcase.

She reached her hand out for them. Why hadn't Sophie come? She could make better sense of this. Still, Sophie was too damn polite sometimes. She'd end up inviting him for coffee -and.

"I'm her lawful father and I would be her, like, trustee or such for the estate money." Rose maintained her quiet. She didn't have much to say anyhow, but the less said, the better.

"It's a opportunity could make her life easy, not like mine."

"How come you need to find her? How come they didn't send a detective or something?" She wasn't sure what was okay to ask.

"'They' is a bunch of people who will get the money if she ain't showed up by September 30 this year. 'They' ain't going to be looking for her. I got a guy here owes me a favor. A bad gambler. I helped him out in a pinch last year. So he owes me interest, you might say. He's been like a detective for me. And for Zak, too," he added. "It's going to make life easy if she gets this inheritance."

A bad gambler helping him.

She thought of Jake talking about all these folks on crowded Easy Street. She saw Zak's name on the papers before her. She was beginning to understand that this was or might be real. The girl had avoided him like blackflies. He hadn't mentioned the mother either. Was she in on this? Rose jotted down the name and phone numbers for the lawyers in Georgia off the top of the papers, the legal names of Zak and the uncle Zak. Sophie or somebody would have to figure out how to deal with it.

Eddie must have read her mind. "Missus, I got to be honest with you. I ain't been no saint. It's the alcohol did me in, but I got the better of that now. Ain't had a drink since September 19 last year. I mean to make it up to her."

Rose didn't make a great confessor. Empathy, compassion, whatever was necessary for that was lacking entirely. "I got to go," Rose said, starting to get up.

"Missus, where's my little girl?" He seemed to say it in a winning way. Now that he'd established a rapport. She held the papers in her hands as if she weren't handing them back. She wanted to see how he dealt with that.

"I'll call you on the telephone," Rose said.

"I better have those," he said, reaching straight across the table and snatching them.

"Ya," Rose said. He was avaricious. Not that he took them, but the way he did.

"I want my girl," he said, his eyes getting slit-like, his tone hardening. "I traveled a long way to find her." Then he said. "There would be a substantial reward for a person who helped us get back together."

Rose felt the solid gun against her side through the purse. Her contempt was nearing complete. Since she'd stood up, she could see Jake and Boody's trouble sense rising. They had an eye on them. She wouldn't need to defend herself.

"Kissmyass," Rose said.

He changed again. "You must care something for her," he said, the implied threat disappeared from his voice. "This here's a big chance for her."

"I got to go," Rose said, "I'll call you." She did not wave at Edith or anyone. She slammed out the door.

Rose managed to walk, one foot in front of the other. He offered money to get his hands on her. The sun was bitterly bright. The sidewalk bounced heat up, making the path almost glassy. Still, for Rose, the news Eddie brought made the ground of her world porous, a pile of loose atoms with nothing in between. She might fall through any second.

She took a route well out of her way, took the bus going south when she should have gone east to the subway, checking behind at every turn to make sure he didn't follow her. Rose had to keep him from knowing where she lived. In case Zak came back. She would, wouldn't she? Of course.

Emerson yesterday, Eddie today. She petted her little gun snuggled at her side in her old lady purse. A gun could be a real pal when you're lacking in confidence. It wasn't much use against the law, but it wouldn't come to that. She'd never used it but to practice a couple times at the shooting place. She would, though, she was convinced, if he tried to hurt Zak. Father, schmather. "I hope he sweats his ass off," she growled as she walked. Then she had a better idea. "I hope he sweats his nuts off and has to go to County to get them sewed back on." She smiled at the absurd meanness of it.

When she got to the subway, where she could keep an eye on the entrance, she stopped to phone Sophie and say she'd met him and she was okay. Sophie was not there. Rose had no patience now. "Tell her not to call. We can talk when I get home," she said. Home. For how long?

These were exactly the complications years of wandering had shaved out of her life. If you get involved with people, life gets messy.

She took the last detour, checking always to see if he followed her. She made a long stop at six corners. Then, somehow, managed to move again.

When she came to Sophie's little house, it felt like she could rest. Her leg was throbbing and the knee hit bone-on-bone for the last couple blocks. She sat her substantial ass in a chair, thought of getting a cool glass of something, but dozed off and on.

When Sophie got home, it was nearly dark, almost 8 o'clock. She approached the darkened living room slowly.

"Are you okay, old lady?"

"Ya. What do you think?"

"I think you look like you have heatstroke," Sophie said, as she moved toward the other chair, first laying out a little footstool for Rose's bad peg. She brought a glass of water, had put ice in it. "What's the news?"

Rose's face registered nothing, but she was smiling inside. No one had fussed over her in years. She used to turn any attempt away with a growl. Here was a new secret she'd kept from herself. She liked it. That hung there with the despair of loss on the other branch, balancing her.

All the way home, she'd been thinking about life. She believed in causality, the idea of necessity in the relation of events. At the same time, there existed in her life and the lives she'd observed a randomness that brought one to a place where chance ruled. Quantum physics, of course, had brought these contradictions into a new light. She was able, weren't we all, to inhabit antipodal views simultaneously, a bilocation in her mind.

The sun was still kept out. The kitchen was comfortable, if a bit warm. A handful of zinnias in their ridiculous colors and intricate anatomy was on the table in a green vase. "Nice," Rose said. She sat, humming tunelessly to herself as she felt the force of what she'd experienced today.

"I couldn't stand the man," she finally said, returning to her daily self.

"Zak's father?"

"Hmmm. He's arrogant and greedy. He flexes his skinny muscles like a wrestler, to scare you. You know the type."

"And..?"

"And I think this is real, this opportunity for Zak."

The thought lay like a snake between them.

"I stopped by an attorney office on six corners. He's Irish, but still. My old neighbors' son works next door. He called these people and they are sending copies of the papers. He thinks it's legit."

Sophie nodded. "If it's legitimate, you're thinking she should go with him, aren't you?"

Rose let her head fall forward until her chin nearly touched her chest. Her eyes were on her fingers that touched each other, testing each other's substance. These are my hands, she thought. Not what they used to be when I was twenty, but today's hands, worn and arthritic and still mine. Not so able to tear the world where it's impenetrable, not so soft to take the hand of a lover, a child. Were they ever? These hands couldn't protect little Grace. Here they were again, hanging useless.

"Otherwise, how can she have the chances she would have this way?"

"Chance?" Sophie caught. Rose heard it then.

"I mean opportunities."

"Yes, but you said chance. Rose," she said urgently, "this is about the money. I don't know. Money can buy opportunity and it can steal it. I don't know if this is something destined or just a fluke. Zak will have to decide."

"Can a girl decide this? Isn't that what adults are here for? Jesus-Maria, what adults she has. By what 'fluke' did she meet us?" Rose was getting upset. Her heart had been under stones for a long time, buried with Little Grace. And it struggled up for this, to be shut down again?

"If it was, what did you say, unrestricted chance, though

you—anybody—has to admit there's no such thing, then it offers her a different life than the one she's known—one that has her father in it. If there was causality in this it escapes me, but we can't know reasons things happen. We have to accept that they happen."

"That what happened? She's left big bags of money. I'm a Polack. You know I like my money. But only if she goes with this desperate man and her mother who doesn't know where she is half the time? That she met us? That she's living god-knows-where with god-knows-who?" Rose was getting confused. She dealt so much better in numbers and ideas. She had not faced the world optimistically. She hardly faced it at all. She'd survived it. She'd been a daughter, a sister, a wife, a mother, even a friend back when she did that kind of thing, bouncing like an atom with no sense of purpose. Grace, yes, her little Grace. Almost purpose. To that one being, she was the most important person. Her mother couldn't save her little Grace from disease. Now, she could finally admit, she chose Zak. Even if it was clear that Zak didn't want her to. That choice only meant she would do everything she could to help her, to protect her. All to find out that, if she loved her, she would have to let her go.

Sophie started some words, but stumbled. Rose wasn't feeling patient.

"Rose, I met with the woman Zak stayed with sometimes."

"Who?"

"Her school friend's mother. Her name is Suzee."

"How did you find that out?"

"It was, I guess, a chance piece of paper."

"Chance."

"I called the number Zak had scribbled down one day when she was on the phone. She probably was doodling. It was a Negro woman from the South side. Her daughter was at Trinity with

Zak. Zak stayed with them for a while toward the end of school."

"That's where she called instead of her mother those times. To her girlfriend's house?"

"I think so—of course, yes. She cares for Zak and to whatever extent she—or we—can help, she's in this. I don't know her opinion about what should happen. It was news to her, at least the inheritance part. She kept her opinion to herself. But now we're in touch. I trust her, Rose. Whatever Zak decides, there are at least two groups of grown-ups she can count on, whom are in touch now. If we can meet her mother, maybe we'll be a trifecta."

"Okay."

Sophie explained about the money Zak had offered and Suzee reluctantly held for her. She'd stopped at the bank and got cash, in case Zak showed up here. Rose couldn't help thinking that crazy as the kid was, she could go anywhere.

"We're all, at least for this moment, in this together."

"If we see her again, we must help her do the right thing," Rose said.

"We will, Rose."

What the hell was the right thing? The sun was sloping. Where was that girl?

The Democratic Convention
Chicago
August 27, 1968

CHAPTER TWENTY-ONE

Sophie
Tradition is Best

A feeling of danger followed Sophie from the moment before she awoke Tuesday morning. Rose had done well. She saw the father, stopped and saw an attorney, and then came home and discussed things rationally. That was as it should be. Rose was surprisingly sane when she wanted to be. Sophie suspected that her "craziness" was somewhat thought out. Unless she had no control over it, which would be the scarier idea. So where were her nerves coming from?

The convention was unnerving. Shown on television last night, and the *Trib* confirmed it, and then some. She found herself checking the news on the small television that was kept in the back office in case of emergency, snowstorm or tornado. The radio was good for those, but the TV was doing a job the radio could not on the convention. Of course, the news, excepting the periodic iron glove of Daley in the Amphitheater, was mostly outside on the streets.

She felt awkward with all this nonsense, these young people being so rude. Something was going wrong and she didn't want any part of it. She wanted the life she'd worked at, where things went as planned, your partner at your side, your job secure because you did it well. The alternative was chaos.

She wanted the predictability she was brought up to expect. She refused to acknowledge that her own life was not that way. Things kept going awry, but that didn't change her needs.

She had a meeting with her superior at work at his request. Sophie had never been a complainer, had done the work that was given her even when she didn't want to. Like that "seminar" last night. It was her job and it necessarily had parts she would not like. She was surprised when he offered a fully administrative position. It would mean moving to a different library, closer to home. It would entail a substantial increase in salary, less contact with the public and more control over programs. Because she was a usually cautious person, she did not let the flattery get to her immediately. She asked for a week to decide and he said that's exactly what he expected she would want. It was reasonable.

Who was she to advise a child? Anyone who was a parent was willing to tell you, no matter what you saw from the outside, that you have no idea what it is to raise a child. Although she did have ideas. Mothers control what their children read, making them choose something within their own aesthetic. It's their right. Sophie didn't think so, but she had to face that the parents own the child. In her heart, she felt the law makes you take better care of your car or at the minimum have insurance against the brakes failing. Their was no insurance required to raise a good child. People did their best or did not and it was, frankly, none of your business. Though what could be more of anyone's business than the next generation being raised seemed clear. Still, it would take certain kinds of parents, who were supremely interested in the child rather than their egos, who would listen to an outsider when they were confused, or worse yet when they were certain.

Sophie felt honored to be offered this new position. She pictured the orderly running of her own branch, within the guidelines for the City Library, of course, but with the possibility of her order. It was a brilliant future.

CHAPTER TWENTY-TWO

Zak
Road Money

That was one hell of a mess Monday. It wasn't showing so much on the TV and the papers were confused about it, but the violence was true. It was weird to be in the middle of it, hearing everything from people crashing at the pad, and then watching it on TV and then, this morning, reading about it. Nobody seemed to have it right, she guessed because each one told the story they could see. Not that Zak saw anything, just they were all so different.

The news guys were really pissed, both from television and the papers. You think even Chicago pigs would know better than to be breaking their cameras, smashing reporter heads like pumpkins.

Zak hated to miss the action that was going down, but reality had hit. It was serious, but they were raucous and silly, marching, singing, chanting: "LBJ, LBJ, how many kids did you kill today?" They were all a part of a worldwide movement to stop the war, put money into schools, not bombs, burning draft cards 'cause "hell no, we won't go." They were making a difference.

Her reality had hit, too. Wherever they were going (not to war, but maybe to San Francisco), it was soon, and she was going to need some green to leave with them. She had no future here. She needed to see Linda Lee again, just one time, hopefully alone. She wanted to be convinced to grow the rest of the way up next to her.

Not likely, and you had to have a backup plan.

She was heading to Sophie's to get a little bread to line her pockets. She came in the yard and said hello to Rose in Polish. She thought that would be a nice touch. Rose seemed surprised to see her, which was okay with Zak. That would keep her off balance, maybe make her find some work for her.

Rose showed her what kind of plants to pull out, the weeds. Rose was all concerned and kept asking her questions until Zak realized that when she left them Sunday night, she was kind of upset. But she wasn't anymore. That was a million years ago. The old gals were just a way to get some bread. It was her roomies her mind was on. Two of them got hurt bad last night. MaryAlice, who was really just a friend of a girlfriend of somebody, who went to DePaul, a real nylons and sweater set kind of girl, got pushed through a plate glass window down on Michigan when the pigs and the soldiers came swarming down the street. She was cut up, not arteries or anything, but hurt pretty good and at Cook County. And Mickey G, who was really one of them, he got beat up all around his head, had to have 35 stitches. He said it was nothing compared to coming back from Nam, legs shot off and all fucked up.

And here was Rose all bugging her about she saw Eddie (who cares?) and this "opportunity" (yeah, to get raped and beat, probably). So Zak just pretended she was living with Linda Lee and she knew everything. It was mighty powerful, the feeling of telling Rose to butt out, that is was a family matter and none of her business.

Zak was light years away from it all now. She had a plan and it didn't include any of that but a ticket to Frisco. That's what she was doing here instead of down in Grant Park with everybody. At least they never bugged her about where she was. They assumed she was around out there somewhere 'cause where else would anybody want to be? She needed to make some money, honey.

Rose wanted her to make a picture of the garden, so Zak took some really cool acrylics Rose had bought for her and some fine paper and she settled herself around the corner of the garage, where she could sketch and take in the orange-blue of the afternoon. She was only in the middle of the beginning.

Then she heard talk and popped her head around the corner. Emerson. Zak just about peed her pants. What was with this moron?

He's got to be connected with my alleged father, she thought. How do I even know he is my father, except Linda Lee told me so? I love so many things about her, but they are things that, given no limits, will kill me. You can't have a mother who thinks everything's all right, even when she's on the skids. This time, skidding back into Eddie's arms. Is he all right? Zak could hardly even spell m–a–y–b–e on that. Except his money got her into the Art Institute, she was sure of that.

But the kids kept telling her that Frisco is full of artists and she'd love that.

If she just got to meet with John Henry before she left. Damn it all.

Zak realized that she was not paying too much attention to what Rose and Emerson were talking about. She, like, couldn't hear them, dig? Rose told her to go get her purse from inside and Zak simply did it. She didn't have any connection to this whole scene. She wondered: What is she going to do, hit him with her purse?

Until Rose dug in that old lady purse and pulled the gun out. The look on Emerson's smirky face was first, of course, the smirk fading. Then Rose shot the garage. Then he went pale as a fish belly. And he left. Smart move, too, because it looked to her like Rose might blow him away.

"That was groovy," Zak said, after he left.

"Ya. He got scared."

"You were going to shoot him."

"Maybe yes. If he put his hand on you."

Zak wasn't aware of how close Emerson had come. It must have been fairly close though. She had a vague wonder if she put down this address, Sophie's, almost without thinking, in a habit of self-protection, at the Art Institute. But no, she didn't remember doing that. Why would she, it was Linda Lee who set that class up. How the hell had Emerson got here?

Zak stayed another hour, not even worried that Emerson would come back nor nothing. She had turned some corner. She got a good enough looking picture together and gave it to Rose, who gave her two twenties. Zak was so happy, she kissed the old dame on the cheek. Then Rose gave her a big wad. Suzee. She was shocked. All that money she gave while she was working, from her Saturday jobs cleaning basements and sweeping sidewalks and such and gave some to Suzee for her keep. All in her hand. She was astounded, and it took her long minutes to ask how Suzee got this money here. She remembered Suzee's hand on her cheek.

Zak wanted Linda Lee to put her hand on her cheek in that way right now. It would change everything. Linda Lee cried a lot, but Zak could see it was the alcohol in her making her cry, not any real life. If they could do away with that, things could still work out. Zak could make it better.

Not now, though. Now, she had to get going downtown to Grant Park. She needed to find her tribe. Her future was with them.

At Logan Square, she used the pay phone to call Suzee. She knows stuff, like Sophie, Zak thought, 'cause she was starting to think again. Sophie isn't much for a kid, though. I get the feeling she can barely stand me. Fuck that.

So she called Suzee, who asks point blank:"Where you staying at?" And Zak tells her the truth. Not where, but the situation.

"You are a smart child. This doesn't sound smart."

"I'm not such a child," Zak says. "I got to protect myself."

"So what are you doing with a bunch of hippies who smoke reefer and don't know how to wash, and are they into freelove?" Whoa! Zak wanted to defend them, but she didn't know that they needed it.

"I got no place else to go to."

"You got here."

"You want me to go to school."

"That's your job. I got mine and you got yours."

"It costs money, Suzee. Hey, thanks for all that money. That was supposed to be to help out. How did you get together with Sophie?"

"That ain't no nevermind," Suzee said. It was the first time Suzee sounded like she was talking to an equal. "We can figure something out. We can start school off with that money you been giving me, if you want."

She explained some of what was happening. That her supposed father is looking for her, with her mother's blessing. And that is no place to be. And she's under age and they can force her to live with them, and Emerson from Social Services on her case. CPS, the works.

"Sounds like you have some big decisions to make. I'm going to talk to you like an adult, now, not like my child. Though if you come home here, you will be busted back down to child, get it?"

"Yes, Maam."

"Does your mama work?"

"No. SSI, she says. But I think the true story is Eddie is paying her to get me back."

"Well, that's not right, unless you are wrong."

"I don't think so, there's, like, evidence."

"If you were my daughter, I'd be out looking for you. Me. Not some cracker social worker. Why does she have them coming around? It's trouble in the making."

"Man, it's a long story. I don't even know it, really."

"I got time to listen."

"I ain't got time to tell," she said.

"Has she herself come looking for you?

"She, uh, loses track." Pause. "I'm scared, Suzee. I don't know what to do." Her voice broke a bit and she liked to slap herself.

"I know, baby. Sometime, we can't have what we want most. I'll come get you if you'll let me. I will take your hand and bring you here."

"But if Social Services is in this? They can bring trouble, you just said it."

"They don't like to work too hard, Zakariah." Zak knew that from way back.

'We can get them to back off if we're smart. But do NOT confront him or them." This was no time to tell her about Rose and the gun. "We just have to make everything scrambled so they don't want to untie the knot."

The other thing. Zak had to say it, for they'd been speaking truth now. "Can I say this to you? You won't get mad? Promise?" When she had assurance, she said: "I am so not black."

"Did you think I didn't notice? I don't care if you're green. You can come stay until forever, when you get to be adult."

"Other people will care." She heard Renee in her head. "I don't want to bring you trouble."

"You let me worry about that." Oh, man, she'd love to. But sometimes, Zak needed to keep an eye out around adults. She'd learned that early on. She still didn't have any idea what she should be looking out for, but look out she did.

"Can I talk to Macy for a minute?"

"Not here." She wanted to tell Macy about Emerson and Rose, about how he turned tail when Rose got fierce. She would bust a gut.

"You go see your mother. See what you can figure out. If you are hellbent on not staying with her, if you feel it's not safe, then you have a place to stay at. You understand?"

"I understand." She had to add it, because they were deep into it. "I can't promise."

"Where else you going to go to, child?"

Zak got cagey again. The less Suzee knew, if she went off, the better for her—and me, she thought. Suzee didn't like lies.

"I'll figure it out."

"We can figure together, if you want. You are still a child."

Zak thought: I ain't never been a child, but she didn't say it, just promised she'd call her after she saw Linda Lee, that much she could do. Not today, though. She needed to get down to Grant Park for the speeches and stuff. Everybody from her pad would be there.

She would be out until 2 AM.

She loved the gun pointed at Emerson's belly.

CHAPTER TWENTY-THREE

Rose
Cowgirl

Rose had started Tuesday itchy. The *Times* was full of the violence in Lincoln Park. She would have searched the photos for Zak, but there was only one with a horse statue and one with the scruffy poet, Allen Ginsberg. Who cared about them? Photographers' cameras smashed, reporters' notebooks taken and many reporters hit by billy clubs. Riot rifles shot. Sixty protestors injured, seventy arrested. Zak one? A priest offered shelter to the protestors and his thanks was a note from a policeman, a member of his parish, that he was leaving the parish because of that. The Yippies asked the UN to send observers. Ginsberg said, "The conditions in Chicago are similar to those in Prague." JesuMaria.

She started to read a book, put the book down. Finally, she went to the garden, coffee in hand. Pulling at weed here, there.

Then, Zak was standing at the gate. See, she said she'd come.

"*Djien dobre*," Zak said. Rose smiled and answered the same. "You got anything for me to do today?"

"Sure." Rose knew she came because she needed the money. She showed her what was weeds and asked her to pull them out.

"It looks nice, all these flowers going," Zak said.

"Maybe you can make me a picture later."

"Yeah."

Rose tried a couple times to find out what Zak was thinking. When they saw her last, she was a mess. "What about that guy?"

"It's groovy. I got a plan."

"You're not worried about that man?"

"Nah. I know what I'm doing. I'm cool."

"Good." Cool. There was nothing good about it. She had no idea what had changed. The girl seemed her old self and they were normal: Rose puttering and Zak moving stuff around as Rose asked her to.

After an hour, two, Rose had to spit out what she'd been chewing. "I met your father."

Zak glared at her for just a few seconds, then said, "What's happening?"

Was she on dope? Stoned, they say. She'd expected a big reaction.

"You didn't tell him where I am?" Zak asked, all innocent.

"I don't know where you are," Rose said, feeling frustration crawl.

Zak turned 14 years worth of cool at her. "I'm here, man. I'm living with my mother, where do you think? That's where a kid lives." Righteous. Rose knew she was lying through her adolescent teeth. "Anyhow, what's it to you? We ain't related. You're nothing to me."

The pain of that was familiar. She was nothing to everyone. "I know that," she said. "We—I—didn't know if your mother did the research about this inheriting, we didn't have the idea you had anyone helping you sort it out. It's real, Zak. It could change your life, open doors for you."

"That's between me and my mother," Zak says.

"Okay, okay." Of course. A mother who doesn't show up at her important event along with this put-your-quarter-in the-slot-and-walk father. Then he comes back to kick the machine every now and then. And she says she's with her mother now. Cool. What the hell was she doing, getting involved in this? It was none of her business. It cut to her heart and beyond, but she put that to the side. Rose went in and brought out some art paper, some acrylics, they were called, to paint with. They continued pulling weeds until Zak went around the corner to make a sketch. None of my goddamned business, Rose muttered.

Until Mr. Emerson shows up on the other side of the waist-high fence. "Mrs. Warshawsky?" he says. Rose doesn't answer him and moves toward the garage. She wants to go around the corner, to warn Zak to get away, but he comes through the gate talking and Zak emerges, looking curious. As soon as Zak sees him, she freezes.

"What are you doing here? There's no school. Did I do something wrong?"

"If it's, let's see, wrong to run away from home. Your parents are concerned."

The look on Zak's face told Rose that that was a laugh.

"Don't you want to keep on with programs like the Art Institute?" He moves toward Zak, who twitches away. "Come with me now."

Zak's body pulls back.

Rose steps in.

"Where you think you're taking her? I don't know you. Are you on the list?" she says just as they said it to her at the Art Institute. It didn't make sense, but it sounded authoritative.

He hands her his card.

"Is this official? This is official business?"

"This is to show you I'm a responsible adult who works in a trusted capacity with the Department of Social Services. You can, um, pass the care of this child to me without worry."

Psia krew, Rose thought. "Let me call them."

"I am 'them.'"

"I want to talk to someone in charge. You need papers to take her."

"You're not Sophie, she must be at work, so you must be Rose?" He put out his hand.

He was used to having access. She knew his kind. What is with these men, they think you shake their hand and they are your friend? "None of your GD business. What do you want?"

"He said you were, let's see, feisty."

"Who said?"

"Never mind."

"Who?"

He smiles. He moves toward the girl and Rose wedges between. "Go inside. Get my purse out." Zak starts to say something, but Rose gives her a look that does not allow discussion. Just like that, she's a kid. She goes.

The two stand squared off.

When Zak hands her purse to Rose, Emerson moves peremptorily toward Zak.

"Stop." In a beautiful moment as he ignores her and moves forward, Rose pulls her gun from the purse, aiming it slightly below his belly button.

He seems amused, but it stops his forward motion. "A bit more than feisty, isn't it? This can be considered, what would you say, criminal?"

"Kidnapping is criminal. I'm protecting property. Get off it."

His hand moves inches, as if he had the right. And Rose turns the gun 35 degrees to her right and shoots a hole in the garage. The noise is huge, the recoil more than she'd bargained for, her hand immediately numbs, her elbow aches. Ouch, goaddamnit, she thinks. Yet her arm stays strong, not enough arthritis or age to stay her intention. The gun is pointing at him again and he's jumped back. The smell of the shot hangs around them.

"Go," she says. He backs out, speechless.

Rose kept her eye on him until he moved out of sight. For long moments, Rose and Zak stood there, the Polish Cowgal and her sidekick, the Kid.

"Shit," said Zak.

"Ya. Shit." There was a not-so-large hole in the side of the garage. Good Lord, where did the bullet go? She strolled out into the alley to see if she hit something—someone. What the hell was she thinking? Because of the way the garage was set obliquely on the land, the shot went through perpendicular walls. The exit hole was more sizable. She had to think how to repair that before Sophie got home. But there was no one dead in the alley, no trail of blood. *Jenii ukochana,* what was she thinking?

Zak was shook up. Rose was shaking from her slippers to the tips of her hair.

"You are some kind of crazy," Zak said. Then she laughed. "I like it. Did you see the look on his mug?"

"Ya. He didn't expect that." Nerves poured out as laughter.

"Did you pull a gun on Eddie?"

"No, why should I? He wasn't anywheres near you."

"Far-fuckin'-out. You were, like, protecting me?"

"No. Ya. No. I wasn't thinking."

"I am fuckin' impressed."

Rose had thought for a while that all old people, women especially, should be issued a gun once they were sixty-five. That would make the punks think different. If you turned to them with a loaded weapon and said, "What do you want, son?" Maybe they would talk among themselves before they came after you and maybe think—no, let's leave her alone–she looks old enough to be packing. That would be rich.

"You better get going," Rose said. "He might come back."

"I can finish this. I don't think he's showing up here soon."

"Ya. He won't call the cops, too. He had no papers," she said. Zak had to go, though, she could see how antsy she was. "Wait, I got something for you." She went in and came out and gave her some money.

Zak counted out two, three, four hundred and fifty dollars. "What's this for?"

"Three hundred is from Suzee."

"What the hell? Suzee? How you know Suzee? Why's she giving me money, she don't have none herself."

"Sophie met her. We stuck our nose in your business. Sorry, we did. Suzee said you gave her money when you were staying at her house."

"That was to pay my keep. She was supposed to use it."

"She gave it to Sophie for you. She didn't think you were coming back. If you go back there, you'll have it." Rose had a mouthful o words to ask where was she going? How could she help? She lost her little Grace, and here was a real life flesh-and-blood child that she could help. Maybe. One who didn't want her at all. "Please," she had to pry the word out, "let me know where you decide to go, what you do. I'll help if I can." Zak shrugged. "You can just call here. I'll stay here until we hear from you. Please. At least call up."

"Okay," Zak said. "Don't shoot nobody."

Rose looked directly at her. "Kissmyasss."

The girl didn't turn at the gate. She walked out as she must. Rose muttered words she hadn't heard come out in years. "I love you, kiddo."

★   ★   ★

When Sophie got home, Rose had to tell her about the day. This might be the straw that broke her back. That was all right, she could leave. If Zak didn't need her here, there was no reason to be in this one place. She knew how to live around. She'd grown soft, but she had hard in her. She wanted help to take care of this girl more than she'd wanted anything in forty years.

Yes, of course, Sophie was upset. Rose saw it in the wrinkles at her eyes, in the forehead lines, the way she refused to look at her.

"I didn't mean to shoot the gun," Rose said. "He was putting his hands on her. She didn't want to go with him."

Sophie barely breathed. "You can't do that," she said.

"Well, I did." Rose didn't think it was so funny as she did when Zak was there. Not only did she have no legal rights, she didn't have a moral foot to stand on. She had spent the afternoon thinking about how she would tell Sophie. She opted, as ever, with straightforward. You can't build up to it or work it into a conversation: I weeded the back garden, talked to Zak. Oh, and then I shot the garage.

The Democratic Convention
Chicago
August 28, 1968

CHAPTER TWENTY-FOUR

Sophie
No Exit

Sophie wasn't at all sure what to do.

Rose had gone berserk. She pointed a gun at that man, shot the garage, and gave Zak $150 of her own money. She wanted to get together with Rose and Suzee and Zak's mother and go over the possibilities for her life. Finally, she saw no specific danger from the man from Social Services or from the factless existence of Zak's mother.

"We are not her parents."

"I know that, do you think I'm..."

Sophie broke in. "In this case, your obsession makes you bordering on stupid."

Rose glowered.

"Sorry. Rose, you shot at a man. Don't give me that look. You shot the garage."

"That's not the man. I wasn't thinking."

"Right."

"If we meet with them..."

Sophie did not recognize herself in this interrupting shrew. "You met Eddie. Thoughtful fellow? I met Suzee, who has no more legal standing than we and could get in trouble for—well, if we are to be honest—for having black skin. And. She sheltered Zak when they were looking for her."

"If we both care about her..."

"She has parents, even if they are not good at it. The law doesn't say you have to be smart or able. You still own the child."

"Maybe they want to help," Rose said.

Sophie didn't bother to answer it. She thought: You are projecting. It's you who wants to help. They want the girl and the money. She let it fall into space.

"I need to get to work."

"Ya," Rose said and sunk into a pile. "You want me to leave?"

"No." She switched to Polish. "I want you to work in the garden and try to have a decent day. Take the bullets out of your gun, figuratively as well as literally. It might be time to reassess. Don't go off anywhere. Sit here or read or be out in the yard. Just wait, for God's sake. You know that this thing is real and Zak would benefit financially and educationally. Put that into your musings."

She couldn't take this any more.

As she made her way to work, she found that she was also unduly upset about the convention. There it was, in the *Trib*. Daley had called out the National Guard. They stood with loaded machine guns in the Loop, barbed wire on the front of their jeeps, to push back the crowds. She had to agree with their general description of the protestors as "the hippies, the Yippies and other nondescripts." Were they a danger? LSD in the water and assassinations? It sounded like Stan's Virgin's talk. Although their habit of referring to everyone in the street or park as "hippies" seemed ludicrous. There were many well-groomed intelligent protestors against both the war and, increasingly, the way this convention was being handled—and more young people from Chicago itself were showing up every day, even if the arrested were "one-third not from Illinois," according to the police, according to the *Trib*. Two-thirds were from Illinois. Newsmen were being beaten, their cameras smashed. One of them was knocked down in the Amphitheater by an Andy Frain security usher. What was this? This shouldn't happen. It was as if the world were coming to an end.

She didn't want her little world to.

After she did her main tasks for her real job, she called Alan. He was an attorney. He had begun to be her friend again, after all this time. He had a cool head and had gotten married, so he wouldn't misunderstand her call. Maybe she could meet him for lunch or after work for a drink. She found the idea of a drink enticing. It was only ten in the morning.

She kept checking the little TV in the back and was horrified as the convention coverage spent as much time and more on the streets than in the hall.

She and Alan met just after work in a near-North side bar and restaurant. They shook hands, which seemed odd yet appropriate. After talk of their jobs, his married life, a few books she was reading, he made an announcement.

"I'm going to be a father," he said. His face was bright with the promise. He had married a woman ten years younger, which gave him that option.

"That's wonderful," she said. Sincerely.

"See, things work out for the best," he answered, referring to their past intimacy. She agreed. She would never be a mother, age the least of the reasons. Talk of a child gave her a way to talk about "her friend," which she hoped he would believe was not her.

"I have a friend..." Alan rolled his eyes. This was one of his least admirable characteristics, his impatient judgement. She decided to go ahead anyway. "...I wanted to ask some questions about. It involves a child." Maybe that would soften him. "My friend has contact with a young teenager, who is, frankly, a runaway, though she sometimes stays with her mother. The mother, it seems, is not able. Now the child is being sought by her father, who doesn't live with them, probably with her mother's consent, because of a will that would benefit her. They have been less than ideal parents. Social Services has sought her and she has stayed with other adults, who took her in when she was having a rough time."

"Are you the one who took her in?" Alan asked.

Sophie felt she could honestly answer that negatively. "It's a friend of mine."

"What's the question?"

What was the question? When Sophie called him, she thought she knew, but it was much harder in person. Did anyone have the right to interfere, to "help" where the child indicated a clear preference to have little to do with her parents' plans or even with her helpers? He was a lawyer, for God's sake. What was she thinking? She still plunged in. "My friend went slightly mad when a Social Services man came to collect the child. He was not in an official capacity, which made her bold and angry, I think. She pulled a gun on him."

Alan gave a low whistle.

"He didn't call the police, which furthered her feeling that he was up to no good."

"The police have their hands full right now," Alan said.

"Or he was not there as an official, but as a friend of the family, which is what my friend thought."

"I would suggest that your friend give it up. Family law is complicated, but this friend of yours is not in the child's family, correct?"

"Yes."

"Are the parents abusive?"

"I don't know. I don't think so."

"Are they damaging her?"

"Yes. Well, not in a specific way."

"Look, Sophie. CPS hardly has time to investigate cases where children are starved, let alone where there's an inheritance some kid decides she doesn't want."

"I'm not talking about Child Protective Services. I'm talking about my friend."

"And you want to know what, exactly? Legally, I assume? Can she threaten someone with a weapon? No, she can't. Can she steal the child away, assuming she has the capacity and wants all that entails? No, she can't. Should she get her nose out of this? Yes, she should."

"What about a will that leaves this child a substantial sum, based on her name and her naming her issue the same?" She went on to explain what she knew about it.

"It sounds highly contestable, if what you understand is the truth under the law. It could be tied up in courts for years."

"If I gave you the information, could you look into it? As a favor?"

"If the parents of the child gave me a dollar, because I couldn't accept it from a minor, I could. I don't really want any part of it, especially if the child is a runaway. I have my future to think about."

This was enough. Whatever generosity he might have buried in there, it was not to be mined. All she was leaving with was a lesser opinion of him. She was done and ready to go home. As she looked around, she saw many people coughing slightly, none of them seemingly noticing that others were. Lincoln Park was not far from here. Her own throat was constricted, eyes pinching. She realized a waft of tear gas had begun to seep into the restaurant.

"Sophie," he put his hand on her forearm, "because we're old friends, I would like to advise you to get as far from this as you can. 'Pulling a gun' on someone is serious. This woman sounds unstable. Is she," he hesitated, "a 'particular' friend of yours? Love is blind, you know." There was a smirk in his voice.

Sophie felt a deep blush, an embarrassed panic, and hoped it didn't show as vividly. She had hoped he was nobler than to make such a reference. How did he even know about her and Barbara? She had never thought of Rose that way, nor would she. "She is passionate about the child," she deflected. "Her child died when she was young and I think this one..." Immediately upon saying it, she wanted to take it back. He had no right to know anything about these good flawed people. "I need to go," she said. "Thanks for your help."

He puffed up a bit, happy to be useful, though, of course, he wasn't. "Let's be careful out there. The hippies are on the warpath."

He was smart in some things, but, though his life looked more orderly than hers, he was simple. Not in a good way. Small-minded bastard. She was glad to escape him again.

She did need to get out of this. Rose would amble along fine, as she did before they knew each other. Zak was probably gone forever, with her big wad of cash from Rose and Suzee, with her protestor friends.

Sophie herself had a new job to look forward to. Her life was gaining its order back, like a quick shot from the hip. She smiled to herself at the synchronicity.

She had done what she could. Now she was done.

CHAPTER TWENTY-FIVE

Zak
Finding Linda Lee

She stood across from her mother's apartment house for quite a time, staring at the windows from left to right, top to bottom. She watched the flat reflections, each mirroring the world above her differently. Light, color, all changed with point of view. Until she finally pulled herself together and marched up to the old wooden front door with its smudged glass and a piece of heavy-gauge metal at the place where the lock entered the frame.

Once she started, she moved without hesitation. Up the tired stairs, up past the smells of frying meat and last night's beans, up past the glad noise of Puerto Rican music, the carpet once entire now catching her heel as she turned the landing and straight up to the door and the key penetrating and a twist of the hand and she was in.

It took a second to register. The apartment was a shambles. Not like usual, though. The fridge door was open and there were cleaning things in the kitchen, a box in the center with cans and spices and their own plates and silverware thrown in it. She looked into the living room from the wide doorway. The daybed was in the middle of the room. There were some dropcloths on the floor near the windows that faced the alley.

Zak took the few steps to her mother's room. Linda Lee's clothes, even her personals, were thrown from the closet and drawers in a pile on the floor. The mattress leaned up against the wall.

She walked in as though walking on water. She bent and then kneeled, touched Linda Lee's dress, the black one with the yellow-printed flowers. She ran her hand over the neckline and she could see Linda Lee's keen clavicles above, her breath making her chest rise and fall just a little, the twist of her torso, the swell of her hips below the waist. She held the dress to her face, took in the lilacs.

A deep purple came over her. And she knew.

She keened in a low howl. Every tear she'd dammed as a child came now. They fell to the floor until she was in a pool and they began to fill the rooms, until she was knee-deep, until her legs were waterlogged, until she was up to her waist, awash in grief. If the windows opened, they would spout like waterfalls down the sides of the sad building and they'd fill the empty-hearted streets. The park would be flooded, the children would have to be moved to rooftops, rowboats would have to come to save them.

No one needed to tell her. She felt it in the clothes. She saw it in the purple black. She smelled it.

Linda Lee was dead.

Zak had always been careful not to cry because crying made her sad. But now what? Right in her face was the saddest thing ever, the lost chance to make things right, the opportunity they had together that they'd thrown away. Unbearable. How would she ever walk out of here? Walk into the rest of her life?

Maybe for hours or maybe for days she sat, the dress crumpled against her, her hand reaching out to touch a fallen lipstick which she spread on her own lips, knowing where it had been, and here that ridiculous pin-on watch her mother always wore to job interviews, one scuffed red heel, a once marvelous ridiculous red hat, crunched now, musky. Her hands played over them like the keys on a piano. The ragtime symphony of her mother's life.

Zak felt the burnt orange-red liveliness in her mother that had made these things look good on her. She felt the gray-brown of Linda Lee's saddened life made stupid by her choices. Or were they choices? Sometimes Zak thought she was gripped.

Zak's lonesome wake grew silent. After sitting quietly for unknowable time, she became aware of little noises in the other room. She stepped quietly to the doorway of the bedroom. A small man was moving the dropcloths. In one hand Zak still held the watch in her downturned palm, her fingers spread over it, their tips lying along the fat flesh of the butt of her hand. From the other, the dress dragged merrily along the ground, its décolletage crushed in her grasp.

"Hey," Zak said, low and assured.

The man twirled. "What you here for? You the girl, the daughter."

"Yeah," Zak said. His English wasn't great, maybe. You never knew with these guys. Sometimes they faked it. He was Polish or something like that.

"She a nice lady," he said. "Too bad." He might have been offering condolences. It was hard to tell.

"Uh-huh," Zak said, pretty sure there was more to come.

"She owe me rent," he said.

The funeral was over.

Zak bent her head to the side. What was she looking at? Self-interest. Sure, her mama had died, probably not in a pretty way, probably not in peace, maybe not violently by anybody's hand, Oh, Christ, Zak was dying herself to know every detail, but for him there was the matter of this money she owed. Now that was important.

It's all a matter of perspective.

"You pay?"

I'm still a kid, she wanted to yell. Don't you have a drop of compassion? Can't you wait until I digest this? Do you know how she died? When? Was it here? Was she alone? Who found her? Where is she now?

"No," Zak said.

"Then get out," he said and moved toward her. "You can't take no things. You pay—you take."

Zak wrapped the dress as a scarf about her throat as though she were Isadora Duncan. And the Mazaratti. "Fuck yourself," she said. He had his hands up as if to take the dress, but she could see he didn't mean to move on her. He was not going to touch these particular things she'd picked. A hammer lay only two feet from her. She suddenly understood how someone picked up a hammer, a stone, a frying pan, and beat the senses out of another human being. "Another senseless murder," they say. Well, it made sense to someone.

"How'd she die?" Zak said, really quiet, really firm.

The man seemed to find his humanity in that moment. "The ambulance came. They say too much drugs."

"Yeah, she did. Was it the police?"

"Coroner. The coroner from the police."

That meant somebody called and said she was dead. "When?"

"Saturday. Night time."

Zak went back into her mother's bedroom. She poked her toe around the stuff her mother used to wear put on her face wrap around her waist strap on her feet. She'd reach for something and then she'd think, no, don't bother with that. The dress was still round her shoulders. There were some photos of them together stuck around the mirror. Linda Lee never lived, even in the car, without a mirror. On the wall she'd tacked up a couple of Zak's drawings. Zak touched the thumbtacks, where Linda Lee's red-nailed thumb had pushed. Her sketches, her art. She unstuck the photos. She loved this one, with Linda lee looking straight into the camera, and Zak, with her body half turning away, her head and neck turned back to the camera, one hand on her mother's shoulder. The drawing Zak had made, copying it, was her favorite.

The drawers were turned out. No pictures from when she was little, no hint that she grew up with this lady.

Zak was a ghost in her mother's life. Now Linda Lee was going to return the favor.

"Did you empty out the drawers and the closet?"

"Nah," the guy said, washing down the windowsills. "It was like that when I get here."

"The mattress too?" Zak asked, perplexed.

"Nah, I did that, just the things was out already. That man your Papa?"

If Zak had any heart left, it would have leapt. But she didn't.

"He say he was?"

The guy shrugged. "He say 'my girl' this and that. You the girl?"

"I don't know. Maybe."

"He say he find the girl and then he will have money to pay."

"He here when my mom died?"

"I don't know, little girl. Rico say he stayed in winter, but he gone and come back a couple months, in and out. He act important, like a cop." Zak didn't say anything. Fuck Eddie, the cheap stupid bastard. "Some men, they act that way. He didn't pay me the rent."

"I don't have no money to give you," Zak said.

"Yah. I know. Okay."

"Okay," Zak said, standing there with her mother's dressed still wrapped around her neck, the watch in her hand, a silly brooch pinned to her chest.

The guy kept working. He acted as if she weren't there. He wasn't being rude, though. He was showing the kind of respect people who have to live on top of each other show.

Zak went out the door. She wanted to know what happened, every detail, but she didn't have the heart to go asking neighbors.

Linda Lee died. She wasn't going to get to see her again.

She dived down the stairs and went to wait for the bus. She dropped her keys from her mother's apartment in the gutter, first one and it sparked the slightest blue when it kissed the hard-formed street, then the other.

How could this be over?

Zak's mind went empty on the bus. She didn't make a decision which to take, just got on it. She was being taken by a tide. She rode north and east and then west again, with no idea where to go. No idea at all.

When she finally seeped through the door at Sophie's house, they both were watching television.

Their faces went from something she didn't understand to relief, to worried scold, to sad upset in the splitting seconds they saw hers.

"I went to see my mother," she said.

"We thought you needed to go somewhere," Sophie told her only hinting at what that must have meant for the past many hours.

"She's dead."

The waters rushed down the streets of the hill town, smashing the walls they passed, twisting nightstand necklaces into tight loops before the power crushed them, broken, against the rocks; the evening table's glassware pulverized; bedside books torn in pieces and drenched—taking everything, everything with them.

Rose put her hands to her face. Sophie opened her arms.

Zak was a sliver in a deluge.

CHAPTER TWENTY-SIX

Rose
Force is Substance

Sophie had come home after work flustered. It was fairly late, and Rose had been wondering where she was. Rose had heated up some spaghetti leftovers, but Sophie didn't even wave her off as she dashed from the back door. Totally out of character, she rushed to the television. When Rose saw what was on, she, too, grew agitated.

"Unbelievable," she heard herself saying again and again. Sophie shushed her. What they were seeing was a Chicago they had never known. The police were slamming protestors, hitting them full force with their nightsticks: wild men.

"Did something happen?" Rose asked.

"Later," Sophie said. "There are tanks on the bridges, soldiers with bayonets, jeeps with cattle catchers...."

Rose thought there might have been a bomb, a disaster, something that started this. But the newscasters didn't act as if this was a reasonable response to a terrible event. Their voices were disbelieving, outraged yet almost whining. They were sincerely angry and helpless.

Every now and then, they would change the channel, only to see more of the same.

"What in God's name...," Sophie muttered.

"I don't know," Rose said. "I don't know."

They fell back into the silence of seeing an accident happen, knowing this was no accident.

"Oh my God," Rose said, as a policeman clubbed a protestor already on the ground, being dragged by two other cops.

From inside the Amphitheatre, Abraham Ribicoff decried the "Gestapo tactics." Daley reacted with a foul face and silenced hollered words. Rose snuck a look to Sophie, but there was no special recognition.

A newsman described the shattered plate glass window at the Hilton last night, where five or six protestors, reporters, someone, had been shoved through by the crush of police.

Whatever was happening, there was no standing on the sidelines, no nuance, no shade of gray.

"It's impossible," Sophie said.

"I'm afraid not."

"We should all be afraid."

The protestors, bloody and beaten, chanted, "The whole world is watching." Their arms pointed in unison toward the police, crying: "Shame, shame, shame."

So much was happening, in their living room, with the stone of the Hilton in the foreground. They watched the events, the on-the-spot analysis. The surprise and outrage of the reporters revved up the realization that this was not acceptable, this was not okay.

The front door opened and Rose looked away, for the first time in half an hour, from the television screen.

When Zak came through the front door with that black and yellow dress wrapped around her neck, Rose was struck dumb. Zak. Every muscle in her body had altered. Every cell on her face was swollen, almost bruised. Rose looked to Sophie, who was still glued to the television. She got up and turned the TV off. Sophie snapped, "What are you doing?"

When she saw Zak, her face went limp.

Rose thought immediately of Eddie. Had he found her? Hurt

her somehow? She didn't want to think how. Thank God she was learning not to blurt out just anything that came to mind because Zak's news was big and directed to a very different place. This would not have tolerated a misunderstanding on Rose's part. Rose was learning (thank you, Sophie) that if you left blank spaces, people hear themselves, grow into themselves better. She thought: I would have been a lousy mother when I was younger.

Zak spoke. Rose covered her face. Sophie stood and Zak fell into her arms.

Zak sat up late into the night with them, wrung with grief. All that they'd seen tonight of their Chicago was twirling in the background, but this was now. This was Zak.

As she told stories, Rose could hear the honed eye of an art-ist. She was a funny girl. She couldn't help, even in her grief, peppering humor through a description of one of Linda Lee's brighter days, when upon finding the janitor cornering Zak to "talk" with her, she smacked the him with her substantial purse. "His hat went flying one way and his stinky cigarillo the other way." As she got lost in her own story, Zak's face brightened and she'd giggled almost as she had with Macy. For a moment, Rose saw the little girl Zak used to be. She also told them terrible sto-ries of a child long ago abandoned by a woman who couldn't find herself. There was no blame in them. Zak spoke as an observant chronicler, stopping for breath when—what—something fright-ened her or might bring the tears on again.

No little girl deserves to be without people who take care of her, Rose kept thinking. She didn't think of herself, of course. If she had only taken better care of her little Grace, how differ-ent life would have been. Microbes, something invisible might always be lurking. It was her colossal failure that she couldn't help her, her endless grief. Even in the photo Stan had brought, which was Zak not so long ago, the child's bright eyes looked to the world as a welcoming place. In denial of, in spite of her experience, she hoped beyond her own reality.

If that woman didn't have Zak, Rose thought, she would have given up long ago. She immediately recognized the melodramatic in her thought. From the stories Zak was telling, Rose knew one thing about Linda Lee. Grief was her passion. People live long and even with joy though they are lost, a raft cut adrift. They love and are loved; they are witty, even elegant. Grief wore the soul away, not the persona. It was an accident of addiction, not a decision, that she had quit.

How could they help this girl, poised on the edge of her possibilities? Rose assessed herself. She was an old woman who'd beaten herself up pretty good in the past ten years. Would she live long? Her twin didn't. Her parents, in their thirties when they had the girls—lived to a decent eighty. There was some chance of longevity. Was she a mental case? It looked that way, but she didn't think so. It was emotions that had put her in the crapper. Funny, she had always thought it was emotion that separated the human animal from other animals—big emotions full of theory, like love and hate. She used to think that animals felt only fear and self-interest, which people did, too, but with an ameliorating underlay of social good, altruism, conscience, honor. Since her going off the edge, and coming back from it, more and more she felt that it was the control of emotions that made "human" different in the kingdom. A lot of people seemed to think as she had, that feelings were what made life real, but she had to nix that idea. They were an ego trip, as the kids say. She didn't think she'd sink into them again. Even the guilt she circled and edged. What about finances, she grilled herself. She had her Social Security coming, but there wasn't a hell of a lot there. For the first time she regretted having given up her house. It would have been worth something.

Sophie was a good woman, and she cared for them, but she was young still, could have another adult life, a someone for herself, a girlfriend if that's what she wanted. Why would she want to tie up with this old fart and a lonely girl? And if she did, then what? She was a librarian, not a millionaire.

Zak had come to them now out of sheer pragmatism. All she could get with them was this life. Not such a much.

Eddie, with this inheritance business, could provide a new reality for the child. It was a different picture, though, without this hapless Linda Lee Zak adored. She could meet the right people, get a good education in art or whatever she turned out to want or be good at. He'd said he turned over a new leaf. Unless this death would make him slide into alcohol. Maybe this was the opportunity Zak needed, this pouring of money over her, a baptism of cash. The deadline was getting close. September—beginning or end? Rose couldn't remember. It was now very late in August. No time but the present to decide.

Rose chided herself. Zak had lost her mother. She would not want to talk about this. Now was the only time to. Rose felt Zak's loss, which, in her own life was far too familiar. She's just a girl. She, too, would go on to laugh and cry, make art, maybe, learn the world. All of life ahead.

The exhausted girl had to go to bed, though she didn't seem to want to. Her eyes were slits and she sat quietly, first on the rug near Sophie's feet, then leaning her back against Rose's ample legs. She rested her head on her knees and nearly fell over. Sophie put her hand on the girl's shoulder as a gentle sign, a release. Soundlessly she rose and kissed each of them once.

Finally, it must have been two in the morning, Rose sat alone with Sophie. They'd never seen Zak cry before tonight. They'd never heard the stories of her torn childhood. They should let it root, this new intimacy. They knew now about the tooth she lost when an eight-year-old girlfriend tried to show Zak how to hit a golf ball in the crowded streets of Chicago, how the club came back and gave her a fat lip, an empty space where her adult front tooth had hardly had time to settle, and how it had earned her the fullness of her mother's attention for an entire day. Linda Lee had screamed, just once, when Zak came through the door and immediately turned into Florence Nightingale, icing the cut, telling Zak not to worry, getting her to the hospital for stitches, the tooth wrapped in a tissue as if it could be replaced by sheer conscientiousness. Zak described that day, her sipping of a malted, trying to get canned chicken noodle soup up a straw with her mother chopping the noodles into pieces nearly small enough to suck through. Her face was filled with delight as she told it. Zak loved her mother. Like no one else. Of course.

The girl had worn herself out with talking her sorrow and mitigated joy. Only a childlike heart could keep them so separate when they lived tangled.

"We got to figure out about this Eddie," Rose said.

"Soon. Maybe not tonight?" Sophie almost pleaded.

"Maybe tonight. I don't know." Rose was restless. She didn't want to make the decision. She was exhausted too. She had to fall into Polish.

"Pure science confirmed that matter and energy are the same," Rose said.

Sophie looked like a bird, which couldn't possibly understand what Rose was driving at. She began to run a pan of soapy water.

"What are you doing?"

"Wiping down the cabinets."

"JesusMaria, you're going to wipe the paint off." All right. That's what Sophie needed to do. Rose went ahead and it had to be in Polish, the words were too hard. She knew her pronunciation in English made her sound stupid. "What had to be abandoned by that new reality or theory, really, they're all theories on which they base a trial, was the ancient idea that force was a cause of motion."

"Hiroshima," said Sophie, the dawn breaking.

"Applied science, yes. It's all based on numbers, though, behind that. They are the absolute reality," Rose said. With full authority. She knew she was jumping. She tried to go to Sophie's track. "But first, New Mexico. Do you know that when they set off the first nuclear reaction, they had no experience, of course, but some, only three per cent of them, had the idea, theoretical because there was no inference to be made, that the reaction might go on into the atmosphere surrounding the earth, enshrouding all we know in a firestorm undreamt of? Never mind that arrogance, never mind that." Rose wiped her fingers across her forehead.

There was no sound but the sound of the water being squished from the rag, the wiping, the rag back in the water, the wringing, the wiping.

"Here's the thing. With that worldly, not theoretical, but in-this-world event, the duality of force and substance became untenable." She spoke as if it were the most important event in the universe. In a way, it was, in the only universe that mattered to humans, their own lives. "All dualities are untrue."

But more. "Old notions were displaced, abandoned, washed away with the new experience," she concluded.

Sophie clearly didn't have it in her. "What old notions are we displacing, Rose?" she asked with quiet desperation. She dropped the cloth.

Now Rose was confused. It was all so clear a minute ago. "We were helping the girl. She's been doing okay with us. Now something has come up." Rose was bowing her head, counting her fingers. "The man is her father. He can offer her things we don't know exist."

Her voice was so low, Sophie nearly had to lean into the breeze of her breath to hear them.

"I think we have to let Zak go."

"Are you sure?" Sophie said with quiet disbelief.

"No, of course not." Rose was irritated.

"Now is not the best time to decide, maybe."

She leapt back into English. "Not this very minute, maybe, but damn soon. Her father is here. He has to get her in September. The mother died. He can take her from us if he wants. If she wants, anyhow, she might pick to go with him."

"She won't."

"They can take her."

Rose didn't kid herself. They. Everyone whose job it was to maintain the status quo. Social Services. Who would understand Zak? How would Zak be better off with them? She and Sophie certainly didn't look good. She was the neighborhood nut. Quite publicly. And, JezusMaria, if they discovered that Sophie was a lesbian, and of course they would, they would have to save the child from perversion. Ill-suited women to fight for the girl. Not much money, they were nobody. If they went up for judgment, they would be found not only lacking, but guilty.

And. They hadn't exactly altered Zak's habits, which, all on their own, would be further witness against them. Zak cursed like a truck driver when provoked. Ameliorated by Sophie's presence, but still. What could be more provoking than a bunch of social workers asking impertinent questions? Zak smoked cigarettes and wore clothes that looked like someone's castoffs, and would leave new ones in the closet with the dust.

No, it would not do to try to work with these people.

"She doesn't like her father," Sophie said. "She called him a 'son-of-a-dogfish' tonight. She said he was 'a piece of biology with a temper.' I don't think he's been a father to her in any way but one."

"We're fishing in a swamp," Rose said. "We aren't going to come up with the King of France."

"You're mixing your metaphors," Sophie said. "I like her, too, Rose."

Rose glared at her.

"I'm old. And broke," Rose said. "And half crazy."

"Not so crazy. Crazy in love, perhaps."

Rose cut that off, none of her business. "I look pretty damn crazy."

"So what? Eddie doesn't sound like any prize package. He hardly knew she existed before this inheritance business." Once Rose set her mind, it would be mighty hard to get her to turn.

"He can take her anyway. Then he has big money. He has the right. You said it. He owns her."

★   ★   ★

Sophie was enraged in her quiet Sophie way.

"Since when do you worry about legal rights? What is the law but a fallible social guide? There's a higher law." She was inundated by a flood of "laws" that had been made that kept her people from owning land, from moving where they pleased, from having certain jobs, and finally from very existence under the Third Reich. Laws were what men made to create order. Whose order and whom they thought their enemy was relevant. Laws were too often fear-based, flawed. She'd been wading in these feelings since she talked to Alan, but now was being engulfed by them.

"He can throw mud on you," Rose said in the flat-out way that only Rose could do. "If this had to go to a court instead of the cops, which is bad enough, he can tell the world you're a 'L.'"

There's no crime in that, Sophie wanted to holler. It's my business. It hurts no one. She knew she would feel differently if that fact, if it really was one, were brought to light. She'd been

comfortable in the darkness. There, it really was her own business. That it had gotten to Alan was beyond expectation. That
she would stand before the world as one was unthinkable. Rose
was coming to this decision out of purer motives than she. It was
apparent in the twist stab of fear Sophie felt. Fears first, as was
probably the case with everyone, world leaders to kindergarten-
ers, and then the theory to justify them. Action was based pri-
marily and still on fear. Did she really think the child would be
better off with her father?

She found herself reasoning out the passing of Zak. The law
was large. A biological father has every right to his child, no matter how absent or even harmful, within the wide law, he may
have been. Of course, that was as it should be.

Was it self-interest clouding her judgment? Sure. Sure it would
be. She was so far from perfect, she couldn't even make out its
spelling from here. Sophie felt a grief she hadn't known since
Barbara's betrayals. This time, she was the betrayer.

"Perhaps you are right," she said.

Rose's eyes were heavy. "I'll call him in the morning," she
answered.

It was late, late and they were beyond sense. They were going
to send the girl off packing. It's true. There was no fighting it.
Sophie hated that they were folding. After all they'd been through
together, they were deciding Zak's future on the basis of money
and the law and fear. She and Rose would no longer know each
other, that was clear. After something like this, a hard decision
that goes against the heart. But she nodded.

As they put their cups into the sink to remain unwashed until
morning, Zak came staggering out to the bathroom. She was
on automatic—blurry, with her eyes nearly shut. When she saw
them, a sleepy grin formed her lips. She came over and rested
her head on top of Sophie's and reached out one hand gently, as

if it were a frame, to touch Rose's face.

It was a gesture that Grace, forever six, had. At once so remi-
niscent and so absent, so tender and so missing all her life since,
that thought suspended and Rose was paralyzed. As soon as Zak
left the room, she was washed in her own tears.

Their dreams tonight would be wordless worry.

CHAPTER TWENTY-SEVEN

Drawing the Desert

The lizard sat staring a lidded stare at the constant sun. He was overwhelmed perhaps by the noon heat or by his having a place in it. He moved not at all.

Zak was his twin in stillness, crouched with her butt an inch above the ground, her legs all double, her outline a praying mantis with its torso twisted up and a ridiculous straw hat stuck on. The sweat was mauve as it ran down her back.

When she'd first approached him, he'd bobbed his head, nodded and did push-ups. Then he stood still, and blood spurt from his eyes. She'd stepped back a foot and squatted, the better to merge with his soft desert gray, his pastels—tan, brown, red, and yellow. The lizard blinked. Zak would not.

She was startled by the vivid starkness of the midday desert, where sunlight bounced with increasing brilliance from sand to sand to cactus. Her quiet sorted out the ochres, the washed-out violets hinted far away. She was afraid to look to the elemental sky, too blue to stare directly into, too bright for any but the native eye to meet. Her own eyes teared from the strange brightness.

She was blessed more and more with symphonic sight. The night rain fell and it was the spectrum of purple she heard. A dust storm blew and she smelled every shade of brown and beige, taupe and musk. The heat was a fast orange-red stripe flying round her eyes, the cold an electric line of blue chilling her bones. This, along with the underpainted magenta hormones jostling every part of her, put her into intense moods.

Nearby was a clapboard building, once paint blue, now sanded and sere. There was no other building around, not a hint of neighborhood. It was a sorry excuse for a museum that had promised ice cold something. Stuck there in 118-degree heat and the only thing passing for shade was scrub brush and the sun-dwarfed shadow of a skeletal rusted green Ford pickup. Zak's sudden hormones and her certainty that she would die like a dog in this heat made her jump up and whoop. She flew around the building three times, her boots kicking up a sandstorm. She collapsed on the sand.

The lizard turned his head to catch the sounds, the muffler of wrinkles at his neck hardly moving.

After she caught her breath, Zak picked her lanky body up and went in the sand-dusted store. It was dark as an Afghani cave after the brilliance outside. She took out her acrylics, her pencils, her paper. She began to draw her desert cohort, "El Torito de la Virgen"—the Virgin's little bull. "Don't tread on me!" Mexicans said of him. "I am the color of the earth. I hold the world. Walk carefully, therefore, that you do not tread on me." It was different, this exacting work of putting to paper the muted, mutable tones of the desert. Subtleties were teaching her a lot about color. She could keep learning forever.

If the car ever ran again.

"Another soda?" said the cowboy who ran the place, awakening from hovering, wobble-headed, over his newspaper.

"Uh-uh," said Zak.

"You got to keep up your fluids out here," he said. "You can get dehydrated easy, little lady."

Zak moved her eyes up from her paper for a second to take him in. No one had come by since they'd been planted there. No one had passed on the road or called on the phone. Waiting on Lowell's tow. She looked back at her paper hornytoad. All in all, she'd rather spend time with the lizard.

Suddenly, she heard the motor turn. She jumped up and streaked toward the car.

"You did it," Zak said, stupid as a rock.

A grinning Sophie rested on a T-shirt in the driver's seat, ram-rod straight so her back didn't touch the vertical part, the hem of her dress pinched between forefinger and thumb. The key, left hanging in the unrelenting light of day, must have been untouchable without intervention.

"Indeed. Why don't you tell that old woman to get over here before the Lord blinks?"

Rose sat at wary rest in sun-diluted shadow around the back. She was deep in herself. She winced as her thumb touched her middle fingers. What an alien place to be. Automatic to her old gardener's hand to cradle vegetation new to her, she didn't know the cholla, the "jumping cactus." So she carried glass-like splinters, stigmata of her ignorance. She tried to focus her eyes to see the fine hairs that had invaded her skin. They were indistinguishable among the tiny cracks put there by years of hard wear.

Her broad glance moved to the empty look of the desert. She didn't know what kind of animals could live here. Plants, she knew, managed just anywhere. Indians had made fat corn ripen ready on the stalk right in the middle of the wavy heat of this Arizona. Hell, wasn't she coming from Chicago, where Trees of Heaven grew out of sewer drains and tortured little weeds scrambled up from the sidewalks' cracks? If that weren't evidence enough, she had seen starved, twisted little trees in the crags of rock mountains. They stood out like flags flying in the harsh wind, dwarfed by the immensity of lack in their immediate world. Surrounded by a meagerness that made life hardly worth the living, they held on with a ferocity that seemed beyond them. Maybe animals, too, had that. Yet they seemed so much more vulnerable to the moment. Look at dinosaurs. People. No, Rose, thought, her money would never be on the animals, certainly not the mammals. Plants had the idea. Slow adaptation.

Zak came flying out through the back door, her notebook and little wooden box of color in her arms. She was grinning like a wave in a pee pot.

"Ço to jest?" Zak had learned that meant "What's happening?"

"Sophie got the car started."

Now Rose awoke to the tap of the internal combustion engine. She smiled and started to move. Her ankles and knees were much better in this heat. The annoying shots of pain had been replaced by a dull ache that was much easier to live with.

After she settled into the car, it lurched westward, the road's asphalt wet with heat.

They were heading to San Francisco eventually. "If you tip the country, all the loose nuts roll to San Francisco," she'd heard. So be it. They were definitely three nuts, or at least two-and-a-half.

Two kidnappers and a willing kid.

An upset life was not unfamiliar to Rose. It seemed it was all her life had been except for those few years with Grace and, of course, when she was a child. Even with her husband and the girls, later with a steady job and owning a house, with thousands of gardens available through catalogs and then picking one, her life had been one change after another, a continuous flow of circumstances. That was the one constant.

Sophie, though. She was time-bound to her house and her job. She was not used to big changes washing over her. *Psia krew*, a lot was required of her to make the decision. Sophie, from Rose's point of view, was a "good girl." She went to schools and ended up in what she was most suited for. She bought a house. She'd played by all the rules.

Except, maybe, that one she broke, the one that made her go with Barbara. Was that such a big deal? Maybe yeah.

If Sophie hadn't done that, she could not possibly have done this. One time, only one time, do you listen to your own rules and allow them to trump the rules that are set for you and you gain the strength to make another decision that looks like a mock to the world.

There were people who would condemn them for taking the girl away. There were people who would put them in prison. They would have to look over their shoulders for a good while, until Zak was eighteen.

So what! Rose threw a challenge out to anyone in the world who might question their decision. By choosing to keep her with them, they were undramatically and quite surely running for their lives. This was not a taking, it was a saving. A saving grace.

Grace, her sweet daughter. Would she approve? Or would she be conservative, fighting to maintain the way things "should" be? In either case, Rose felt that this was her ode to Grace's life unlived. This child would have a chance to be what she wanted to become. This child's life would be lived.

★   ★   ★

The night Zak discovered that she'd lost her mother, Rose had gone to bed with the imprint of that sleepy, newly sweet hand framing her face. She and Sophie had stood eye to eye before they went to their beds and rested their foreheads one against the other's. They said nothing as they separated.

In the morning, Zak had slept long and hard.

The two women met in the kitchen.

Each had come to a conclusion.

In keeping with her own, Sophie grabbed her tea and

immediately got on the phone.

All Rose had to do was wait for Zak to wake. She sat warming her swollen joints by wrapping her fingers around her Eight-O-Clock.

After a while Sophie came in, poured herself another cup from the teapot and sat square across the table.

"I called the people in Georgia directly. And my friend, Alan. It's a strange will, one that he repeated can easily, even understandably, be contested. Leaving everything to an heir that bears the same name. The attorneys back there don't even know that Zak is a girl. They think she's a young man. But Alan said she doesn't have to be male if there's no specific mention of that, just a supposition about a child he never met."

"It means she might not get the money?" Rose asked, tracing the colors carved onto the table.

"It means it can be contested. Alan says that unless they can prove the old man was mentally incapacitated, not just eccentric, it should hold. The Georgia attorneys say he was unusual but not unable. If Zak presents herself, the money and stocks and land are most likely, in the ninety-something percentile, hers, in trust, until she's twenty-one, at which time the estate will become hers solely. Some of it is questionable, like her having to name any issue the same name, a few other items. Without any guarantees, they tell me it's an enforceable will."

It was true. Again.

Everything Eddie had said and more. Zak's great uncle, a narcissist of the first order, had left his entire fortune to Zak, except for the part reserved for his foundation, which had as its sole purpose the dissemination of his thousands of pages of his discourse.

"Ya," Rose said. She knew she was glowering. "I'm not mad at you." It was her brand of apology for the look she couldn't keep off her face.

"Of course not," Sophie answered.

When Zak finally got up, it was as if from a trance, puffy-eyed and looking as though she hadn't slept at all.

Rose would have to wait until Zak seemed able to be in this world.

*　　*　　*

"So, shall we continue on to Albuquerque as we planned?" Sophie asked.

"Sure," Rose said.

"Why not?" Zak piped up from the back seat.

"Well. I'm thinking…. We're supposed to meet Stan in four days. He has the final papers for us. That should give us time to head down there and back. Or we could stay around the area. Or head over to Salt Lake City."

"I don't want to be by no Mormons," Rose said.

"Yeah, they hate Catholics," Zak added. "They hate Jews, too."

"Maybe I shouldn't point it out, but no one here is very Catholic."

"Rose is," Zak said.

"Not exactly." Rose was a cultural rather than a theological Catholic, a concept she learned from the way Sophie was Jewish. Washing up in the church basement didn't make her devout. The incense, the Latin, the vestments, the altar cloths, the connection to the ancient past, were what her religion had given her. But all that was changed now, since Vatican II. It was all guitars and "Kumbaya."

"I would call myself a secular humanist," she said in Polish.

"You don't believe in God now?" Sophie asked in English.

Zak was looking at one and then the other.

"Probably."

In Polish, Sophie said, "Agnostic?"

"I don't think so."

"That sounds agnostic." Sophie smiled.

Rose couldn't explain. She believed in a kind of mass consciousness, a repository for all that people learned about being alive. Of course, there was something else absolutely unexplainable. Where, otherwise, would art come from? Genius? The reality that stayed in our minds after someone died? But a God who dabbled in everyday experiences? No, that wasn't true. God didn't sit down and have tea with people. That's what other people were there for. If you met them correctly, you met God. She was aware of leaving Zak out. In English, she said: "It's about learning how to be decent." She knew it was a poor summation.

"Like kids," Zak piped in. "Little kids."

"Maybe yeah," Rose said. Interiorly, she went on: Something like the way kids learn. If you make a mistake, you simply try another way. We are stupid a lot. Greedy for love, angry in a world that doesn't honor us, too proud to learn, too lazy to work effectively. Self is all we know. A kid, if we are doing our job, learns how to better her self and every other self.

If something is right, it furthers you, and it doesn't hurt anyone else, not in a big way. Simple—so simple, we make it complicated. What you want, what I want. They don't always jive, but there are right ways to resolve them. Churches and governments and, less and less, people you meet on the street don't think about vice or virtue. Pragmatism is the religion of the day. Even those saying Jesus-this and Jesus—they are only forcing their view of the world on others. "I" is the world we live in. And then something like those kids at the convention happens. Crazy, challenging everything, fighting the order imposed by the "haves." Planned chaos as a backdrop for financial prurience. It restores your faith. A virtue, if memory served, faith.

And hope—another one.

"Mormons are too sure of themselves," Rose said. "They judge everyone."

"Catholics, too," Sophie said.

"Roger," said Zak.

"Any maniac in any religion judges everyone," Rose conceded. "Why don't we just go to Albuquerque?"

As they turned toward Albuquerque, Zak piped up from the back seat. "I can't believe you gave your house to Suzee."

"I didn't 'give' it to her. She's earning it by taking care of the rental. Eventually, if we don't return within five years, I'll sign the rest over to her. Until or if we do, she gets a part of the rent each month for her work. Thanks to that crazy will of your great uncle's and Alan, we figured out that we could do that. I'm getting a substantial sum of the worth out in a mortgage, since mine was paid off. "You and Your Finances" gave me the idea and I implemented it, with Alan's help. It gave us a good nest egg. So, when Stan meets us with the final papers, it's done."

'And I have the job waiting in San Francisco."

"Too bad Suzee and them couldn't move to that house. It's nice."

"It wouldn't be so nice for them," Sophie said, "unfortunately."

"Yeah, I know. There's nobody black around for five miles, maybe ten. Macy wouldn't like that."

The neighbors wouldn't like them either, Rose thought. Sophie had taught her not to say just anything that passed through her head. Sophie had also made her promise to get rid of the gun. But after this little trip. It didn't seem crazy to have it on the road.

"I don't think it will be too hard for Suzee all the way on the South side. Stan will help her manage, since it's his people from the soup kitchen, Boody and her gentleman and their little baby and her old girlfriend, Zee, who will be living there."

"That's weird," said Zak.

"We're weird," Rose said.

"If you hadn't noticed," Sophie added.

★   ★   ★

When Zak finally came out of her semi-coma that sad emotion-spent morning, Rose asked her to talk more deeply with them.

"This is something we need to talk about. We don't want to, but.... Wait before you jump all over me." Zak looked confused. "It's hard to explain how....." Rose looked to Sophie to carry on.

"You know about the will that has you as heir?"

"Shit, yeah," Zak said.

"It is real, Zak. I know Rose told you. I've checked further into it. It can set you up for life."

"Like 'Life in prison.'"

Rose felt weak, hesitant. It's not like a garden. If something's wrong, you take it out. You throw it away. You plant it somewhere else. This. This. This decision Zak made could be wrong. The child didn't have the experience she needed to make this decision.

"I think you should go with him, Zak," Rose whispered.

"Oh, brother of Jesus," Zak said. "He could sweet-talk Linda Lee, but how'd he get around you, Rose?"

"It's true, the will. He says he don't drink anymore. That can change a man."

"Eddie is a lyin' sack of shit."

"The chance of being with you inspired him."

"Bullfuckinshit," Zak said. Sophie didn't make a move to correct her. Zak stood up and knocked the chair back, her fists hanging at her sides. "He left Linda Lee on the floor."

Silence.

"He knew?" It was Rose. "When, I'm sorry Zak, it's important, when did your mother die?"

"Saturday on Sunday, at night," Zak said. "He went through her stuff Sunday. That's why she didn't come. That's why he sent Emerson. That landlord told me," Zak said cold and hard. "He ain't inspired to shit." Her eyes turned inward and Rose knew she was there again, seeing it, feeling it.

He knew. That sonofabitch sat there with Rose talking about wills and his dear daughter and the whole time he knew. Her eyes met Sophie's which were wide and round. The Penrose Triangle, Rose realized in a flash. The optical illusion that could be drawn and looked logically possible, but could not be made. She had turned Eddie into a social Penrose Triangle.

"Fuck him," Rose said.

"Try to keep your language together, Zak," Sophie said. She did not direct it to Rose. "I know it's hard, but when things are hardest, that's the time for it." Rose gave her a shivering look.

Zak went out to have a cigarette. No one tried to stop her.

Sophie started to say something. "I...." It was hard for her to think this, but she knew it was true, "I love her."

Rose's glare subsided. Her lips parted, slack.

"I know. It's surprising." Especially to Sophie. Barbara, who'd hated social togetherness, while loving some aspect of presenting herself with Sophie, who loved the freedom to let whim, where it fed her alone, rule in personal life, had always said Sophie had hard defenses. Barbara wanted the bowls of their skull, those wonderful protective devices that were meant to keep brains entire and able, to melt. Sophie respected why these lovely skulls were there. She appreciated that they did their work so exquisitely while giving the mind all the space it needed to roam. Barbara had wanted the intimacy of blood, wanted to be known from cell to nerve. At the same time she'd wanted privacy the way a teenager does. It had made Sophie schizoid. She thought that push-and-pull had disabled her ability to love. Was money so important that they should pack Zak off with a callous DNA donor, to somewhere in the South, for God's sake, just because of the weight of it? She watched her own fears rise. Just because she was afraid was no reason not to go on.

'Rose, I'm never going to have kids. I have no family anymore. But you. And her, now."

In a flash, Sophie was taking over as guardian. She had sorted out all that's "correct" and "legal" and "responsible" as Rose had. The news of Eddie's perfidy was the muscle she needed to wrestle it all down and come out, as Rose so wanted to after feeling that soft touch along her jawline, in the same place. Like a flock of birds turning in midair without outward signal, they turned and headed together.

He had the right. He had money. He had nothing.

★   ★   ★

"Just a few more days until we meet Stan," Sophie said.

Rose thought of evolution, the interdependence of living things that move toward a common, though each selfish, goal. Maybe mammals were not quite doomed.

There was a coming together in life. Sometimes, not every day, but now and then, this glimpse. The perfect order of numbers—that world of the thoughtfully explained—would smash up against wild color—a kind of ecstasy, and each would partake of the other, some elements of the other. And something inexplicably sweet could occur.

She'd have to think about it.

Oh Lord, deliver us.

We can succeed only by concert. . . . The dogmas of the quiet past are inadequate to the stormy present. The occasion is piled high with difficulty, and we must rise with the occasion. As our case is new so we must think anew and act anew. We must disenthrall ourselves. . . .

—*President Abraham Lincoln's Message to Congress December 1, 1862*

ACKNOWLEDGMENTS

There were quite a few years I courted New York in hopes of having this novel and the ones to come published by a large publishing house. With the changes in publishing, I realized my work might not be a big seller, a realization that some very good agents helped me understand. I decided to self-publish. But self needs to be defined.

Self is not me or I. It's a community of smart, thoughtful people who cheered me on, sometimes with only a phrase, often with much more. Some of those came from fine literary agents who didn't need to be kind, but praised the manuscript while regretting that they felt they would not be able to sell it and so could not represent me. More came from able and persistent readers, who read it in many revisions: Julie Alexander, who paints abstract poems; Beth Farrow whose keen brilliance and quiet care are invaluable; Davis Oldham, writer, teacher, editor, a prince. Other readers, with their suggestions and careful criticisms guided me to the finish: astute and generous Nassim Assefi (who has written *Aria* and forthcoming novel with working title *Say I Am You*), the appreciative Carolyn Allen, Cha Davis, and uplifting supporters Ellen Sturgis and Linda Summers, Pat Dawson, and Gitana Garofalo.

Lisa Borders, editor and author in her own right, helped me to find the way to keep these characters in the light. Thanks to sometime copy editor, Marjorie Charney, to Sheri Simonson for her graphic help, and to Mark Kornblum, website guru. A special holler to talented and touching artist Pam Keeley, who provided the cover drawing and to Dana Scheurholz, extraordinary photographer.

A writer is made, not born. A careful writer is foremost a reader. Among the countless novels which have lifted me into worlds I thought I could not imagine, are, above all, Bulgakov's *The Master and Margarita*, Robinson's *Housekeeping*, Barnes' *Nightwood* and, more recently, Mitchell's *Cloud Atlas*, Strout's *Olive Kitteridge*. Any stories of Alice Munro and Amy Bloom are a blessing and a lesson. These are writers who work at it and then work more, and produce work beyond themselves. I could not have written without having seen these landscapes.

Thanks to the the State of Washington Artist Trust for showing confidence in my work with their grant for literature. The King County Arts Council (now called 4ARTS) also supported me. Each of these awards came at times when I was turning my head away, thinking I had no right to write. They renewed me. And a sweet thanks to teacher and playwright, Ki Gottberg, who told me to go ahead and try for them and, so, kept Seattle from counting yet another unemployed real estate agent.

And thanks, Miss Bernadette Coles of Madonna High School.